Aiden—Vested Interest #2 by Melanie Moreland
Copyright © 2018 Moreland Books Inc.

Registration # 1148533
All rights reserved
ISBN: 978-1-988610-05-4

Edited and Proofed by:
D. Beck
Lisa Hollett, Silently Correcting Your Grammar
Jodi Duggan

Cover design by
Melissa Ringuette, Monark Design Services

Interior Design & Formatting by
Christine Borgford, Type A Formatting

NEW YORK TIMES AND *USA TODAY* BESTSELLING AUTHOR
MELANIE MORELAND

DEDICATION

Karen
This one is for you.
As my PA, you make my professional life easier.
As my friend, you make my world brighter.
I love you for both.
You fought for Aiden when he was only
a few lines in a chapter.
You've loved him the longest, so he is yours.
Officially.

And as always,
My Matthew,
Without whom I am lost.
Always yours.

PROLOGUE

IT STARTED THE way it always did. Voices, shouting, flashes of panic. Broken fragments of memories, images that blurred and blended into each other.

"You're just like your father. Worthless."

"He can't read? What a surprise. He's always been so stupid."

"I'm not paying for anything extra for him. If he can't keep up, that's his problem."

I was running, frightened, and out of breath. I needed to hide, to get away. Rocks hit my legs, and one even cutting into my neck. I felt the wet of blood as it seeped down the back of my shirt. I rounded the corner, ducking into the alley and behind the dumpster. I held my breath, trying to stay silent.

The running feet stopped, the voices angry.

"Where did he go?"

"Do you think he's in the alley?"

"No, the little bastard is scared of his own shadow, he'd never go there.

Let's keep looking."

Like a miracle, they moved on, but I stayed huddled, knowing they could come back. Knowing that even if I avoided them today, tomorrow they would find me.

My body shook as it recalled the number of beatings I'd taken at school. On the playground. At home. I could hear my gasps of air and feel the panic setting in. It wasn't real, but I was useless to stop the barrage of fear coursing through me.

Slap.

"You worthless piece of shit! All you do is cause me disappointment!"

"Please, Momma, not the belt . . ." I sobbed.

"You'll get that and more, you ingrate! I wish you'd never been born!"

The pain from her strike was so vivid, I felt my body jerk in reflex. I heard my own shout. Still, I couldn't break through the grip keeping me trapped in the past.

The room was bright, the décor familiar. I realized I was in Greg's office on that fateful day, staring at him holding a gun to his chin. Except, this time, it wasn't him holding the gun. It was me. I had the gun pressed to my throat, staring at Bentley. He shook his head.

"You're such a coward."

"I don't want to do this," I begged. "Help me."

"I'll be glad when you're gone. You've been nothing but a pain in my ass. I've put up with you long enough."

"No, Bent—we're friends! You said so!"

He shrugged his shoulder dismissively. "No, you were useful, but I'm done. You're a waste of space and the world would be better off without you."

He turned, walking away and ignoring my pleas.

The room felt cold, the air making me shiver. I looked around. I was alone, abandoned by one of the few people I thought I could trust. I shut my eyes, pressing the cold steel to my skin.

"Stop."

My eyes flew open at the sound of her voice. Cami stood in front of me.

"Don't do this."

"I have no choice."

"You do." She extended her hand. "Come with me."

"No. I'm not what you need. I'm not what anyone needs."

"If you do this, you'll never find out."

I shook my head, pressing the gun closer.

I felt her leave. The darkness surrounded me. I squeezed the trigger.

With a loud gasp, I bolted upright in bed. I drew in much-needed oxygen, desperate to try to tamp down my panic. Swinging my legs over the edge of the bed, I fumbled with the light, snapped it on, and glanced around the room. Still terrified, I ran my hands over my torso and head, feeling for the blood, the hole left by the gun. There was nothing except a sheen of sweat covering my entire body.

Desperately thirsty, I reached for the water bottle on the nightstand, drained it, and tossed the bottle to the side. I hung my head, feeling my breathing return to normal and my heart rate slow down.

It was a nightmare. Not the first and certainly not the last I would have.

However, this one was different from before. More intense than ever. Vivid with the last image of Greg. I knew his death was still on my mind. It lingered on the edges, drilling itself down into my psyche and coming out when I tried to sleep.

The last time I'd had a really bad dream, I'd woken beside Cami. She had soothed me. Held me close and comforted me until I fell asleep again. When I was wrapped in her embrace, the terror hadn't returned.

Tonight, I was alone, and I knew, without a doubt, it would come back. Repeatedly, until I dragged myself from my bed and started my day.

But that was how it had to be because, nightmare or not, the message of the dream was correct and always would be.

I *was* worthless, and she would never be beside me again. She deserved so much more than I could ever be for her.

I rose and grabbed a pair of sweat pants. I'd work out, then head into the office. At least there, I could be something other than what

4 MELANIE MORELAND

I was in my dreams.

I could be Aiden, friend to Bentley and Maddox. Part of a successful company. Respected by many, admired by some. Wealthy, humorous, and without a care in the world.

It was a great cover. No one ever looked past it to my real self.

The one I kept hidden.

CHAPTER 1

AIDEN

I INHALED THE scent of new car, looking around in appreciation at the interior of the custom-made extended SUV that BAM had purchased. Two rows of seats, facing each other, so I no longer had to ride up front when the three of us traveled together on longer trips. Rich, thick leather seats, lots of leg and headroom, and thanks to Reid, decked out with every technological innovation possible. It was a comfortable way to travel, including a third row of seats that was easy to access or could be folded down for luggage. I had overseen the design myself, making sure it met all our specifications.

Bentley slid into the back across from me before I could get out and open the door. He dropped his briefcase on the seat beside him and took the cup of coffee I held out with a nod of thanks. We both sipped in silence for a moment. He appraised the interior of the vehicle, looking pleased.

"I like this one. Rides smooth."

I grinned. "It does. Frank likes driving it too."

Frank flashed a thumbs-up, making Bentley chuckle.

"Good job, Aiden."

He sighed, leaning his head back against the smooth leather and crossing his leg over his knee. The movement caused his pants to ride up, exposing his socks. I was unable to stop the grin that pulled at my mouth.

He was wearing bright red socks with purple and blue triangles. His tie was the same bright red. Unable to resist, I tapped his foot with mine.

"Nice socks."

He opened one eye, the glare evident. "Shut up."

"I've never seen you looking so . . . *jaunty*."

He sat up, tugging down his pant leg. "Fuck off. Emmy picked them out. She says I need some color besides blue and gray." He brushed imaginary lint off his knee. "She assures me they're hip."

"They match your tie. Very coordinated."

"Aiden," he warned.

I held up my hands. "What? All I said was you looked jaunty. It's good to try new things."

"Drop it."

"Sure." I drained my coffee. "You know, a red pocket square would finish the ensemble. I bet Maddox has one you could borrow. Make you even hipper."

"I'm gonna hip check you right into next week."

"I'd like to see you try."

He lifted his newspaper with a smirk. "Or I'll tell Emmy you made fun of her choices, and she'll cut off the scone train."

"Bastard. That's below the belt."

He pulled his jacket away, showing me the highly polished belt he was sporting. "It's new too. Will I add that to the list to tell Emmy?"

Our eyes met, both glaring, until I saw his lips quirk. Then we were both laughing. He picked up his coffee and finished it. "I told her I would try."

I chuckled. "Honest. I like the socks. It's just something I expect from Maddox—not you."

"She wanted me to have them, and I had to wear them. You should see the other pair. Freaking polka dots with so many colors my head ached." He stroked the silk around his neck. "The tie, at least, I can handle."

"No, she's right. The socks are hip."

"But let's face it. I'm not hip."

"You're better than you were. Emmy will make sure you're cool." I smirked at him. "Maybe one day, you'll be as cool as me."

It was Bentley's turn to roll his eyes. "My greatest aspiration."

I leaned back, crossing my arms behind my head. "Yep. I know."

"You should have seen her face when she asked the cost of the socks. I thought she was going to have a coronary."

"She's not used to money the way you are, Bent."

"I know. I have the feeling she never will be." He laughed. "She was googling sock care all evening. I keep telling her to stay off the damn internet, but women . . ."

"Especially your woman. She's addicted."

The SUV stopped and Maddox climbed in, holding a tray of coffees along with a bag of donuts. He glanced around the vehicle with a low whistle. "Nice, Aiden. Very nice."

"I know." I smirked, leaned over, and snagged the bag and another cup. The three of us lived on caffeine. It didn't matter which cup I grabbed—we all took it the same way. Light on the cream, no sugar.

"Greedy fucker. Maybe those are for me," Maddox growled, trying to snatch back the bag.

I reached in and grabbed a double chocolate with a grin. I knew those were his favorite. I took a big bite.

"You snooze, you lose."

"Gross. Chew with your mouth closed. It looks like you're full of shit."

"Well," Bentley drawled, "if it walks like a duck, and quacks like a duck . . ."

Maddox threw back his head in laughter, and I grinned at them. I loved it when we were together and just being ourselves.

I tossed the bag at Bentley. "Quack."

He handed the bag back to Maddox. "You pick first."

I snorted. Always the gentleman. So proper. Maddox grabbed a second double chocolate donut and handed the bag to Bentley who grinned and pulled out the third one. Maddox knew us all too well. He leaned forward and dropped the bag beside Frank. "One for you too."

"Thank you, Mr. Maddox. I do love me a good donut."

We all chuckled. No matter what we did, he insisted on calling us Mr. before our names. At first, it was Mr. Ridge, Mr. Callaghan, and Mr. Riley. He had finally agreed to use our first names, but he refused to drop the Mr.

For a few minutes, there was silence as we sipped and chewed. Bentley once again crossed his leg, and I nudged Maddox's foot, lifting my eyebrow toward Bent. Maddox followed my line of sight, his own eyebrows rising when he saw what I was trying to show him.

Of the three of us, Maddox was the most stylish. Bentley was classic: dark suits, white shirts, silk ties. I hated suits—they felt constrictive, even when tailored to my broad shoulders. I preferred T-shirts and my leather jacket, but for the office, I opted for dress shirts and pants, only suffering a suit when absolutely necessary. However, Maddox always went all out. Vests, patterns, pocket squares, funky shoes. He would love the addition to Bentley's wardrobe.

Maddox remained silent, sliding his glasses up his nose, and tapping on his cheek the way he always did while thinking.

"Nice footwear, Bent. Very . . . *expressive*."

"Don't start."

"Just saying. Colorful. Unexpected. Emmy, I assume?"

"Maybe I picked them out. You ever think of that?"

Maddox shook his head, not hiding his smirk. "Maybe I dressed in drag last night and got freaky with a clown."

Bentley shrugged. "I always suspected you had some sort of circus fetish. Bound to come out."

I began to laugh, slapping my knee. "Bentley made a joke! Come out! Closet! Get it, Mad Dog?"

"Yeah, Bentley made a funny. Let's alert the media."

We all began to laugh, the sound of our amusement filling the car. I could hear Frank's low chuckles from the front. He always liked it when the three of us started in on each other.

Maddox wiped his eyes. "Seriously, what's with the socks?"

"Emmy's influence."

"She's trying to make him hip."

Maddox shook his head. "You can't make someone hip. Either you are or you're not. I hate to break it to you, Bent, you *are not.*"

"I suppose you are?"

Maddox lifted his legs, setting them on the seat beside me. He yanked up his pant legs. "I am."

Bentley looked horrified. "What the hell are those?"

"These are what us hip people wear." His socks were even brighter than Bentley's—blues, greens, yellows—and two different patterns.

"You call those hip?"

"Yep."

"They don't match!"

"Exactly. The colors are the same, and their designs are similar, but no, that's the idea. They aren't mirror images. They're mismatched on purpose."

Bentley snorted. "On purpose? Looks like you got dressed in the dark." He raised one eyebrow. "Were you feeling along the floor for your socks after the clown incident, Maddox? That's the closest you could get to a matching pair? You needed to get out before the red nose started glowing again?"

"Fuck you, asshole. At least I buy my own socks. My girlfriend doesn't have to pick them out for me."

"At least I have a girlfriend. I'm not bumping uglies with a clown."

Maddox sat back with a grin. "Maybe I'm not either. I might not have gotten dressed in the dark, but I wasn't alone when I woke up."

I reached out and we fist-bumped. "Listen to Mad Dog. Getting himself a bone!"

"More like a boner." He winked. "Of epic proportions. The lady in question may not be able to put on *her* socks this morning, if you catch my drift."

Another fist bump.

Bentley rolled his eyes. "You two are ridiculous." He eyed Maddox. "Anyone we know?"

Maddox shook his head. "I never kiss and tell."

"Unless it's a clown."

He winked. "Unless it's a clown."

Chuckling, I changed the subject, not wanting to delve into Maddox's personal life. They would want to delve into mine next. That wasn't happening, especially after last night.

"You're seriously interested in this property, Bentley? It's a summer resort—not our usual style," Maddox queried, sipping his coffee.

"I'm interested in the land. I think we could do something special with it. The resort is old and outdated, but the land is prime. I wanted you both to see it."

Maddox glanced at me. "Hit me."

I pulled off my sunglasses and rubbed my eyes as I gathered my thoughts. Before I could speak, Bentley narrowed his eyes. "Aiden, are you all right?"

"I'm fine."

"You look exhausted."

Maddox studied me, and I shifted in my seat, uncomfortable at the worried looks on their faces. I needed to shut that shit down—and fast.

"Maybe you're not the only one scratching the itch, Mad Dog."

"You were with someone last night?"

I lifted one shoulder, dismissing the question. "Like you, I don't kiss and tell. Now, can we move on to business?" I forced a smirk to my face. "Unless you want to sit around and braid each other's hair and talk girlie shit."

Bentley groaned, rubbing a hand over his face. "Spare me. I have enough of that now. Do they ever make a move without consulting each other? I swear she has Cami on speed dial. This morning it was about what color *tights* she should wear with her dress. I told her black, but she had to call Cami."

"And?"

"Apparently, nude was the decision. Black was too—" he held up his fingers in quotations "—harsh."

"This is the woman you let pick your socks?" Maddox muttered.

"Fuck you."

"You first."

"No thanks, Emmy took care of that as well." Bentley settled back in his seat, his grin wide and wicked. "That, my friends, is the reason I put up with the constant consultations."

"Sex."

He shook his head. "Sex with *Emmy*." Even though his voice was teasing, there was no doubt about his feelings. His eyes were warm and his contentment shone through. I felt a flash of jealousy at his obvious happiness, but I tamped it down. He deserved to be happy.

He studied me for a minute, then flicked his hand. "Okay. Back to the business at hand."

Inwardly, I sighed with relief. Business, I could handle. Bentley's inquisition, not so much.

"Huge lot, over five acres, prime waterfront. Been in his family for years, but none of them live in the province now, and they don't want the responsibility of a resort. The owner is retiring to be closer to his kids. He reached out to us—the land isn't even officially up for sale."

"Any reason why he reached out to us in particular?" Maddox asked.

"His granddaughter, Jane Whitby, interned with us a couple of years ago. She told him how awesome I was to her."

Maddox raised his eyebrow. "*You* were?"

Bentley chuckled. "I remember Jane. She was bright. Efficient."

I nodded. "Sandy loved her. We gave her a bonus and a great reference when she left for Calgary. She told her grandfather we would do right by him if we were interested."

Maddox nodded. "Great. That was nice of her to think of us."

"Anyway, from the pictures I saw, the land is the prize. The buildings need to be demolished. Far too much work to renovate, but it could be sweet if we built. I can already think of a dozen investors who would want in."

"If the numbers work," Maddox mused.

"This remains between us," Bentley cautioned. "If we go ahead, nothing anywhere but verbal conversations between the three of us until the papers are signed."

"We're safe, Bent. We've overhauled everything—all our systems are tight. Reid has all that shit under control. No one is getting through his systems," I assured him. "No one is spying anymore."

He sighed, staring out the window. I knew the betrayal of his lawyer and friend, Greg, had shaken him. Bentley had become overcautious with everything. Emails, texts, phone calls. He would relax eventually, and I knew I had to be patient.

"For now, keep it between us," he stated.

"Okay."

Maddox spoke up. "I thought Muskoka was the place to be for resorts."

I leaned forward, shaking my head. "Think about it, Mad. By noon every Friday, Highway 400 is backed up with people trying to head up north. One accident and you're stuck for hours. Then heading home Sunday is the same. The reason people want to escape the city is to relax. By the time you get there, you're tense. It takes a full day to adjust, then you have to head back and you're faced with the same thing. Once again, you fight the traffic and crowds. So, it's all for nothing. You're right back to being tense."

Bentley spoke. "Aiden is right. We researched it thoroughly. Muskoka is awesome, but it's gotten ridiculous. The very things you're looking to escape follow you. The crowds, the traffic, the expense. Port Albany is still small and not as developed. Great views, nice lakes, and still peaceful for the most part. Marketed in the right way, I think it would sell extremely well, whether we keep it in BAM or form an investment group."

"We're pretty tied up with Ridge Towers—can we take on another project?" Maddox queried.

Bentley shrugged. "Let's not get ahead of ourselves. Let's see the land, find out what he's looking for, and decide if we're interested. We can always buy and hold it until we decide."

Maddox and I agreed. "Good plan."

CHAPTER 2

AIDEN

BENTLEY ALWAYS CHANGED when he was interested in something. No one else would notice, unless you knew him. He spoke a little faster and used his hands more. His gaze never stayed in one spot, but instead, moved rapidly, taking in everything as he spoke.

At the moment, he was on fire. As he spoke with Jed Whitby, I knew he was already forming an offer. Maddox wandered around, stopping every few feet to take in the view. It was stunning. I pulled off my sunglasses to peruse the vast expanse of water. It was a warmer day, with a light breeze. I could imagine how it would feel under the heat of the sun, sitting with a beer, enjoying the view.

"Fucking awesome," Maddox murmured beside me.

"Bent wants it."

"No shit. I want it."

"That makes three of us."

"This is a fucking no-brainer. Whether we keep it, build it, or do some of both, we need to buy this place."

I studied the property. "I wonder what's going on with the pieces on either side?"

Jed appeared beside me with a chuckle. "You'll find out in about twenty minutes. I told my neighbors I was selling, and they want in on the action."

I inhaled hard at that information. The land formed a wide U configuration. If we obtained all three parcels, the possibilities were staggering. I met Maddox's gaze, and I knew he was thinking the same thing.

Jed slapped my shoulder. "Look around and come inside for coffee. I warn you, my wife always told me it was tar. And that was when she was alive to oversee how many grounds I put in the pot."

I smiled. "Fair warning."

He made his way toward the main house, leaning heavily on his cane. He had told us his health was the main reason he was selling.

"Too much physical work in the season and difficult to find kids to hire anymore," he explained to us. *"They want tech jobs and things they can do while sitting on their asses, texting all day."*

We all chuckled at his description because he was correct.

"It's lonely in the off-season. My wife and I did this together. Without her, it's not the same. My daughter has a nice place for me, and her kids are there. Jane is close too, so it's time to sell."

Bentley stood, contemplative, and stroked his chin, while Maddox tapped his cheek, looking thoughtful. I knew they were both going through offers in their heads. I already had a number in mine. I had memorized everything about the area and the values of the properties. As Bentley's right-hand man, and vice president of the company, my role was unique. Not only did I oversee all the security for the company and Bentley, but I was also involved in all aspects of our acquisitions, as well as legwork for the large projects we took on. Maddox was our numbers man, and he knew our finances inside and out. I was sure if I asked him, he could tell me our bank balances to the penny.

Ridge Towers was a huge project, both in scope and financially, but I knew we were on track with it. We were on budget, ahead of schedule, and the interest in it was already positive. Once we hired the right marketing team, sales would explode. Originally dubbed Bentley Ridge Estates after a joke from Emmy, we had decided to stick with Ridge Towers, agreeing the name worked with the location. It was going to be an extraordinary piece of our company's holdings.

We watched Jed walk into the house before anyone spoke.

"That was unexpected," Bent mused. "All three properties?"

"I know." I snorted. "I thought *this* piece was impressive."

"If we can get all the land, we can't pass this up," Bentley stated. "Even if we break it up and resell, we'll make a fortune." He paused. "I don't want to play games with these people. No lowballing. We'll listen to them and make a good offer. Wrap it up fast."

I admired that about Bentley. He was never out to cheat anyone. He was fair in his dealings, especially when it came to his interaction with people. Shrewd and intense, but always honest. He had been from the day I'd met him.

"You have all the figures in your head, Aiden?"

"Yep."

"I assume you know the stats on the adjoining properties?"

I gave him a scathing look, and he chuckled. "Just checking. Hit me with numbers."

I threw out figures for each parcel, and he nodded. "That's what I was thinking. We need to do some more due diligence, but I think you're right. Maddox?"

"As always, my boy nailed it."

"Can we handle it financially?"

Maddox smirked. "Easily."

"Then let's go and listen to what they have to say."

⌒

I RUBBED MY temples, the words running together, worse than usual, on the page in front of me. Nothing was recognizable. None of the usual markers I could concentrate on and work with appeared. I glanced at my watch and winced. I had been at this for over two hours and had accomplished nothing. The notes I had were the highlights from the exceedingly unusual business meeting we'd had with the three owners of the properties, Bentley's musings, and a few points Maddox had made earlier.

We had been quiet in the SUV. As usual, once Bentley got an idea, he was silent, working through the details in his head. Maddox had been busy on the phone, and I clutched the file folder Jed had stuffed into my hand, the paper covered in coffee cup rings and worn around the edges. Once we hit the office, we went our separate ways, with the plan to talk it over in the morning. I had hoped to break down the document more, but I'd failed.

Nothing new there.

Bentley walked in, tugged at his tie, and sat in front of me. He studied my face for a moment, then purposefully leaned forward.

"What's going on?"

"I tried, Bent." I indicated the sheets on my desk, shame coloring my voice. "I can't-I can't do anything with this information. I'm sorry."

"There is nothing to be sorry for—don't even go there. Jesus, Aiden. Have you been at it since we got back?"

"Yeah."

He shook his head. "I glanced at it earlier. I could barely make sense of it myself. His writing is chicken scratch, and there's no business terminology to focus on. Sandy will type it up for us tonight, and we'll go through it tomorrow. All of us." He rubbed the back of his neck. "Did you not get my message?"

I picked up my phone. "Shit. I had it on mute while we talked to Jed. I forgot to switch it back on."

"I called and told you to give it to Sandy. I knew you'd stress over this too much."

"I hate how you have to dumb things down for me."

"I am not fucking *dumbing* things down. Stop with that shit. You're smarter than I am, for God's sake. You just process it in a different fashion."

I shrugged, not believing him.

He scowled. "Aiden, what's going on with you?"

Denial tripped off my tongue fast. It was second nature to me now. "Nothing."

He tilted his head. "Your boss isn't asking—your friend is," he informed me quietly. "Why are you so down on yourself lately? The nightmares—are they back? You look exhausted."

I couldn't meet his concerned gaze. "Nothing new and nothing I can't handle."

"You're lying."

My head snapped up.

"You forget how well I know you, Aiden."

"Leave it, Bent. I'm handling it."

He sighed. "I wish you'd go and talk to Chloe, the counselor we've been seeing. She's been amazing with Emmy and me. I think you'd find it helpful."

"I don't want to talk about my past. I want to forget it."

He shook his head. "You *can't* forget your past. It shapes you, and if you don't deal with it, it haunts you forever. That's what I've discovered. Running away doesn't fix anything. Talking it out, getting some help does."

I scrubbed my face, wanting the subject closed. "Look, I'll think about it. Just leave it right now, okay?" I picked up the papers in front of me. "We need to figure out how to make these people happy and buy this land."

He knew when to let it go, so he changed the subject. "That was some of the most beautiful property I've seen in a long time."

"I agree. The views are spectacular. I wanted to pull up a chair with a beer and just look at the water."

He sat back, running his fingers along the crease of his pants. "Have you ever wanted a place outside the city?"

I pursed my lips. We all lived in very different locations. Bentley had the house filled with antiques, reflecting his old-fashioned manners and upbringing. Maddox lived in the penthouse of a condo building, high over the city, all clean lines, and modern. My loft in the warehouse district was open, with brick walls and wood floors, plain and utilitarian. We all enjoyed city living, simply in different ways.

"I never thought about it until today," I admitted. "Something about that place . . ."

"I know. The openness and the views. Made me think."

"Yeah."

He stood, holding out his hands for the papers. "Sandy will clean these up, and we'll talk it through tomorrow." He snorted. "We have to be sure to include the fact that we won't remove Mrs. C's crabapple trees for four years."

I chuckled. I had liked Jed's neighbor, Mrs. Cartwright. Bossy and direct, she was determined. Plus, she was an awesome baker. I had devoured half a dozen of Mrs. C's, as she insisted we call her, oatmeal raisin cookies. They were stellar. They were also the perfect antidote to the insidious brew Jed had plied us with. Tar was being kind. Adding milk made no difference. It remained blacker than the bowels of hell and tasted like burned asphalt. However, we all drank it as we listened, me memorizing the details of the conversation. A far easier task than deciphering the documents Jed gave us.

"Don't forget we have to let Mr. Wilcox stay in his house for one last summer." Jed's other neighbor had stipulated that condition.

"How could I? He was damned adamant about it." Bentley shook his head in amusement.

"Their demands, such as they were, are all workable. Bizarre, but workable."

"If we decide to go ahead, we'll give them what they want. We can do the offers this week once we hash it out. You and Maddox can work them up together."

"Yep."

"Great. Unexpected, but great. The potential . . ." Bentley stared out the window. "It's astronomical."

"You're right."

His phone buzzed and he glanced down, grinning as he read the screen. "You still okay for tonight?"

"Tonight?" I repeated blankly.

He sighed. "You're starting your self-defense lessons with Emmy and Cami? Ring a bell?"

My heart rate picked up at the sound of Cami's name. Bentley hadn't been happy about Emmy wanting to learn self-defense but had agreed it was smart and asked me to do it, rather than have her go to a stranger. It wasn't a surprise when Cami said she wanted to learn as well.

"Right. Of course. But we can't use the gym here at the office. That pipe that leaked last week is still being fixed. It's a mess down there. We'll need to replace the floor once it's repaired." I frowned. "Dee isn't taking part?"

"No, she's working a lot of overtime on some case. She told Emmy she would maybe join in later."

"Okay. I can always make plans with her when she's available."

"Thanks, Aiden. I appreciate you doing this for me. For them. You're the only one I trust enough. You want to use the gym in my place?"

I couldn't help the feeling of satisfaction his words gave me. I knew how much Emmy meant to him, and his trust meant a great deal. "No, you have too many machines. I need open space. They can come to the loft. I have a punching bag and everything we need."

"Okay. I'll bring them over later. Six?"

Bentley was my main priority during the day, but I didn't have to accompany him in the car all the time anymore. It was convenient for us to go together since Frank went right by my place to get Bentley and parking in Toronto was a bitch. But some days, I drove myself into the office. We took it day by day, but I was always ready should he need me. In the evenings, he used his own car, unless he was attending a function with crowds of people and we felt it was better to have me on hand. When he and Emmy were alone in the evening, he was fine. He was smart and strong, and I had taught him enough moves that he could protect them if need be, and he liked the privacy.

"Fine. But you need to stay out of the way."

"Why?"

"You'll be all protective and make Emmy tense. I need to do this my way. You can pick them up later."

"Emmy was wondering about Mexican after. Dee can join us around eight if we're interested in a night out with the girls."

Maddox strolled into the office. "Beers, tacos, and pretty girls? I'm in. I'll text Dee and tell her I'll pick her up so she doesn't have to take the subway."

Bentley and I shared a look, both of us wondering how often he texted Dee. Or saw her. However, we knew it was useless to ask. He would shut down. It made me think, though, perhaps she was who he was with last night. Maddox was a straight shooter, and he didn't play the field. If he were interested in Dee, she would be the only one he would be seeing.

"Aiden?"

I shrugged, feigning indifference. "I guess."

"Okay, I'll let her know."

I stared out the window, fighting the reaction I felt about seeing Cami. She was Emmy's best friend. I liked hanging with Bentley. He liked hanging with his girl, and she liked bringing along her friends. I was doing my job by helping Bentley. It was smart to teach Cami some defensive moves too. Afterward, it meant nothing, just people enjoying some time together. Like Maddox said. Beers, tacos, and pretty girls. It was all good.

Fun. Lighthearted.

At least, that was what I kept telling myself.

⌒

WHEN BENTLEY MET Emmy, Cami Wilson crashed into my life like a wrecking ball. From the moment I saw her, kissing her was a temptation, fucking her was a fantasy, and hurting her was inevitable.

Smart, funny, and gorgeous, she was difficult to resist. Especially when she made her feelings known—since she had no problem expressing herself to me. The difference between Bentley and me was the fact that he was ready for a permanent connection, and I wasn't. I told Cami up front I didn't do relationships, particularly long-term ones, and I didn't want to start something with her that had no chance of going anywhere. She didn't seem fazed by my words, and we had started an unconventional affair. By that, I meant she was perfect, and I was an ass. I called her on occasion, we texted, hung out with Emmy and Bent, often with Dee and Maddox joining us. In the darkness of Bentley's movie theater, I held her hand, pulled her onto my lap to kiss her when no one could see. Snuck away to fuck her on occasion, and every so often, met up with her for coffee or lunch, but we never went on an official date. It was rare that we saw each other except when we were in the company of friends, and we both understood the rules. There was no PDA in front of them, nothing to indicate we were anything besides friends. I never discussed Cami with Bentley or Maddox; although from the looks I received from Bentley and Emmy at times, I was certain Cami didn't follow my silence is golden rule.

Cami tried to reach out to me. She would text and invite me places or ask me over for dinner at her apartment. She would check up on me and listen if I had a bad day and wanted to talk. When we were together, she was warm, affectionate, and always patient, never pushing me for more than I could give. In bed, she was passionate and strong. We fit together. However, there was no *us*. There never could be. She was persistent, but I was determined not to allow her to become too embedded into my life. I wasn't capable of what she was looking for. Love came with pain and rejection. The only thing that followed when I allowed myself to care was disappointment and regret. I had enough of that to last me a lifetime.

I thought back to our first time together. It had been brewing below the surface for both of us, and the night Emmy had been kidnapped, Bentley and I'd had a huge argument, which threw me off-balance. I was anxious, drowning in guilt, and seeking something.

What it was, I didn't know until I ran into Cami.

Fueled by anger and a need to escape, I went upstairs, taking the steps two at a time, and there she was, as if she had been waiting for me to show up. She was upset and emotional, and I knew what I needed. What we both needed. Before she could blink, I had her against the wall, kissing her like a drowning man, desperate for air, and she was right there with me. Somehow, I knew she was what I needed to get through that moment. She would be the one thing that would calm me. I needed to lose myself with her. Only Cami.

Minutes later, we were naked and in her bed.

She was everything I had imagined and more. Her skin was like silk, stretched smooth over her bones, and it glowed ivory in the dim light. I sat back on my heels, staring down at her perfection. Her breasts were full, the nipples taut and ready for my mouth. Her waist was narrow, and her hips fit in my hands as if made for me. Her wavy hair spread out over the pillow, ink spilling on white paper, the pink highlights bright in the dark. Her green eyes were hooded, radiating back at me the want and need I felt. There was no shyness; in fact, she lifted her arms over her head, her legs falling open, showing me her soft, pink center.

"You're so fucking beautiful," I whispered against her breasts, capturing a hardened nipple in my mouth and swirling my tongue around it. She whimpered, arching her back to get closer to my mouth.

We spent long minutes exploring each other. Her hands felt like heaven on my overheated skin as she touched me. I had never known lips as soft as hers as she traced the ink on my arm, nor had I ever wanted anyone as much, as she explored my torso. Her mouth was wicked and hot when she wrapped her lips around my shaft and tongued the head of my cock. I hissed with pleasure, sliding deep into her mouth, until it became too much and I pulled back, wanting to finish inside her.

"My turn." I grinned.

The small group of freckles that always teased me at the base of her neck was thoroughly licked. I pulled her hand to my mouth, kissed her wrist and made my way up her arm, slow and teasing, tasting and nibbling as I went before I bit down on the curve of her neck. We kissed for endless moments, frantic and wild, then slow and gentle, until she was pleading with me for more. I eased her onto her stomach, gliding my hand down her spine, tracing the delicate ridges and curves, following my fingers with my mouth. I cupped and stroked her luscious ass, biting the right cheek, then sliding my fingers between her legs, groaning at how ready she was for me.

"Like this, baby? You want me like this?" I demanded, pumping into her with my fingers. "You want my cock?"

"Yes."

I reached for my pants and grabbed the condom from my wallet. In one smooth move, I was buried so deep inside her, I moaned. I wrapped my hands around her waist, lifting her up onto my thighs. I grabbed her chin, turning her face, and kissed her as I began to move, holding her flush to my body. She grabbed my hair and tugged as we fucked. It was intense and profound. Hard and fast. Exactly what we both needed. She tightened around me, her breathing rapid, her low moans telling me she was close. Our kisses became frantic, our movements hurried. She came, her pussy milking my cock like a fist, and she gasped my name. I exploded inside her, groaning and cursing until we were both spent.

I slid us both down onto the mattress, pulling her close. It should have felt uncomfortable. Normally, when I was with someone, I itched to leave as soon as we were done. But with Cami, I wanted to be close.

"Stay for a while," she whispered. "You need some sleep."

"I have to get back."

She rolled over, facing me. I sighed as she began to stroke my hair, and I leaned into her caress. "Just a little while."

I was exhausted, both physically and emotionally. I gave in and tugged her to my chest, falling asleep until I woke from a gripping nightmare a short time later, trembling violently.

"I'm here," she whispered. "Right here, Aiden." She stroked my hair again. "You're okay. I have you."

It made me feel safer than I had in my entire life.

I shook my head at my thoughts. It was odd how often she skipped through my mind. How the thought of her could bring a smile to my lips when I least expected it. It was useless and crazy to think of her, but at times, I couldn't stop myself.

I grabbed my things. I'd make sure Bentley got home, then head to the loft and prepare myself for the whirlwind that was Emmy and Cami.

Especially Cami.

CHAPTER 3

AIDEN

"NO, EMMY." I repositioned her hands. "Never make a fist with your thumb tucked inside. One good crack and you'll break it." I recurled her fist. "Like this."

"It feels weird."

"So will a cast." I smirked. "Now, try again. Remember what I told you."

She adjusted her stance, shoulders back, head high, ready to strike.

"I'm going to come at you. What are my weak points?"

"Eyes, nose, neck, knees."

"Okay, let's go."

We sparred a little, and I was pleased with her efforts. She was tiny, which was what made Bentley the most anxious about the training, but I could show her how to use that to her advantage. The important thing was to teach her how to defend herself, although I hoped she never had to use those skills. I wasn't sure Bentley would recover if she did.

We went at it for a while, until sweat covered Emmy's forehead and her breathing grew faster. I raised my hand, indicating time was up for now.

"Okay, good job. I want you to practice some more and use the bag a little, while I do this with Cami. Just like I showed you earlier."

"Should I wear gloves?"

"No. I just want you to tap it. Don't hit it hard—you're not strength training or a boxer. Get the feel of using your fists. It can help you learn to feel the power of your hits. But we need to start off slow."

She moved over to the bag, studying it before she started. Bentley, who was working in the corner, doing his best not to distract her, watched her movements but stayed away, letting her concentrate.

I braced myself and waved Cami over. She had been jabbing at the bag while I worked with Emmy, so she was already warmed up and ready. We faced each other, and I struggled to keep my face impassive. She was taller than Emmy, her body curvier. I knew those curves, and the sports bra with a cropped mesh top over it did little to hide her assets. The sliver of skin between the short top and her tight yoga pants begged to be licked. She looked sexy with her hair pulled up, today's streaks multicolored with blue, pink, and purple. They shone under the lights like a rainbow. I never knew what color they'd be when I saw her. It was always a surprise.

"Nice hair," I teased. "Reminds me of Bentley's socks. Jaunty."

Emmy laughed, and Bentley threw out a curse from across the room. Cami shrugged her shoulders, not seeming to be affected by my words.

"I was going for sexy, but I'll take what I can get."

I had to bite my tongue not to tell her, or show her, how sexy she was tonight. I tamped down my feelings and adjusted her stance, patient as I went through the same instructions I had given Emmy. It was obvious Cami had been paying attention, because she needed little help. I ignored the part of me that was disappointed I couldn't keep touching her.

I tested how much she'd been listening. "What are your strongest weapons?"

"The same as your most sensitive. Elbows, knees, and head."

"And?"

"The element of surprise."

"Good. Remember that."

We faced off, and I had to admit, I was impressed. She didn't get in many moves, but she did manage to avoid me getting my hands on her very often. When she appeared winded, I stepped back.

"Okay, now—"

A yelp and crash from behind me made me spin around. Emmy was on the floor, the bag swinging in the air. Bent was on his feet and moving toward her instantly. I joined him, dropping to my knees beside her.

"What happened?"

"I tried to do one of the roundy type kicks. I missed."

"You're not ready for a roundhouse kick, Emmy. Far from it. That's a whole other type of training."

"I saw it on the internet. It looked easy."

I snorted, and Bentley rolled his eyes.

"How many times do I have to tell you to stay off Google?" he demanded.

Emmy chuckled.

"Are you hurt?" Bentley asked, running his hand over her legs.

"I think I twisted my foot a little when I fell."

I picked up her foot and ran my fingers over her ankle, testing it. "It's not broken, but I think it's a mild sprain."

Bentley muttered a curse, and Emmy shook her head. "Relax, Rigid. I've had worse."

"Enough for tonight." He helped her to her feet, frowning when she winced.

"I think we'll take a rain check on the tacos too."

"I wanted tacos," she protested. "It's just a sore foot!"

I spoke up. "Go home, ice your foot and put it up, so it doesn't swell. Take some Tylenol. We'll finish here and pick up a whole bunch of tacos and come to your place. Does that work?"

Emmy's smile was wide. "Perfect. I want some nachos too, Tree Trunk."

I laughed. "Deal."

She gasped when Bentley swung her up into his arms. "Put me down. I can walk!"

"Except you don't have to." He indicated the desk he'd been working at. "Will you bring the laptop when you come?"

"Yep."

"I'll bring your stuff, Emmy," Cami offered. "Let Bentley look after you. We'll be along in a little while."

They left, and I chuckled as I listened to her telling Bentley to put her down or she would use her new skills on him. He ignored her instructions, demanding she stop struggling or he might drop her. When she threatened again, he informed her she had no new skills yet and to be quiet. She was busy telling him off when the elevator doors closed, cutting off their conversation. It entertained me to hear her berate him and his overprotective nature. It was something she brought out in him.

Cami laughed in amusement. "He's gonna listen to it all the way home."

"He's going to tell her no more lessons."

"She'll ignore him."

"I know."

Our eyes met, and I had to look away. Cami had such an intense gaze. It was as if she saw right through me to the person I kept hidden below the surface. The one few people ever saw. I cleared my throat. "Do you want to keep going or call it a night and go get the tacos?"

She shook her head, her ponytail swinging wildly. "No, Bentley will have to fuss for a while. Emmy tells me that's how he handles his worry over her. Let's keep going and give them a little time."

"Okay."

"How about I come after you this time?" Playfully, she put up her fists and bounced on the balls of her feet. "You ready for me to take you down?"

I smirked as she circled me. She looked as if she were getting ready for a WWE fight instead of learning to defend herself against an attack. Still, I couldn't resist the temptation to see what she would try. She stopped moving, challenging me with her look. I, in turn, circled her and bent low to her ear, teasing her. "Bring it on, baby."

She spun, stepped back, and searched for an opening, constantly on the move. She was graceful, her muscles tensing as she danced, her movements sensuous and fluid. I tried to ignore the way my body reacted to her. Her shirt was damp and clung to her breasts, her nipples straining under the material. My erection kicked behind my sweats, and my desire began to overtake my good sense. She wasn't a threat to me physically, but she was dangerous in other ways. Teasingly, I jabbed my fist toward her. "Come on, tough girl. Show me what you got."

I had to swallow when she tugged her shirt over her head and flung it away. Her sports bra was purple and had a zipper down the front. The word "handy" ran through my head. I knew what she was doing, so with a wink, I yanked my damp shirt over my head and sent it flying as well. Two could play at that game.

We circled and sparred, her attempts to land any touches proving fruitless. I smacked her ass a couple of times, which seemed to agitate and spur her on, making me smile.

"Is that all you got, little girl? Not so tough, after all, are you?"

Narrowing her eyes, she lunged, missed, then stumbled, and gasped, bending at the waist. I dropped my arms and leaned over her, concerned. "What? What happened?"

She took me by surprise when she grabbed my wrist, spun me around, and bent it behind my back. "Gotcha!" She laughed.

In a fast move, I pivoted, yanked her back, and pulled her flush to my chest. "Never let your guard down," I hissed in her ear.

She melted against me and slipped her hand between us, palming my growing erection. "No," she whispered. "You never do."

I ignored the double meaning to her words.

I dropped my head to her neck, licking at her exposed skin. She tasted salty and sweet all at once. She moaned low in her throat as I slid my hand over her sports bra and tugged the zipper down, then cupped her breast, teasing the tight nipple.

Using her ponytail, I angled her head to the side, exposing her neck more. I nipped at the tender flesh. "You've been taunting me this whole time, haven't you? Teasing me with these tits of yours, wanting me to touch them. Touch *you*."

"Yes." She panted, gripping my cock harder, making me groan.

I shouted as she wrapped her foot around my ankle, sending us both to the floor. She scrambled over me, straddling my hips, a mischievous grin on her face.

"I won."

I arched up, pushing my erection into her heat. Her eyes fluttered shut, and I smirked as I flipped her, hovering over her on the mat, our gazes locked in a frenzy of need.

"I think we can call it a draw."

I crashed my mouth to hers, kissing her hard. Our tongues dueled for control as she gripped my shoulders, pulling me closer, her nails a sharp prickle on my skin. I bit her bottom lip in warning, soothing the burn with my tongue. I kissed, licked, and nipped my way down her neck, tonguing her hard nipples, then lifted her hips so I could tear away her yoga pants and sneakers. Using her bare feet, she pushed my sweats out of the way, and my cock sprang free, slapping against my stomach.

"I fucking love it when you're commando," she said, wrapping her hand around me, stroking her thumb over the sensitive crown. I shuddered at the pleasure of her touch.

"Just like I loved the zipper on your bra, baby. Convenient," I retorted, sinking two fingers into her. "*Jesus*, you're so wet."

She arched into me, breathing out my name. I pressed my thumb to her clit, teasing the nub, and tried not to come at the sight of her under me. Her skin glowed, her hair had come loose, a bright explosion of colors around her face. Her green eyes burned with the intensity of her need and her chest moved rapidly as she gasped for air. She kept working me, stroking and twisting her hand around the head of my cock, making me shiver.

I wanted inside her. Now.

As if she knew, she wrapped her legs around me. "Take me."

I dragged my cock through her wetness, the feel of her all-consuming.

"Condom," I managed to get out through gritted teeth.

Where the fuck were my condoms?

She cupped my face. "I haven't been with anyone else, Aiden. There wasn't anyone before you for over a year. I'm safe." She swallowed. "I'm on birth control."

I froze, looking down at her. I had never had sex without protection. *Did I want this?*

I hadn't been with anyone either. But her trust in me was overwhelming.

"I'm safe too," I assured her. "There's been only you for a long time."

"I want you so much. Please."

I moved again, nudging at her entrance.

Jesus, the heat of her.

Had I ever wanted anyone as much as I wanted her in this moment?

She arched, and I slid forward a little more.

The answer was no. I never had. I wanted this with her. Only her.

I slammed into her body, making us both shout.

Nothing prepared me for it. The heat and sensation of her—the way she gripped me. She matched my thrusts, clinging to me tightly. I pushed and pulled. She gave and took. Our bodies moved in long, rolling waves, the pleasure so great my eyes stung.

I kissed her, drowning in the sensations. Never wanting it to end. She stiffened, crying out my name, and all too soon, I followed her, ecstasy snapping at my spine. I came hard, thrusting relentlessly, her name falling from my lips until I collapsed on top of her.

Until we were nothing except a mass of entwined arms and legs, our bodies pressed so tight to each other, I couldn't tell where she ended and I began.

For a few, unthinking moments, I was good with that. Then, as usual, reality—and my doubts—crept in, and I knew I had to move.

It was harder to separate myself from her this time. Somehow, I got to my feet and offered her my hand. "You grab a shower while I order tacos."

"You could join me."

"I think we've joined enough tonight, Cami."

I ignored the flash of hurt in her eyes and bent over to grab her clothes. "I assume you have something to change into in your bag."

"Yes."

I picked up her bra and swung it on my finger, trying to tease her. "Maybe something a little less provocative next time so we don't end up in this predicament again."

She grabbed the bra from my hand. "God forbid."

I stopped her from walking away. "Hey."

"What?" she snapped.

"I'm sorry, okay? I just . . ." I huffed out a breath. "I find this part hard. I don't know what to say or do."

She shook her head, her expression softening. "How many times do I have to tell you I don't expect anything? You made yourself very clear when we started."

"Yet, I always feel awkward."

"Just what a girl wants to hear after mind-blowing sex."

My lips quirked. "Mind-blowing?"

"Well, it was. You're kinda being a mood-killer here."

I held up my hands. "Sorry." I flicked my finger to my head with a wink. "I feel the same. Mind—officially blown."

She walked toward the bathroom, glancing over her shoulder. "You should join me in the shower. Maybe your mind won't be the only thing blown tonight."

I gaped at her. I heard the shower come on and made a decision.

Or, at least, my cock made it for me.

I hurried to join her in the shower. Tacos could wait another few minutes.

CHAPTER 4

CAMI

OUR SHOWER TOOK longer than planned, and Aiden hadn't ordered the tacos, deciding we would just wait for them since they were always fast. He was quiet on the drive to the restaurant. I didn't try to push him, even though I wanted him to talk to me. He kept everything to himself. His thoughts and feelings were so deeply concealed that unless a person bothered to look into his eyes and see the hidden pain, they accepted the outward package. Strong, cocky, and playful. He was all that, but inside, there was more. He had a damaged soul, and as much as I wanted to help him, he had to want that from me.

I wasn't sure he ever would.

We pulled into the parking lot as my phone buzzed. I looked at the message with a frown.

"Bentley says Emmy fell asleep, and he's asking for a rain check on tacos. Maddox already told him that he and Dee weren't coming since she's still at work." I sighed. "She's always at work these days, it seems."

"Something big happening?"

"It's a case she's researching for a new lawyer with the firm. I don't know all the details, but it involves a huge property and estate dispute out west. She'll be going for the court case too."

"Huh. So she isn't home much?"

"No. I feel as if I hardly see her anymore." I didn't bother adding I thought Maddox saw more of her than I did since I knew Aiden wouldn't talk about his friend or his private life. I tamped down my disappointment, knowing my time with Aiden was over. I reached for my seat belt, pausing. "If it isn't a problem, could you drop me home or at the closest subway stop?"

"What are you talking about?"

I indicated the rain that was falling steadily. "I don't feel like walking too far to catch a ride home. My coat isn't waterproof."

"You're not hungry?"

"Yeah, I am. I just assumed . . ." I let the words trail off, unable to state I knew he wouldn't want to have dinner with me alone. It would be like a date, and we weren't dating. He'd made that very clear.

"You assumed wrong. It's *tacos*, Cami. We can grab some food and eat, then I'll drive you home." He shook his head in disgust. "As if I would drop you off at the subway, whether it's raining or not. I'm not *that* much of an asshole." He got out of the car and ducked his head down into the doorway. "You coming?"

I could only nod.

Inside, we grabbed a table, and Aiden didn't even open his menu. He ordered nachos and more tacos than I thought we could eat, then added two house special margaritas. I lifted my eyebrows in surprise.

"Those things are lethal."

"Just one." He grinned. "I have some work to do when I get home."

"It'll be late. Can't it wait until tomorrow? Is Bentley that much of a slave driver?"

"Why would you think it's Bentley? Maybe I'm not good at my job."

"Don't be ridiculous, Aiden," I scoffed. "I've seen you in action. I've heard Bentley and Maddox talk about you. Emmy thinks you're the cat's meow."

His eyes darkened, and he leaned forward, his voice low. "What about you, Cami? Aside from being an asshole that would fuck you, then drop you off at night in the rain to catch the subway home, what do you think of me?"

I studied him briefly. His dark, curly hair was still damp from the shower. He kept his beard trimmed tight to his skin, but it was thick and soft under my fingers when I touched him. His shoulders were broad as he leaned forward, resting his thick arms on the table. His eyes, as always, captivated me. They were so unique and stunning with one brown and one green iris. They showed his true emotions— but only if I looked beyond the nonchalant façade he presented to the world. They spoke to me now, my incorrect presumption still upsetting him.

"I don't think you're an asshole on any level, Aiden—"

The drinks and nachos arriving interrupted me. We ate and drank in silence, Aiden frowning as his gaze flitted around the restaurant. He looked uncomfortable and on edge. I drew in a long breath.

"I'm sorry I assumed something I shouldn't have earlier. I know you have rules, and I didn't want you to think you *had* to have dinner with me."

His gaze softened as he looked at me, his shoulders loosening. "I'm sorry you felt I would rather eat alone than with you." He shook his head. "I never meant to make you think that way. I just don't want to give you false hope."

"You're not. I'm fine."

"You're a great girl, Cami. I enjoy spending time with you."

I held up my hand, not wanting to hear it again. His idea of time spent together and mine were two different things. "I know. You've said it already. Please just—"

"I wish I could give you more. It's never going to happen, though. It's not how I'm built."

I took a long drink of my margarita, wanting to ask him why. To make him explain what made him feel that way, and to tell him why I saw him differently. However, I knew it was useless, so I changed the subject.

"What is it you have to do tonight? A new deal?"

He waited until our waiter cleared away the empty nacho plates and the massive platter of tacos was placed in front of us. He dug in, eating two tacos before taking a break. He wiped his mouth and sipped his drink.

"Yes. An amazing opportunity fell into our lap earlier. Some prime lakefront. Three parcels, and the owners have a"—he grinned so wide, his eyes crinkled—"*unique* set of demands. Sandy transcribed them into a document, and I have to go through it tonight and be prepared for our meeting tomorrow."

"You can't do it in the morning?"

He ate three more tacos, used his napkin again, and hesitated. He looked wary, then shook his head with a heavy sigh. "I couldn't be ready in time."

"I'm sorry?"

He drained his margarita glass, then reached for the water, downing a large amount. He studied me before he spoke, his voice quiet. "I have dyslexia, Cami. I don't read very fast, and when the document isn't in a certain format, it takes me longer to read and absorb the content. In fact, there are times I *can't* read it because nothing makes sense. It's as if the letters move as I try to read. That happened today. The lists Jed, one of the sellers, wrote out were like a foreign language to me. No matter how hard I tried, I couldn't decipher the words." He looked down, running his finger over the edge of his plate repeatedly. "I felt like shit, as if I were letting Bent and Mad Dog down."

I was shocked at his revelation. He had never once told me anything personal about himself. I thought about the way he always bypassed a menu. How he didn't keep score when we went bowling. The way he used a computer, studying the screen intently, mouthing things silently. It all made sense to me now. I swallowed before I replied. I didn't want him to see how much his words affected me.

"I think you're being too hard on yourself. I doubt they felt that way."

"No, they never do. Bentley was awesome as usual. He said it was chicken scratch to him as well and he would have Sandy decipher it and type it up for me. I'll study it tonight and have it memorized for tomorrow."

"Sandy is good at deciphering chicken scratch?"

"Her father was a doctor, as well as her husband. So is her grandson. She insists she's an ace at it."

"Ah, that makes sense. Reading it after it's typed helps you?"

He ate another taco, finishing off the platter. I still had two left of the four he had pushed on my plate, but I was much more interested in his story than eating.

"It does. There's a font that seems to help me see the words clearer—why, I don't know, but I discovered it in university, thanks to Maddox. He and Bentley knew about my dyslexia and some of my coping mechanisms. He wanted to help and asked me if I was willing to let him try."

"You agreed, I take it."

"I trusted him. He explained how adding a row of numbers is harder if they aren't lined up in a similar fashion, and he wondered if a different font and spacing might help me, given some of my other preferences. It took us a while, but he was right. It's not perfect and I still struggle, but it helps."

"He's a good friend."

"They both are. He and Bentley formatted all my documents during university to help. They went with me to talk to my professors about what I needed. After, Bentley made sure every document in the office used that font and all the documents are formatted the same way. Plans, contracts, emails—everything. He does everything he can to make it easier on me. He even requests paperwork from clients and other people to be sent using that font. If not, Sandy redoes them for me." He was quiet for a moment, then cleared his throat. "I was embarrassed at first, but he has never judged me, not once, and I appreciate his efforts."

I resolved to hug Bentley a little harder the next time I saw him. My already good opinion of him grew immensely.

"You said something about memorizing?"

He raked a hand through his hair. "I have no idea why I'm telling you this."

"Please don't stop."

"When I was younger, I developed some sort of trick, I suppose you could call it, that I use now more than ever. Most of the documents we use have the same wording. I find words that I know and can recognize, and I can figure out the rest of the page. Once I do, it's locked in." He tapped his head. "If there are changes, I can tell by finding my key words. I look for what is new or missing, rather than having to relearn the whole document. Once I read it, I can recall the entire thing. The same with conversations. I concentrate in a different manner from other people, and I can remember details most would forget. Bentley and Maddox know I can do these things, and they rely on me."

"That must feel good."

He lifted his shoulder, self-conscious. "Are you going to eat those last tacos?"

I pushed my plate toward him. "No. They're yours."

"You didn't eat much. Are you sure you're okay?"

"I'm good."

I was fascinated watching him eat. He dove in, chewing fast, yet he wasn't rude or messy. His table manners were impeccable, but he still ate quickly, almost defensively, as if someone were going to take his food away. I had a feeling he ate that way for a reason and I was dying to ask, but I was afraid he would stop talking altogether, so I kept my mouth shut.

"Is it the same for everyone with dyslexia?"

"No. There are many forms, and it affects people differently. My case isn't as bad as some are, and I was able to bluff my way through school for a long time. I still do that when I have to, but I don't like it." He sighed. "I envy people who love to read. It's such a chore for me."

"Do you listen to audiobooks?"

"Yes. I enjoy hearing someone read out loud. It's also a learning tool for me when I can follow along with the book."

I made a mental note of that, then pressed on.

"So you'll read the lists when you get home?"

"Yes. I want to be prepared for tomorrow. Bentley doesn't want to wait on this and take a chance someone else will get wind of the land going up for sale."

"It's that great an opportunity?"

"The property is awesome." He pulled out his phone and swiped the screen. "Look at those views."

I went through the photos. "Those are breathtaking."

"Makes me want to buy the land myself and build a place." He chuckled.

The image of him on a porch, a beer in hand, as he stared out over the water came into my head. The fact that I was beside him resting my head on his shoulder and enjoying the view brought me up short. Neither was going to happen. I had to stop fooling myself.

Forcing a grin, I handed back his phone. "Are you sure I can be trusted with this information? Maybe I'll run and scoop you. Break in to my piggy bank for the down payment."

He laughed, his head thrown back and his shoulders shaking. "I think you're a safe bet." His face became serious. "If I didn't trust you I wouldn't have told you about my dyslexia, Cami. It's rare I talk about it to anyone."

I met his gaze. It was honest and open, although still wary. As if he were worried I would judge him.

"I think you've overcome something in an amazing fashion, Aiden. You've taken a challenge and learned to use it to your advantage.

That's to be praised, not hidden."

"It's personal."

"It must have been difficult growing up. Was your family helpful?"

His face changed to a blank expression. His gaze dropped and his body stiffened. He spoke one word, the tone of his voice cold and distant. "No."

He stood. "I'll pay the bill. It's time to go."

He strode away without another word or glance, leaving me in shock.

I guessed our conversation was over.

I WAS TIRED and sore the next morning. It was still raining, the dreary clouds matching my somber mood.

Aiden had been quiet and tense as he drove me home, although he'd walked me to my door and made sure I got inside.

I turned to him before opening the door, laying my hand on his arm.

"Aiden, I'm sorry if I overstepped. I didn't mean to upset you."

He looked at my hand, then shook his head. "I just . . . I don't talk about it, okay?"

"Okay."

He surprised me by pressing a kiss to my forehead, then turning and walking to his car.

He had never done that before tonight.

I had barely slept all night, tossing and turning. Dee was up and out of the apartment early, and I spent some time researching dyslexia. I had no idea how many people it touched, the varying degrees of severity, and how it affected everyone in such a different manner. My admiration for Aiden only grew with the way he handled it and himself. The main thing that bothered me was how ashamed he felt, as if he believed that somehow it was his fault.

Once at school, I yanked open my locker door, pulling out notebooks and sketchpads, grumbling to myself. I had hoped my umbrella was there. I'd searched everywhere at home and texted Emmy to see if I had left it at her place, but she said no. Dee didn't have it, so I hoped it was in my locker. I loved that umbrella. I had bought it at a one-of-a-kind craft fair, and I adored the brilliant pattern of irises, my favorite flower, that exploded when I opened it. It was double-sided, so I saw the flowers inside as well. It felt as if I were walking in a garden as it poured all around me. I racked my brain, the sinking feeling I had of leaving it on a bus or subway by accident settling into my chest. I wiped a hand on my shirt, feeling the damp of my skin. The rain wasn't letting up anytime soon. Luckily, Emmy and Bent had picked me up not long after I'd left the apartment, saving me from being completely drenched. I sighed, realizing I would have to buy another umbrella, although it wouldn't help today. I'd get a cheap one in Chinatown on the weekend.

"Hey, Cami!"

I turned, fixing a smile on my face at one of my fellow students. "Hi, Louisa."

"Miserable day out, eh?"

I pushed the damp hair away from my forehead, remembering the feel of Aiden's lips as they brushed along my skin. I hoped he was all right this morning. I wished I could check on him, but I knew he would either ignore me or get annoyed by my concern and be brusque if he responded.

Louisa was staring me expectantly.

"Oh yeah, ugly day."

"You should have an umbrella."

I wanted to snort at her words, but I only shrugged. I had learned Louisa didn't have much of a sense of humor. We were in a class project group together, and I'd discovered she had a habit of pouting when she didn't get her way and was often passive-aggressive. She barely spoke during discussions, but then she would email everyone with long, detailed explanations of why she didn't like something we had discussed or planned. I assumed she was shy and felt more comfortable addressing her thoughts via email, but it got a little annoying.

Still, she seemed like a kind, somewhat lonely person, and I did my best to be friendly, although she didn't make it easy at times. She sought me out, no matter how often I tried to dissuade her without being rude.

"I guess I lost it."

She dug into her bag and handed me a small umbrella. "Use this one."

"What about you?"

"I have another one."

"Thank you," I said sincerely. "I appreciate it." I turned, sliding the umbrella into my locker for later. My keys fell out of my locker, and before I could move, Louisa bent over and picked them up. My keychain glittered in the light, the leather and crystals spelling out my name.

"That's pretty."

I smiled in acknowledgment. "Emmy made it for me."

Her smile fell, and she shoved the keys into my hand, tugging her book bag higher on her shoulder.

"She's like your best friend or something?"

"She *is* my best friend."

"Oh." She scowled, glancing down.

Perplexed, I went back to digging in my locker, looking for a set of pencils I wanted. I shoved things around, finally locating them. I shut the door and turned to see Louisa staring at me hopefully. Obviously, she was waiting for an answer to something, and I had missed her question.

"I'm sorry, what did you say?"

"I asked if you would have coffee with me tomorrow?"

"I'm swamped," I stated, stalling. I didn't want to have coffee with Louisa. We didn't have enough in common to be friends the way I thought she wanted to be.

"You kind of owe me," she replied, her voice terse. She cleared her throat. "I mean, it's just coffee, right?"

"I owe you?"

"You said you'd come to my birthday party, and you never showed. You said you'd make it up to me."

I passed a weary hand over my face. Her birthday party had been when Emmy was kidnapped. I'd forgotten about everything else during that time and the few days that had followed it, except what was happening with Emmy. I never told anyone what had occurred, and Emmy never discussed it. People thought we'd both been ill with the flu. It was too private to discuss with casual acquaintances.

"Sure," I agreed, wanting to get it over with since I knew she would keep asking. "Coffee tomorrow."

"Okay, I'll text you tonight and confirm!" She spun on her heel and hurried away.

I shut my locker, muttering to myself as I hurried to class.

"Yep. Great."

CHAPTER 5

AIDEN

BENTLEY ARRIVED AT the office, striding in dressed in one of his dark suits. His tie today was gray, and I was certain his socks were the same black they usually were. No happy Emmy socks today.

I had come in hours earlier, busy at my desk working through the documents. After dropping Cami at home, I couldn't concentrate and instead tried to sleep, which was an epic failure. The nightmares had been stronger than ever, and I was more exhausted than I could remember feeling in my entire life.

Bent had refused to let me come get him with Frank, insisting it was unnecessary, and I was too tired to argue with him. He sat down in front of me, frowning.

"You look like I feel."

"Awesome, you mean?"

"Like shit."

I waved my hand. "How's Emmy's ankle?"

He rolled his eyes at my deflection.

"A little tender, but fine."

"Good. We'll try again next week. Maybe you can convince her to stop self-teaching shit off the internet."

He shrugged. "I highly doubt it, but I'll try." He narrowed his eyes. "We picked Cami up a couple of blocks from her place this morning. She looked remarkably similar to how you look today. Is that a coincidence?"

Cami looked tired? I felt a spark of concern in my chest at his words. *Was she unwell? Had I upset her last night, and she couldn't sleep?*

I cleared my throat. "I have no idea. We had some tacos, and I drove her home."

"You had dinner together?"

"We had *tacos*. Just a couple of friends having tacos on a Tuesday. No big deal. We were already there when you texted. It seemed stupid not to eat."

Before Bentley could respond, Reid sauntered in, a huge grin on his face. He flung himself in the chair beside Bentley. "Hey, morning."

Bentley eyed him with disdain. "Don't I pay you enough for you to come into the office not looking like an unmade bed?"

I snickered. Reid was a good-looking kid, but he didn't seem to care about his appearance. He was tall and lanky, almost as if he hadn't grown into his body, his thick, dark hair too long and in constant disarray. He brushed it off his face, a constant habit I was sure he was unaware he had. He wore thick, black glasses, which highlighted his hazel eyes and heavy brows. His normal state of dress included torn jeans and a vintage rock band T-shirt, a total deviation from the normal dress code of the office, but for Reid, Bentley allowed it. Today, though, his hair was wilder than normal, there was stubble on his chin, and his clothes looked as though he had slept in them. He was a mess, but his expression was filled with excitement.

"I didn't come into work, Bent. I never left. I was up all night talking to one of the guys over at Unwired about the cool stuff we're working on for the condo towers. This is gonna be epic shit, man.

These places are gonna be sick with the things they can do once we're done. Security, music, lighting, even which shower heads you want to use, everything at the touch of a button. No wires, no shit to deal with. We started talking about a new idea, and I had to start writing the code for the programs." He shook his head. "Epic shit."

Bentley and I shared an amused glance.

Reid was an untapped genius I had been lucky enough to stumble across. Because of his criminal record, no one would touch him, but there was something about him that made me want to have him on our side. He had been forthcoming, open, and honest in his initial interview and even more so in his second. He impressed both Maddox and me, even with his oversharing of some personal details, and we had been correct in our instinct he would be a good fit here. We had grown closer, and I knew his entire history now, which only made me more protective of him as I would be with a younger brother. He had proven himself invaluable to us, to Bentley, especially, and he had secured a lifelong contract with our company. Reid, the little shit, took full advantage of it.

"Glad to hear my money is being well spent," Bentley stated dryly.

Reid stood and scratched his stomach, not remotely concerned about Bentley's tone of voice.

"Yep. In fact, I'm gonna go to my office and take a shower in that private bathroom you made sure I had. Damn thing is bigger than my apartment, I swear. I'll even change into clean clothes. I think Sandy brought my laundry back yesterday, so there must be some stuff in the closet."

"Sandy does your laundry?" I sputtered. "That's not her job."

He shrugged. "I didn't ask her to, but she said something about boys being boys and me needing looking after." He grinned. "Who am I to argue with her?"

"Do not take advantage of her kindness," I warned. "Sandy deserves our respect."

He became serious. "Those flowers on her desk are my thanks every week. I bring her coffee, and also upgraded every computer in her house and installed some wicked speakers in her kitchen. For an old broad she has awesome taste in music."

Then he turned and left, waving over his shoulder.

I looked at Bentley. "The kid has no boundaries."

He smirked. "The *kid* is twenty-five. Same age as Cami. Do you think of her as a kid?"

I shook my head. "She's way ahead of him. I guess he's still growing up. I wonder if his time in jail figures into that."

"I think women are always ahead of us, maturity wise. As for the jail time, I imagine it does. It must affect a person in some profound way." He paused. "You were right, though. He's a great hire. Despite his casualness, he's a good addition." He tapped his fingers on the arm of the chair. "The two of you are similar in some ways."

"Yeah, we are."

"You like him."

"I do. He's had it rough, and I understand that."

"A common bond."

"Yes."

"I think he's here for the long haul."

"He is. Did you know about the laundry?"

"Yes. Sandy told me he was helpless, and she is very fond of him. She says he reminds her of us at that age, except he's worse. I think she likes to mother him a little since he is on his own. She uses the machines downstairs and leaves the clothes in his closet once a week. She thinks she gets the better deal. Apparently, the speakers rock the *old broad's* world."

I started to laugh. The kid had no filter.

"What would we do without her?"

"No idea."

Maddox walked in, laptop in hand.

"Do without whom?"

"Sandy."

He sat, crossing his legs. "I don't even want to think about that happening."

"Neither does Reid."

He grinned. "Our resident troublemaker. I saw some of the code he was writing earlier. He explained the concept. The kid is brilliant. Fucking brilliant." He chuckled. "Even if he looks like a monkey's ass most of the time. He'll grow into himself. We all did."

He was right; we did. Each in our own way.

Bentley rapped on the desk. "Okay. Enough of boy wonder. Back to the business at hand."

I flipped open the folder. "Everything looks good. Did you get my email, Maddox?"

"I did. At four in the morning," he added. "Ever heard of sleep?"

"I was in bed early," I lied. "I woke up and sent this out. Do you have numbers?"

He rolled his eyes, opening his laptop. "We can afford to buy all three pieces of property. Even if we carry them for a few years, we're fine. We'll make money, no matter what we decide to do. We barely have to dip into our holdings for it, actually—which is good, considering the money we're soaking into Ridge Towers."

"Are we over on the project?"

"Nothing out of hand. I always pad the numbers, expecting some unforeseen issues."

Bentley looked over the documents I handed him. "Should we offer this as an investment-potential project?"

"I know a few people who would jump at the chance," Maddox stated. "Some calls and I could secure financing so none of our money is tied up."

"No," I exclaimed. "I want this to be ours. In fact . . ." I drew in a sharp breath. "I want to buy one of the pieces myself."

"What are you talking about?" Maddox demanded.

"I've been thinking about it all night. I liked it there. I'd like to keep a small piece and build something for myself."

Bentley closed the file and set it on the desk. He crossed his leg, swinging his foot as he stared at me. I prepared myself for his refusal.

Instead, he shocked me.

"I said the same thing to Emmy last night. What piece were you interested in buying?"

Maddox gaped at us. "What the effing hell?"

I ignored him. "Mrs. C's property. It's the smallest and it's all I'd need."

"I was thinking about Mr. Wilcox's place."

"So, what, leave the middle piece—the most valuable—and do what with it?" Maddox interrupted, his voice hard. "Leave it to rot so you two have some sort of weekend getaway? BAM isn't going to invest in worthless land."

Bentley frowned. "Relax, Maddox. I still plan to develop it. A small, exclusive resort or maybe some high-end rental cottages."

"We could fit in six, plus a main building," I said matter-of-factly.

"We can double or triple that with the other properties," Maddox snapped. "It's crazy to use that for personal shit. Find another piece of property if you have to, and leave this one like we discussed."

Bentley's voice was deceptively soft. "Let me remind you, I have the final say on what BAM does or does not do, Maddox. We went in thinking we were only going to buy the one piece. If I decide to purchase one piece and Aiden the other, then nothing is lost here. Our original idea is intact—or BAM could buy it all and lease the parcels to Aiden and me. There are lots of ways we could work this concept."

Maddox didn't back down. "What if I want a piece? Did you ever think of that?"

"Is that what's upsetting you? Then we can buy it all, rezone, and rethink. Build to a smaller scale. BAM will own what we don't want personally." Bentley met my confused gaze.

The outburst was out of character for Maddox. "I suppose I didn't think you were interested in a cottage by the water, given how much you love urban living," Bentley said.

Maddox stood, snapping his laptop shut. "It wasn't something I thought you'd be interested in either, so I guess we're both surprised."

"Is that what you want?"

"It's not the point. I don't like being out of the loop on plans."

I spoke up, hating the tension that had descended on the room. "There are no plans, Mad Dog. We're discussing an idea. There was something about that view yesterday. It made me question if it was something I would like for the future, and the more I thought about it, the more I realized I did want it. If it's an issue, I'll find somewhere else. I'm not sure I'm even ready for a cottage or what I'd do with one, to be honest. It's just . . ."

Bentley finished my thought. "That view. The peacefulness of the place."

"Yeah."

Maddox shook his head, his annoyance obvious. "You two let me know when you decide. We can take it on fully or the one piece only. Either way, we're good."

Bentley stood as well. "Where are you going?"

"Back to my office."

"We're not finished here."

"I am. You two let me know what you want." He strode out, shutting the door behind him with a firm thud.

Bentley sat down heavily. "What was that all about?"

"I have no idea. I've never seen or heard him so defensive." I snorted. "Maybe over me teasing him about what he's wearing, but not over a piece of property."

"I should go talk to him."

"No. Leave him. He'll come to us when he's ready."

"What do we do in the meantime?"

"Make an offer, but for all three parcels now. We can decide later on what to do with them." I chuckled. "He can upsell to me if that's what he wants. Make us a profit."

"We're solid. I saw our month-end numbers. We made a record profit last year, and we're on track to beat it this year, even with the expenditures for Ridge Towers."

"I know. It's not money worrying him."

"What is it, then?"

I shrugged. That was the mystery. One we would have to figure out.

⌒

I ENTERED BENTLEY'S office, my arms full of blueprints. He was on the phone but waved me in. He scowled into the receiver.

"Really? Are you sure that's what you want, Emmy? You know we could go—"

Emmy had obviously cut him off. Resting his head on his hand, he listened to whatever she was saying then nodded.

"Okay, baby. I'll pick you up in forty-five minutes."

She responded, and her words made him smile.

"I love you too."

He hung up, tossed his phone on the desk with a groan, and leaned his head back.

"Problem?"

"Emmy wants to go out for dinner."

"You love taking her out."

He cracked one eye open. "To Swiss Chalet."

I tried not to laugh. Swiss Chalet was one of my favorites too, but it didn't rank up there for Bentley.

"I could afford to fly her to Paris, have dinner, and be back in time for school tomorrow, and she wants Swiss Chalet." He paused, rubbing his temple. "Plus, she has a coupon that expires today. She insists we use it."

"Nothing wrong with a coupon."

"That's what she says. 'Just because you have a lot of money, Bentley, doesn't mean you should waste it,'" he quoted. "As if a dollar fifty is going to break me."

I sat down, unable to stop my laughter. "She keeps you on your toes."

"That she does. Constantly challenging me. Speaking of

which . . ." He indicated the door with a tilt of his head. "Has Maddox been out of his office all day?"

"Nope."

"What should we do? Send Sandy in to talk to him? He always listens to her."

Sandy walked in, carrying a six-pack of Guinness and a pizza box. "Do not even try, young man. I brought this for you, Aiden. You, Bentley, have a date with your girl, and Aiden, you are marching yourself into that office and talking to Maddox. How the two of you haven't figured this out yet is a mystery. For such smart men, you are exceedingly obtuse." She placed the pizza and beer on the desk. "Frank is waiting for you, Bentley." She pointed at me. "You have a job to do. Now fix this, Aiden."

After glaring at us, she marched out.

Bent and I exchanged glances. He stood, adjusting his sleeves. "We have our instructions. Although I think I'd take Maddox over Swiss Chalet."

"Not a chance."

He picked up his phone, tucking it into his pocket. "Once you figure this out, let me know what's going on."

I picked up the beer and pizza, with no clue as to what I needed to do. "Okay."

We separated in the hallway. Outside Maddox's door, I paused. I couldn't remember the last time it was shut, and I wasn't sure if I should knock or just go in. The problem was solved when the door swung open and Maddox froze, clearly surprised to see me. He had on his coat, messenger bag in hand, and he was obviously planning to leave.

"Hey."

"What's up?" he asked.

"I was hungry. Thought I'd share."

"I was heading home."

I held up the beer. "I have Guinness."

He pursed his lips. "Sandy sent you, didn't she?"

"What makes you say that?"

"She always orders from DelVecchio's. When you get pizza, it's from Santora's."

"I have beer," I repeated.

"Fine." He huffed. "I skipped lunch, so I'm hungry. Is Bent joining us?"

"No. Emmy had a coupon for Swiss Chalet. It expires today, and she told him they had to use it. He was *thrilled*."

He blinked, then started to laugh. "That girl is fucking priceless." He shrugged off his coat. "Give me a beer."

WE DEVOURED THE pizza in silence. It wasn't until we sat back and opened a second beer that I spoke. I kept it simple, because that was how we did things.

"What the fuck was that earlier?"

He reclined back, sipping his beer. "Anyone ever tell you you're like a bulldozer? No tact."

"I don't need tact. I need an answer. What's going on? Neither Bent nor I understand." I leaned forward. "We want to understand, so talk to me."

"Can we chalk it up to a bad day and leave it at that?"

"No. We're not leaving here until you talk." I took a long drink, then set down the bottle. "It's a piece of property I want to buy. It's not the first and won't be the last. Bentley bought his property from the company. You bought one of our condos. Why is this different?"

He sighed and scrubbed his face. "It's not, not really. It just hit me."

"What did?"

"What it represents." He stood and paced the room. "Fuck, Aiden. So many things have changed in the past few months. Six months ago, we were focused entirely on the business. All of us. It's all we had. It was ours. Now Bentley spends most of his free time with Emmy, you're looking at a piece of property miles outside the city—where the fuck does that leave me?"

"What are you talking about?"

He sat down, grabbed his beer, and took a long pull. "Bentley's building a life with Emmy. It's great and how it should be. I'm happy for him. You're gonna build some cottage and be gone on weekends, and in the summer, probably some nights. Less time here. Once Bentley builds a place, you two will be there, and I'll be here. We hardly see each other anymore outside the office now. It'll be even less then." He laughed without humor. "Wow, saying it out loud, I sound like a whiny little bitch."

He was correct. Our lives had changed, and we didn't see each other as much. Bent was busy, and I seemed to spend most of my time alone. Still, his confession surprised me. "You think we're leaving you behind or something?"

He drained his beer. "I suppose. It's stupid, but I feel left out."

"Buy a piece and join us, then."

He shook his head. "Bentley was right. I'm not a cottage guy. I'd buy another condo at Ridge Towers before a cottage."

"Then you can visit whenever you want. Mad Dog, we're family. Whether I live one mile or twenty miles away, nothing changes. I don't plan to live there full time. I just want a place to go to sometimes, somewhere open and peaceful. I remember the odd time my parents would take us to the lake. I loved going—the sounds, the smell of the water, the feel of the sand under my feet. The blue sky and the openness. It was one of the rare times I felt happy as a kid. Something felt right when we were there."

I held out my hands, unsure how to explain. "We aren't leaving you out, Mad. We're just adding another place to get together."

His shoulders slouched. "I know. I fucking know that, but for some reason, it upset me. I can't explain it." He leaned back, rubbing his temple. "But I get it. You should have a place you love. Bentley deserves it as well. I'm sorry for my outburst. I'll call Bent later and apologize."

"We don't need an apology. We need to know you're okay. Is there, ah, anything you want to talk about?"

He snorted. "You want me to kick off my shoes, lie back on the sofa, and spill my guts?"

"I'd rather you didn't. Your socks freak me out a little."

We laughed, and I spoke seriously. "Really, do you need to talk?"

"About?"

I bit the bullet. "Is there something going on between you and Dee?"

"What makes you ask that?"

"Curious. The two of you seem pretty tight when we're all together. It made me wonder."

"Wonder? How? What are you wondering?"

I relaxed back, draping my arm over the edge of the chair. "That's a lot of deflection for a simple question."

"Let me ask you something, then. What's the deal with you and Cami? You spend a lot of time together."

"We're friends," I replied promptly. "I'm helping her learn self-defense with Emmy because Bent asked me to do a favor for him."

"And that's all?"

I shot him a look. "That's all it will ever be."

He met my gaze. "Yes. That is *all* it will ever be."

"So you and Dee are just friends?"

A look of sadness and longing passed over his face, then he cleared his throat. "Yes. She's helped me with some legal stuff, and I gave her some accounting advice. We enjoy each other's company on occasion. We're just like you and Cami. Friends."

Our gazes locked. We were both lying, and neither of us would give an inch.

"Okay, then. Nothing else you want to talk about?"

"No, *nothing*." He was silent for several seconds, then sighed. "I can't, Aiden. I just can't."

His quiet words said it all. Neither of us could say it out loud.

I cleared my throat. "Okay. But we're good?"

He nodded, looking grateful I didn't push it. "Yeah. Honestly, I was just in a bad mood, and it caught me off guard. All the changes and unexpected things happening lately. Deals, moves, new people." He paused and shrugged, appearing sheepish. "You know I need time to adjust."

I knew that about him. Maddox needed order, even more than Bentley did. I glanced around his office. Everything was in its place. There were no papers scattered about, no unwashed mugs, and no files waiting to be put away. The exact opposite of my area.

"Nothing is going to happen right away. We'll proceed however you think is best."

"I drafted up two plans. I think what's best is to have BAM buy the land, and then we decide. You and Bent can buy or lease what you want, and we can develop the rest once a decision has been made."

"Sounds good." I drained my bottle. "You okay now, Mad Dog?"

He glanced over my shoulder. "Yeah. It's all good."

Once again, I knew he was lying.

CHAPTER 6

AIDEN

I WAS UNSETTLED after my conversation with Maddox. He was hiding something—the same way I was. However, I had to respect his right to privacy the way he respected mine. We both had issues we chose to deal with in different ways.

I offered to go to a movie with him, but he'd asked for a rain check and had headed out a while ago, leaving me alone in the office.

I stared out the window at the busy sights of the city. Even at seven in the evening, the streets were crowded, the sidewalks bustling. I was restless and didn't know what to do. I could go home and work out or hit my local bar and have a drink, but neither appealed to me.

I picked up my phone, dialing a number I knew by heart.

Cami's voice was breathless and surprised when she answered.

"Hi."

"Hey, you busy?"

"No."

"Wanna take a ride with me?"

"Yes."

"I'll be there in twenty." I hung up and grabbed my keys, refusing to listen to the voice in my head that told me it was a slippery slope I was standing on.

For tonight, I just wanted the voice to shut the fuck up.

⌢

SHE LOOKED PRETTY when I picked her up. Her dark hair loose and swinging around her shoulders, the highlights still bright with their rainbow hues. Dressed in leggings and a hoodie, without a trace of makeup on, she was casual and effortlessly sexy.

Before I realized what I was doing, I leaned over and pressed a kiss to her forehead.

"Thanks for coming."

She smiled. Cami was one of those people whose happiness poured out of her. Her smile was wide, lighting her face and making her captivating green eyes sparkle. Bentley described it once as beaming. He was right. She was like a sunbeam. My own sunshine.

Reaching over, she squeezed my hand. "Anytime."

Her one word somehow made things right in my world.

We stopped and got coffee, then headed to the highway. She never asked where we were going; she just seemed happy to be going with me. I felt the same way about having her in the car.

"How are your classes going?"

Cami went to the same design school as Emmy, except she was taking fashion design, while Emmy took graphic design. I had seen some of Cami's work, and I knew she was talented and loved the creative process.

"They're good. Finals are soon, and I'm looking forward to the break."

"Are you working all summer at Glad Rags?"

I had first met Cami at the high-end boutique when Bentley had been looking for a birthday gift for Emmy.

"Yes." She sighed.

"You don't like it?"

"It's fine. I make good commission, and my boss is great. It's just a lot of demanding women at times." She proceeded to do a few imitations of a few encounters that occurred at the store, which made me laugh. "But it's not forever. Once I graduate, I hope to get hired on with a clothing company and work my way up."

"Sounds like a plan."

"I don't come in this direction often," she said, changing the subject. "I didn't realize how many wineries there are out this way."

"I know. There's a whole bunch. Lots of great ones."

"I should tell Emmy. We could do a tour or something. That would be fun."

"Bent likes wine. I'll talk to him, and we'll arrange a trip for all of us. Sandy will handle the details. She loves that sort of thing."

She looked over, her expression delighted. "Really?"

"Yeah." I chuckled. "Bentley can spring for the limo to take us."

She giggled and looked away. I glanced down at her hand resting on the seat, the urge to cover it with mine strong. I cleared my throat and focused on the road, gripping the steering wheel a little tighter.

She reached over and turned the satellite radio to a classical station, the lush music filling the cabin of the car.

"I like this car," she mused.

"Me too. It's a Lincoln MKZ. Roomy and quiet." I laughed. "Unlike my motorcycle."

Her eyes widened. "You drive a motorcycle? Aiden, that's dangerous!"

"No, I'm careful. I have it parked at a friend's garage in Grimsby. I hate driving it in Toronto traffic. It's so congested, and there's a ton of assholes on the roads. It takes away all the fun of driving something so powerful. So I leave it there, and I drive it on less traveled roads." I paused. "I love the exhilaration and the power. Have you ever been on one?"

"No."

The thought of her behind me, her arms around my waist, and her breasts pressed to my back filled my head. "I'll take you one day."

"Is it scary?"

"No, I'll make sure you're safe."

She smiled and looked away. "Okay."

"Until then, you can relax in this car. It's very safe."

She trailed her fingers along the luxuriant leather of the upholstery. "Decadent."

"Not as decadent as Bentley's Jaguar."

"I've never been in a Jaguar."

"It's awesome. I tried to convince him to buy a Bentley because I thought that would be funny saying Bentley's Bentley, but he wasn't as amused by it as I was at the time."

She chuckled. "You are a nut."

"He used another word."

"I bet he did." She was quiet, taking a sip of her coffee. "He likes expensive things."

I shrugged. "He's used to them. He came from money. I'm still adjusting."

"Do you ever resent him?"

Her question surprised me. "Resent Bentley? The guy who took a chance and shared a house with me, accepted me the way I was, and did everything he could to make my life easier? Gave me a job I love and made me very rich while doing so? Why would I?"

"He's your boss. Always at the top. Always in control."

I changed lanes, thinking about her question. "BAM is Bentley's. His concept, his passion, his ideas. He offered us equal shares, but we refused."

"Oh?"

"Bentley has what we need as a leader. He's decisive. Clearheaded. Fair. Yeah, he's the majority shareholder, but with that comes a tremendous amount of responsibility and stress. Neither Maddox nor I was interested in that sort of pressure. We both love what we do, but Bentley is the heart and soul of the company. Mad Dog and I talked about it, and we gave him a counter offer. I own twenty-five percent, Maddox owns twenty-four. Neither of us can outvote Bent, and that's how we wanted it. To show him how much we trust him. He trusted us enough to know if we accepted his offer, we could outvote him, if we ever chose to do so. I think, once he thought about it more, he realized our idea was the right way to go."

"Wow."

"I trust Bentley completely. With business decisions, with everything. The three of us have a weird relationship that works. My job description for a VP is the oddest ever written, I think."

"Yes, I don't know many VPs who do security detail as well."

I shrugged. "It's what we both wanted. Like I said, weird, but we just mesh." I chuckled.

"Do you ever disagree?"

I thought about this morning and grimaced. "Rarely."

"What? Your face looked funny."

I pulled into the driveway at Mrs. C's and parked the car. I winked at Cami. "My face always looks funny, Sunshine. In answer to your question, no, I don't resent Bent. I admire him, respect the hell out of him, and I love him like a brother. I'm happy to follow his lead because he never makes me feel as if I'm anything but equal in his decisions."

Then I was curious. "Do you resent Emmy?"

I wasn't sure which shocked her more—my question or my sudden nickname for her. She blinked, then spoke. "What?"

I shrugged. "Her life has changed drastically since she met Bentley. She's living in a great place, and she'll never worry about money again."

She frowned. "First off, she'd live with Bentley over Al's or anywhere else. She loves him, not his money. And second, she deserves the happiness."

"You don't see her as often. Do you resent that?"

"No. I miss her, but I understand. People's lives change. We're still close, and that won't change. We'll figure it all out."

"You approve of Bentley, then."

"He's amazing. The whole package. Sweet and sexy, strong and caring. He's so good to her—how can I not approve?"

A strange feeling rippled through my chest. For the first time ever, I *was* jealous of Bentley. But not for his money. It was because Cami held him in such high esteem.

"I see. Sounds as if you're a big fan."

"I am. Because he's made my best friend happy. He's not my type, though." She peeked across the seat at me with a wink.

"Oh?" I asked, meeting her gaze, needing to hear what she had to say.

"No. I like muscles and tattoos. Beautiful eyes. And men who pick me up and drive me to the lake." She slid out of the car. "Especially when they have funny faces."

I was laughing as I pushed open my door.

I suddenly felt ten feet tall.

Bentley who?

"THIS IS BEAUTIFUL," Cami declared and turned to look at me, delighted. "No wonder you want to keep this place!"

I grinned at her enthusiasm and squeezed her fingers. Somehow, our hands had become clasped together as we walked around and I showed her the property. Mrs. C. wasn't home, but she had given me permission to come out and look around. She had told me to feel free to sit on the porch and that she had left me something on the table. First, I was pointing out all the things I loved about the place to Cami, who listened, enraptured. Like me, she couldn't tear her gaze away from the vast expanse of water or the way the sun looked reflected on the surface of the lake.

"Can you imagine what this looks like during a storm?" she asked. "I bet it's mesmerizing with the water kicking up on the sand and the sky looming over it."

"I know."

"And those apple trees. I bet they would make awesome jelly and pies."

"There are peach trees on the property Bent likes over there. Jed says he has strawberry and raspberry bushes. They share all the fruit between the three neighbors."

"That's awesome."

"They all bought at the same time years ago. Raised their families here, lost their spouses. None of them wants to stay on without the others."

"Wow." She met my eyes. "Sort of like the three of you."

"Yeah, I suppose."

"You need to buy this place, Aiden. No matter what Maddox thinks. He'll come around."

I had shocked myself and told her what had occurred earlier—both this morning and when I spoke to Maddox. She had listened and offered her opinion on the subject.

"I understand what he's saying. He's worried about losing his family." She sighed. "No one wants to be left behind, Aiden."

Something about her words made my chest ache. She sounded sad.

"Did that happen to you, Sunshine?"

"My dad left us for a new family. He walked away as if we meant nothing. My mom—she never recovered." She glanced away, brushing her cheek. "Dee stepped in and became my world. My rock. She's always been there. My mom died when I was still young, but she had checked out long before that."

"So they both left you."

She inhaled slowly and patted my shoulder, meeting my gaze. The bereft look in her eyes made mine sting. "Yes. I understand how Maddox is feeling. You and Bentley need to make sure he understands. It's important."

"We will." Unable to stop myself, I slid my arms around her, holding her close. She burrowed into my chest, her head under my chin. She was tall for a woman, but at 6'7", I towered over her. It felt right somehow, offering comfort. She had done it for me so often; it was good to return the gesture.

We held each other silently for a minute. Then she pulled back with a smile. She still looked sad, but not as vulnerable as she had appeared. I hated seeing her that way—she was always strong.

"Why did you start calling me Sunshine?"

"It suits you. When you smile, you beam. Like a ray of sunshine."

She held out her hand, giving me one of her beams. "Show me more."

Grasping it, I grinned. "My pleasure."

I showed her everything. Jed was home and told us to feel free to look around, and Mr. Wilcox was fine with us walking the property too. "Your Mr. Ridge said you were coming with an offer tomorrow. I have a feeling it won't be ours much longer."

I grinned and clapped his shoulder. He offered coffee, but I politely declined, making Cami giggle when I described the thick sludge he considered drinkable.

"We'll be awake for days," I assured her.

When we got back to Mrs. C's porch, there was a plate waiting, piled high with oatmeal raisin cookies under the plastic wrap. "Now, *these* I can recommend."

She bit into one with a hum. "Delicious."

We sat, enjoying the view and watching the sun disappear. The light faded, the view of the horizon diminishing, yet it was still beautiful. The warm air was calming, the water lapping against the shore and the breeze swirling around us the only sounds. After finishing the cookies, we strolled to the car. We glanced out over the water, hardly able to see where it started and the night sky began. The twinkling light of the stars was the only difference.

"Thank you for bringing me here."

I was shocked by how much I had enjoyed the evening. Part of me had thought I would get her there and fuck her on the beach or in the back seat of my car to ease the stress. But I was strangely content with her quiet company. Her mere presence smoothed the rough edges that kept me tense all day. It was an unusual feeling for me. However, I was sincere when I replied.

"Thank you for coming."

Our eyes locked in the dimness. Her green irises were bright and open. Without a thought, I pulled her into my arms and kissed her. Her mouth was soft underneath mine. She tasted like cinnamon and sweetness. Like Cami.

Like home, a voice whispered.

I pulled her closer, intensifying the kiss. She wound her arms around my neck, teasing my hair, and sighing into my mouth. There was no groping or rushing. Only sensation.

The coolness of the night air. The feel of her curves molded to my body. The silkiness of her hair fisted in my hand.

The total, complete *rightness* of the moment.

Until she spoke, her quiet words like a shotgun blast in my head. The same words used before that were nothing but a lie that almost destroyed me.

"I care about you, Aiden. I care about you so much."

⌒

CAMI

I OPENED ANOTHER drawer, searching in vain for my scarf. It wasn't here. It wasn't anywhere. I racked my brain, trying to remember when I had worn it last. I hurried down the hall, knocking on Dee's door.

"Come in," she called.

I poked my head inside. She was pulling on a blazer, appearing put-together and professional as she always did when heading into the office.

"Hey, you didn't by chance borrow my scarf? The yellow one with the irises on it?"

She smiled indulgently. "No, I didn't. Can't find it?"

I opened the door wider and leaned on the frame. "No. I'm having a streak of bad luck. First my favorite umbrella, now my scarf."

"Bad luck comes in threes. Watch out. Goodness knows what you'll lose next."

She snapped her fingers. "You had it on last week when your project group was here."

"Right. Maybe it slipped between the cushions on the sofa." I ran to the living room, checking the sofa and chair, searching under the cushions and on the floor.

Dee came in, laying her briefcase on the table. "No luck?"

"No."

"Maybe you wore it one day to school, and it's in your locker?"

"It wasn't there when I looked for my umbrella."

She poured us each a cup of coffee and sat down across from me. She patted my hand. "I'm sure you'll find it."

She studied me over the rim of her cup. "What's wrong, baby sister? You look exhausted. I heard you pacing in the night."

"I couldn't sleep. Big project on my mind. I worked on it for a while." Not wanting her to continue, I changed the subject. "How's your research?"

"Oh, what a mess. This clan has more issues than the royal family. They're fighting over everything in the will, including property. The whole thing is quite the situation. It's not simply land out west. They have some all over the country, and it's like a free-for-all with disputes." She shook her head. "I should never have recommended Bill Winston to Bentley. Since Bentley hired him away from the firm, I've lost the lawyer with the most knowledge about property law and land disputes. I find his replacement . . . lacking."

I smiled. Bentley had decided to hire a permanent in-house lawyer and asked Dee for a recommendation. Once he and Aiden had interviewed Bill, an offer came fast, and Bill was happily ensconced in his new office at BAM. He was everything they needed: trustworthy, dependable, and loyal. After what happened with Greg, they were taking no chances. Bill had his own department, and he told Dee he loved his new job. His wife did too, since he was home more with her and the kids.

"I'm sure Bentley would have no objection to you picking Bill's brain for a few hours. He kinda owes you."

She laughed. "I am going to call him today. No one knows property law like Bill. He'll help me sort through some of the details so I know what to do next and craft my recommendations."

"When do you expect it to wrap up?"

"I have no idea. I'm away for several days next week to do some more research in Calgary. I'm hoping soon, though."

"I miss having you around."

She stood and kissed my head. "Me too, kiddo. But it will be over soon, and maybe we can do a trip or something. The three of us girls. A weekend away, maybe? Somewhere fun?"

"I'd like that. Emmy would too, I'm sure."

"Okay, you talk to her about it, and we'll plan it as soon as this is done. My treat. I'm getting a bonus for this work."

"Thank you."

"No thanks needed. When you're a hotshot clothing designer, you can treat me."

She left with a wave. As soon as the door shut, I slumped in my seat, pulling my phone from my pocket. My last text to Aiden sat unanswered.

> *I don't know what I said to upset you, but I am sorry. Please talk to me.*

After one of the nicest evenings I had ever spent with him, he had kissed me. It wasn't our usual, passion-filled, rip-your-clothes-off-now kind of kiss. It had been filled with something new. A fledgling emotion I thought we both felt had permeated the entire evening. Until I told him how much I cared. He had jerked back as if I had shot him, tense and upset. I'd tried to reach out, but he caught my hand, holding it away from him. The look in his eyes broke my heart. Anguished, he was lost in some memory in his head, no longer with me, but stuck in the past.

Silently, he led me to the car, waiting until I buckled up before shutting the door. He stood by his door briefly, his shoulders slumped, inhaling deeply. Then he slid in, started the car, and drove us back to Toronto. After changing the station, he turned up the music and was utterly silent. I tried to figure out what to say, but every time I looked at his profile, the tense set of his jaw warned me to stay quiet. At my building, he shut off the engine, the silence screaming between us.

"Aiden, I—"

He held up his hand. "Thank you for coming with me tonight. I'll watch you walk in."

"But—"

Once again, he interrupted me. "Good night, Cami." Then he leaned over and pressed a gentle kiss to my head.

It felt like goodbye.

I hesitated, then opened the door. I hunched down and looked at him, my voice filled with regret. "That was one of the nicest evenings I've had in a long time, Aiden. I'm sorry I ruined it."

He shook his head, not meeting my eyes. "You didn't. This is on me." He fell silent.

Defeated, I shut the door and walked up the steps, dragging my feet. The tears in my eyes made finding the keyhole difficult. Finally, the key slid in, and I opened the door, shutting it tight behind me.

His car pulled away, leaving me alone and confused.

I hadn't slept all night, the evening playing on a loop in my head. The way he smiled. How my hand felt wrapped in his. How small and protected I felt when he held me. The emotion in his kiss.

The pain in his eyes. I would never forget the anguish.

I sat, lost in my thoughts, startling when my phone buzzed with a text from Emmy, reminding me about meeting for coffee. Glancing at the clock, I knew I wasn't going to make it. At that point, I'd be lucky to make class on time. I stood, feeling drained, and wished I could just stay home and hide for the day in bed. I didn't have that luxury, though. Returning to my bedroom, I grabbed my purple scarf, wrapped it around my neck, remembering Dee's words.

"Bad luck comes in threes. Watch out. Goodness knows what you'll lose next."

I had a feeling I'd already lost my three.

My umbrella, my scarf, and the biggest loss of all—Aiden.

⌒

"ARE YOU LISTENING to me?"

I glanced up from my cold coffee, shaking my head to clear it. I blinked at Louisa, trying in desperation to pick up the thread of our conversation.

Or lecture was more like it.

She wasn't happy I'd been late. I'd already postponed coffee once, and I knew I couldn't miss another date. She had sulked the entire time at our project group at my place last week until I made a point of asking *her* for coffee this time. Then she settled in and worked, even helping to serve coffee and insisting on staying behind and tidying up. I had to admit, when she wasn't being whiny or stuck-up, she could be pleasant. But that wasn't very often. She liked to complain—the way she was right at that moment.

"I mean, really, why drag me out for coffee if you are going to ignore me? Good friends don't do that."

It was on the tip of my tongue to remind her I hadn't dragged her anywhere and that we were school chums, not good friends. But it seemed unkind. So I patted her hand and smiled apologetically.

"I'm sorry, Louisa. I didn't sleep well last night, and today I lost my favorite scarf, couldn't locate my notes in my locker, missed Emmy this morning, and was late for class. I'm a bit distracted."

"Is Emmy angry with you?"

I shrugged. "Annoyed a little, but she knows I had a bad morning. I just hate letting her down."

"She should be more understanding."

"It was my fault." I defended Emmy. "And she's fine."

Louisa blinked. "Oh. Okay." She blurted out, "You can borrow my notes."

"Really?"

"Sure." She dug into her bag. "I'm like you. I still write them out."

I took her notebook, flipping through it. The book was precise. "Wow, your handwriting is so neat. Mine looks like chicken scratch."

"I rewrite them all. I like them neat."

"Ah, that explains it. I'll copy them and give this back to you." I went to grab my bag and knocked over my cup, spilling coffee everywhere.

I gasped and she shrieked, jumping up to avoid the coffee.

"Oh no, my notes!"

"I'm so sorry." I grabbed some tissues, lifting the notebook, blotting up the liquid. "Look, it's not too bad, just the cover, and the edge of the paper. I'll replace it, okay?"

"Fine," she huffed. "But you should take better care of other people's things."

I scowled. "It was an accident." I offered her the book, not liking her tone. "I'll ask someone else if you prefer."

Her expression changed from sullen and pissed to contrite. "No, it's fine. It's just a book, right? Keep it and use it. I'll start a fresh one since it's ruined." She stood, picking up her knapsack. "I'll get that from you on Monday. You can give me a new one when we have coffee again next week." She hurried away with a fast wave over her shoulder, leaving me confused.

When had I agreed to coffee next week?

I glanced down at the "ruined" notebook. A few splashes of coffee on the cover. I flipped through the pages. None of the notes were affected.

With a sigh, I stood and added it to my bag. Everyone was different. If a new fifty-cent notebook made her happy, I would get her one. I'd also tell her I wasn't having coffee with her next week.

No doubt, she'd be angry with me.

But that wasn't anything new for me lately.

Especially not today.

CHAPTER 7

AIDEN

MADDOX LOOKED PERPLEXED and tapped the pages in front of him. "This is more than we discussed, Bentley."

Bent ran a hand through his hair. "I know. Not a lot, though."

"No, but why, if I may ask?"

He and Bentley had talked and cleared the air. I let them do it in private, knowing Maddox needed that, the same way he had with me. I had no doubt Bentley had been as surprised as I was to find out how Maddox had been feeling. However, he had assured Maddox nothing was further from the truth, and we were not moving away or leaving him out. We spoke afterward, and we all made a commitment to see each other more often—the way we used to. It was only when I thought about it that I realized I had missed the time we used to spend just hanging as friends, watching a movie or game in Bentley's media room, or working out together.

We were looking over the final offers for the lakefront properties.

I had already seen them, so I knew about the figures. I looked forward to Maddox's reaction to the reasoning behind the increased offers.

"I told Emmy about my ideas and the people we met and why they're selling their property." He lifted one shoulder. "She was touched by the stories."

"And?"

He rubbed his face roughly. "She told me this was their life savings and not to underpay them."

"Our offer was fair market value."

"And this isn't much over the value. I—*we*—can afford it. You can charge me the difference if I buy the property."

Maddox looked at the papers, then at me, a smile already tugging on his lips. I needed the amusement today. "So the girl who insists you use a *coupon* at Swiss Chalet had no issue with you losing a few hundred grand to a business deal."

"I'm aware it's unusual."

"Are you aware you are totally pussy-whipped?" Maddox responded dryly.

He started to laugh. I joined in, then after he glared at us, so did Bentley.

"Cut me some slack. I can't say no to that girl," Bentley huffed. "She won't let me spend money on her, so if this makes her happy and she thinks I'm a better person, I don't care."

Maddox wiped his eyes. "Life is so much more interesting now that she's around."

"Amen to that."

I pulled out my phone. "Can I call Jed and tell him we're sending them an offer?"

Maddox shut the file. "Yes. Tell him he'll be pleased."

⌒

"GOOD, EMMY. YOU'VE been practicing."

She nodded enthusiastically, wild tendrils of hair swirling around her face. She was sweating hard, and her cheeks glowed red from exertion. She looked proud of herself.

"I've been using Bentley's gym every day."

I heard him snort in the corner. "Every day," he agreed. "My last Emmy-free zone gone. Boom!" He chuckled.

"I don't use your den."

"Much."

"Well, your sofa is comfortable. It smells like you in there, and I like it."

He stood, shut his laptop, and sauntered over. There was an expression of adoration on his face as he tucked one of her stray curls behind her ear. "I like it when you're in there too."

"I like it when I distract you." She winked.

He leaned down, brushing his lips to hers. "I like that too. That's the best part."

"Okay, enough." I clapped my hands. "I don't need you eye-fucking each other in my place."

"We're not eye-fucking," Bentley retorted.

"Yeah, Tree Trunk. We're planning. There's a difference."

I groaned and laughed, despite my mood. It had been dark for the past few days. Even the news that the sellers had accepted our offers for the lake property hadn't cheered me up.

I wasn't surprised Cami hadn't shown up tonight with Emmy. I hadn't responded to her texts or spoken with her since the night at the lake.

I'd had a bad reaction to her words. They had hit home, reminding me of a painful time in my life. And instead of brushing it off, I had dwelled. I had shut her out and wallowed the past few days. I had to admit, a huge part of me hoped she would be here with Emmy, but another part of me knew she wouldn't show up tonight.

"Aiden?"

I pushed my thoughts away. "Sorry, what did you ask?"

"If you were coming for tacos."

"No, I had my fill last week, and I ate before you came tonight.

The rest of you go without me." I didn't want to go and cause Cami to miss time with Emmy.

"It's only us three. Maddox is at some accounting thing, Dee is away for a few days, and Cami just isn't up to going," Emmy stated. "She's at home, resting."

All my protective instincts kicked in. "Resting? Is she ill?"

She glanced at Bentley, then at me. "You didn't know?"

"Know what? What happened?" I demanded to know.

"Cami was jostled going down the stairs at school yesterday and she fell. She hit her knee and landed on her shoulder. She was pretty shaken up, and she told me she aches all over. That's why she wasn't here tonight. I thought she must have told you since you didn't ask."

"I-I assumed she had another commitment," I sputtered.

Cami was hurt.

"Did she see a doctor?"

"They saw her at the clinic. The X-rays showed nothing was broken. They gave her a prescription for some painkillers and told her to use ice."

"They suggested therapy to help, didn't they? Some massage for the aching muscles?"

"She doesn't have coverage. She was going to look something up on the internet." She grabbed my forearm. "Maybe you could send her some stuff, Aiden. Some exercises to help her? You know about that sort of thing, right?"

"For sure."

I met Bentley's eyes. He tilted his chin down in understanding.

"Okay, Emmy. Let's go. I'm starved."

They took their stuff and left, waving goodbyes. I hurried to my bathroom, grabbed some things I'd need, then went into the kitchen to get my icepacks. I picked up the phone and called my favorite Chinese place and ordered some hot and sour soup. It was Cami's favorite.

Then I ran to the car without a second thought.

She was hurt. She needed me.

⌒

CAMI WAS SHOCKED when she opened her door. I could see the pain etched in the pinched look on her face.

"Aiden?"

"May I come in?"

"Why?" she asked, the one word saturated in a quiet sadness.

"I came to help."

"How did you know?"

"Emmy."

She hesitated, and I waited, expecting a shake of her head and for the door to shut in my face. I was pleased when she stepped back, opening the door wider.

Inside, I unloaded my bags in the kitchen and took her the container of soup. "I want you to eat, then I'll look at your shoulder."

"I don't understand why you . . . why you're here."

I opened the soup and handed it to her with a spoon. I sat across from her with a container for myself. "I took physical therapy as well as business at university. I also have my massage therapy license. I constantly take courses to keep up with changes in treatments. I can help with your pain."

She looked down into her soup. "Oh."

"Cami, look at me."

She glanced up, her gaze conflicted.

"Please let me do this for you."

"Okay." She spoke in a soft voice, dipping her spoon into her soup, wincing as she lifted it to her mouth. I had to stop myself from reaching out and feeding her myself.

"What happened? How did you fall?"

"It was the rush between classes. The stairway was full as usual, and someone knocked the girl behind me. She fell into me but caught herself on the railing. My arms were full, and I went down. It was only a few steps, but I landed on my right shoulder. I was lucky and glad I didn't hurt anyone else."

I didn't care about anyone else, but I didn't tell her. "Emmy says your knee and shoulder hurt?"

"Yes."

"Are you taking the painkillers?"

She shook her head. "They make me sleepy."

"That's part of their job. You need to rest and heal."

She didn't respond.

"Are you in pain?"

She hesitated. "I . . ."

"Sunshine?" I prompted. "Are you in pain?"

"Please don't call me that," she whispered. "I think it means more than it does, and"—she lifted her tear-filled eyes to mine—"it hurts, Aiden."

"I don't mean to hurt you." I dragged a hand through my hair. "I'm sorry. The other night caught me off guard, and I overreacted."

"What did I do?"

"Nothing, Cami. You did nothing. It's me. I told you I don't do relationships. I'm not built that way."

"I think, if you gave yourself a chance, you could. If you talked to me, let me help you . . ."

Her voice trailed off as I shook my head.

"I like you, Cami. I like spending time with you. I like being *with* you. I think you're amazing. But the rest . . . it's not going to happen," I told her, keeping my tone gentle. "I'm being as honest as I can be with you."

She stirred her soup. "So friends with benefits is what you're saying?"

"We can be friends without the benefits part, if that makes it easier on you," I offered, hating myself, knowing how much more she wanted. How much more she deserved. "I like hanging with you. You really are a ray of sunshine in my life."

"I like hanging with you too."

"Eat your soup. Let me look after you tonight. We can talk about it later."

She sighed and picked up her spoon. "Okay."

After we ate, I made sure she took some painkillers. Then she lay on the sofa and let me look at her knee. It was bruised and swollen, and I worked on it for a while, stimulating the blood flow and trying to ease the muscle stiffness. After, I rubbed some anti-inflammatory cream into the skin and wrapped it in an ice bag.

"I want that elevated as much as possible and iced every hour tomorrow for twenty minutes at a time."

I eased her onto a pile of cushions on the floor and sat her between my legs. "Let me see your shoulder."

She tugged her shirt over her head, the movements slow and jerky. The skin was mottled with bruises on the top of her arm, and as I ran my fingers over her skin, I could feel the pull and tightness of her muscles. She shivered at my touch.

"Are you cold?"

"No."

"Try to relax. I won't hurt you. I promise."

I tried not to dwell on the fact that I hurt her constantly in another manner.

She sighed, and her shoulders dropped. I spread some coconut oil on her skin and began to knead her neck. After a few minutes, she began to relax, leaning back into the sofa. I was careful as I worked the trapezius muscles, easing the tension created by the fall. I moved up her neck, my fingers sliding on the slick skin, pushing my thumb into the tight spots at the base. She moaned low, but it wasn't a sound of pain. I felt her tension begin to drain away and her arms relaxed, her hands resting on my feet.

I stopped for a moment and grabbed my phone, hitting a soothing playlist. The quiet notes filled the air, helping her to loosen up even more. I didn't talk; instead, I listened to her breathing. I knew when I found a more tender area by the hitch I could hear on occasion as my hands moved across her back. She would sigh when it felt good, and I made sure to linger longer on those areas.

"So nice," she whispered. "It feels so nice."

"Is the pain going away?"

"Yes."

"Okay, we'll keep going."

"I like the music. It reminds me of when I was little."

I added some more oil to my hands. "Oh?"

"Dee would sing me to sleep some nights. She has a beautiful voice." Cami sighed as I found another sore area, silent until the pain was gone and my touch only conveyed pleasure. "She still does sometimes if I've had a bad day."

"You two are very close."

"It was only her and me, to be honest. Like I told you before, my mom was there in body, but she checked out emotionally after my dad left us. She never got over him walking out. I was nine when it happened. A year later, she got sick with cancer and died." Her voice was so low I had to strain to hear it. "She refused treatment. She had no will to live—not even for Dee and me. She deteriorated fast, and then there was just us."

"And your father?"

"Still didn't want either of us. Dee was my family."

Gently, I tilted up her head, sliding my hands to the base of her throat. A tear caught the light as it slid down her cheek. I spread my fingers wide over her clavicle, easing away the tension there.

"I'm sorry, Cami."

She reached up, patting my hand. "It's okay. Dee has been there for me all my life. She's my rock."

I cradled her head, tilting it to one side then the other, soothing and lessening the pain. Then I began again on her shoulders.

I knew when she fell asleep. Her body slackened, leaning into my leg, her hands lax on my feet. Her breathing was slow and quiet. I kept massaging her neck until I was sure she was in a deep sleep. Using caution, I widened my knees, stood, and maneuvered until I could turn around in front of her to look down at her sleeping form.

Her head rested against the sofa. I could see the bruising on her arm, and I crouched to add some anti-inflammatory cream to help with the swelling around the area. I was careful not to wake her or press too hard. Her torso was bare, her shirt a pile on her lap. Her perfect breasts were on display, yet I felt no lust—nothing but an intense sense, *a need*, to care for her. Gently, I scooped her up, carried her to her room, and placed her on the bed, drawing her covers up to keep her warm.

As I studied her, I noticed there were no colors in her hair. The rich, glossy chestnut color gleamed in the dim light. She must not have been able to add her streaks in with her sore shoulder, and I found, as pretty as her hair was without them, I missed the bright bursts of color.

Her eyes fluttered open, and I stroked her forehead. "Go back to sleep."

"Thank you," she breathed out, her eyes drifting closed.

"I'll be right here."

"M'kay."

"I WON'T BE in tomorrow. Can you manage?"

Bentley paused, his breathing on the line all I could hear. I heard a door shut, and he spoke. "What are you doing, Aiden?"

"She's hurt and alone, Bent. I can't just leave her. Her knee and shoulder need ice every hour. She can't do it."

"Emmy would come spend the day with her."

"It's fine. I have it covered. I checked the schedule. Tomorrow is all day in-house, no meetings, nothing. I'm as close as the phone."

"Why are you so insistent on being there for her? You rush over there when you hear she's hurt, yet you refuse to let her into your life. What's going on with you?"

I had no idea what to tell him.

"Talk to me, Aiden."

I sighed heavily into the phone. "I can't, Bent. I can't explain any of it to you. I just need to be here for her tomorrow. I need you to understand that and give me a break right now."

"Are you leading her on?"

"*No*. I've been honest with her. I just . . ."

He let the silence linger, then asked, "Just what?"

"I don't know," I admitted. "She ties me up in knots. She makes me want things I can't have. To be something I can never be." I eased back onto the cushions and scrubbed my hand across my beard. "But I can't seem to stay away from her, no matter how hard I try."

"Maybe you should stop trying. Why don't you give yourself a break, Aiden? You want this girl? Go for it. Put yourself out there. Forget the shit you think you know, and reach out. I guarantee she will meet you halfway. More, knowing Cami. She'll slam right into you and engulf you."

I shut my eyes, wishing it were that easy. Wishing I were brave enough.

"I won't be in tomorrow, okay?" I repeated.

He sighed. "Yes, that's fine."

"Call me if you need anything."

"Aiden—"

I cut him off. "Night, Bent. Thanks."

I hung up, his words on repeat in my head.

"*Engulf you.*"

That was what I was afraid of.

I STAYED ON the sofa, getting up to check on Cami often. I woke her once to give her more pain pills, rub cream into her injured areas, and wrap ice around her arm and shoulder. She was groggy, incoherent, and cuter than she had ever been with her disjointed mutterings and squeaks of alarm as the ice hit her skin. But the swelling was going down, and I knew the pain pills helped her to sleep. I stayed until she was asleep again and headed back to the living room.

I didn't sleep much, too worried about Cami needing something to get much rest. I was sipping coffee when she got up, stumbling into the kitchen, confused.

She had on a sweatshirt I recognized.

"Nice shirt."

She looked down, and I swore she blushed. Cami never blushed.

"You loaned it to me that night we went for tacos and I got wet."

I remembered. After we ate and ran back to the car, she was soaked. I'd given her the sweatshirt from my gym bag in the back and had forgotten all about it.

She tugged on the sleeves. "I'll wash it and give it back."

I waved my hand. "It's fine. I have plenty of sweatshirts. Keep it."

She poured herself a coffee, still moving stiffly, although not as much as the night prior. She sat beside me, taking a sip.

"Thank you for last night and for staying."

"How are you feeling?"

"A little better."

"Well, we'll keep up with the massage and ice today, and by tomorrow, you'll be much better."

She set down her mug. "You're-you're planning to stay here today? What about work? I have to go to school."

"No. We're both staying here. The leg needs to be up, and you need to let the shoulder rest. I'm working from here. And by that, I mean sitting on your sofa beside you while we watch movies. You can grab notes from someone tomorrow. We're both vegging today."

"But Bentley . . ."

"He'll call me if he needs something. Believe it or not, we can function without each other. All three of us are quite independent when we want to be."

"You don't have to do this for me, Aiden."

"Yeah, I do." I drew in a deep breath. "Even more than that, I want to."

She gazed at me, the sunshine back in her eyes. "Yeah?"

"Yes."

"Okay."

After breakfast, she had a shower, and I rubbed cream into the sore areas, pleased to see the swelling going down.

"No streaks again, Cami?" I asked, looking at her damp hair. "They aren't permanent?"

"No. My hair is too dark, and I would have to bleach it out. I use a colored wax product. I like to change it up."

"I've noticed." I chuckled. "I never know what to expect."

"Do you, ah, like them?"

I had to stop myself from telling her I liked everything about her.

"Yes. They suit you."

"My shoulder hurt too much the last couple of days to add them in."

"It'll get better."

She smiled. "It already has."

"Good. Now, pain pills for you, and we're having a hooky day."

"What does that entail?"

"Movies, popcorn, and lots of naps."

She sighed, sounding content. "Okay."

CHAPTER 8

AIDEN

EVEN THOUGH SHE protested, I made her take more painkillers, and she slept. We watched a movie, and it seemed natural to sit on the sofa with her head on my knee. I massaged her neck and shoulder until she fell asleep, then indulged myself and ran my fingers through her long, thick hair. It was soft on my skin. I answered a few texts from Maddox and Bent, but I had no desire to move, or to find some task to do as I normally would if I were alone. Even when the movie ended, I didn't move.

I was strangely content with her.

With Cami beside me, the silence didn't seem as loud.

Instead, it felt comfortable. There was a sense of peace I'd never associated with quiet before. No voices in my head reminding me what a failure I was. No memories tearing at the edges of my mind, making me anxious.

I stared down at her sleeping form, silently thanking her for her unknown gift. Leaning back, I allowed my eyes to shut and my thoughts to drift, enjoying the unexpected moment.

A while later, Cami stirred. She sat up, grimacing.

"I fell asleep again."

"It's fine. You need to heal."

"This must be boring for you, Aiden. All I do is fall asleep on you."

"No," I answered, running a hand over my head. "I'm finding it quite relaxing, to be honest. It's a pleasant surprise."

"I don't understand."

"Silence was all I had growing up, Cami. Everyone ignored me, for the most part. My bedroom was in the basement away from the rest of my family. I spent most of my time alone." I laughed bitterly. "It's not like today where kids are surrounded by distractions—streaming music, phones, tablets, a TV in their room, video games. I was just alone. Reading wasn't a good option, although I did try. I didn't have much for toys or entertainment. So there was just silence. I grew to hate it. Yet today, with you, I'm enjoying the peaceful time."

"It was the opposite for me," she whispered, shifting closer. "There was never any silence. Before my dad left, all they did was fight. I hated the screaming and yelling. My mom would throw things, and my dad would slam doors. My mom wasn't very stable—mentally. She obsessed over things, especially my dad. When he walked out, she lost it." Cami shut her eyes, shaking her head at the memories. "After he left, she began listening to music at all hours. Loud, angry music. She blared the TV and talked all the time. Yelled at us. Especially me."

"Why you?"

"I wasn't planned. I was a big oops for them. She told me once I was a 'mistake.' She never should have had me, because I ruined her marriage."

"That's a shitty thing to say to a kid."

She slid her hand over to mine, entwining our fingers. "We've both had shitty things said to us, haven't we?"

"Yeah."

"But I had Dee. She tried to comfort me, told me my mom was

sick and didn't mean what she said. Dee didn't know Mom had said it before."

"I'm sorry."

She shrugged, the action causing a grimace of pain to cross her face. "I didn't want Dee to know."

"You know you weren't the cause of their breakup, right?"

"I know. My mom drove him away with her crazy behavior. She refused help, and he couldn't handle it. I never understood why he left us behind, though." She cleared her throat. "I guess we just weren't enough for him. He got a new family."

My heart ached for her. I squeezed her hand. "That's on him, not you. It sounds as if we both got the short end of the stick when it came to parents."

She wiped away a stray tear. "Thank God for Dee. She protected me whenever she could. She would sing me to sleep and make sure I was okay." She bit her lip, looking at me. "You didn't have anyone."

"No."

"Aiden—"

It was too close and too personal. I pulled back my hand and stood. "I'm starving, so I'm going to order pizza. Then more pills for you."

"So I'll sleep and not bother you?" she asked, hurt showing in her eyes.

I traced her cheek, hating the pain I saw, pain I knew I caused from shutting her out yet again. "No, so you can heal. I'm going to do some range of motion exercises with you, then rub you down. Believe me, you'll want both the pills and the sleep." I softened my voice. "I'm not good at this, Cami. I'm not trying to be an asshole. My past . . ." I huffed out a long breath of air. "My past needs to stay in the past."

She hesitated, the sadness remaining in her gaze, but she didn't push. "Okay. The local pizza number is on the fridge. It's down the block. We usually pick it up, but I think they deliver."

"I'll go get it. I could do with some fresh air and exercise."

I had to get away from her. Those green eyes saw too much and made me feel too much. I couldn't allow that to happen.

⌒

CAMI SNORED WHEN she was extremely tired. A strange little snorting sound that I found amusing. She had been quiet during lunch, but I had gotten her to smile with a few Maddox and Bentley stories. Those always made her grin. After eating, some light exercises, and another massage, she had fallen asleep once again. I carried her to her room and placed her on the bed, needing to do a few things for Bentley.

I pulled her door shut and walked to the kitchen to grab a water. I was glad my laptop had been in my trunk, and I'd brought it up with me when I picked up the pizza. I worked for a while, pausing when I heard a quiet knock on the door. It was, in fact, so quiet I wasn't sure it was Cami's door until I heard it again.

I strode to the door, opening it swiftly. A girl stepped back at the suddenness of the movement, her eyes wide and startled.

"Oh, ah, I was looking for Cami." She glanced at the door. "Do I have the wrong apartment?"

"No. She's resting."

"Oh, um . . ." She thrust out a pad of paper. "She wasn't in class this morning. I took notes for her."

"That was nice of you. Did you want to come in? She'll wake up soon, I'm sure."

She nodded a bit wildly, and I opened the door wider. She skirted around me, and I followed her to the living room. She perched on the chair as if ready to bolt at any moment, and I sat across from her. Trying to make her more comfortable, I stretched out my hand. "I'm Aiden."

She looked at my hand, then shook it fast, her skin cold and clammy. "Louisa."

I held up the pad. "This will help her a lot. She was worried about missing class."

She scowled, her fingers flexing. "I always take notes for her. She should have known I would help her out. I *always* do."

She seemed almost defensive, as if Cami had affronted her by being worried.

"She's on some strong pain medication. She might not be thinking straight."

That seemed to mollify her.

She inched closer to the edge of her chair. "I heard she'd been hurt."

"She fell down the stairs. She'll be okay in a couple of days."

I'll make sure of it, I thought grimly.

"It was my fault," she whispered.

My eyebrows shot up in surprise. "Pardon me?"

"She had my notebook, and I needed it back. If I hadn't insisted she meet me to give it back, then she wouldn't have fallen."

"I don't think you can blame yourself for an accident. Cami doesn't hold you responsible."

She frowned, seeming to think it over. Then she blurted, "Are you her boyfriend?"

I inhaled hard at her question. "Ah, no. We're friends. I came over to make sure she was all right."

"Oh. Don't you work?"

I chuckled. She was a strange little thing. Small and pale, she seemed to have unnaturally dark hair for her complexion. She had purple highlights similar to Cami's, but they weren't as attractive somehow. Maybe it was her expression. Dour, as if nothing pleased her. She seemed ill at ease in her own skin. Plus, she was all over the place emotionally.

She had been shy, defensive, regretful, and now curious. All in the span of about five minutes. The words *high maintenance* came to mind.

"I work with Emmy's boyfriend. I assume you know Emmy?"

Her face changed, and she glowered. "Emmy should be here. If she were a *real* friend, she would be. I came all the way here to bring Cami notes!"

I didn't like the distaste I could hear in her tone. "Emmy *is* her friend, and I'm very fond of her. I came to help out, so they don't both miss school."

She let out a strange noise, somewhere between a huff and a curse. I racked my brain, trying to figure out if Cami had ever mentioned her. She didn't seem like the kind of person Cami would be friends with. She was very high-strung.

"What did you say your last name was again?" I asked.

"I didn't."

Before I could say anything else, she jumped up out of her chair. "I have to go." She grabbed the pad of paper from my hand. "I'll keep this in case she can't come tomorrow, and I'll add to it. That's what a real friend does."

Before I could react, she bolted out the door, leaving it open behind her.

I stared after her, confused, and got up to shut the door.

Cami came down the hall, scratching her head and looking sleepy. "Did I hear voices?"

I locked the door. "Yeah, a friend from school came to drop off some notes for you."

"That was nice. Who was it?"

"Louisa?" I asked, watching her face.

"Oh. I'm surprised she came here on her own. She complains about coming for our group because it's a long walk from the bus."

"You're only half a block from the subway."

"She hates the subway. She doesn't like to be underground."

I sat down, observing her closely as she took a seat, slowly, but not as stiff as yesterday.

"You know her well?"

"No. She's a bit . . ."

"Odd?" I finished. "I think I scared her. She bolted out of here like a frightened rabbit."

"Were you being Mr. Security?"

"No." I chuckled. "We were just talking. I did ask her what her last name was, though. She left."

"She doesn't like talking to strangers. I'm shocked she came in once she saw you."

"She didn't stay long, and she stayed as far away as possible. What is her last name, by the way?"

Her brow furrowed. "Um, Ken . . . No, Ker-something." She snapped her fingers. "Kershaw."

"She was high-strung."

Cami yawned. "Relax, Aiden, she always is. But for the most part, she is kind. Where are the notes?"

"Oh, she, ah, took them back to add to them in case you didn't go to school tomorrow."

"I don't have class with her tomorrow." She looked perplexed. "Like I said, odd. I'll get them when I see her in class next time."

"Does she change her highlights like you do as well?"

"She doesn't have highlights."

"She did today. Two thick purple ones."

"Those must stand out in her hair. It's such a pale brown."

"Dark. Her hair was dark. Like yours."

Cami looked shocked. "Wow. That must be new."

"It looked strange on her. Like it didn't fit, somehow."

"I guess it was time for a change. We girls like that, you know. She's unusual, but she's still a girl."

I smiled since I would never understand the way women thought. I hadn't changed the way I looked in years. They seemed to like to reinvent themselves often.

"Are you good friends?"

"No, just schoolmates. I have coffee with her on occasion. She seems lonely, and I hate being mean."

For some reason, I was glad. It didn't surprise me that Cami was kind, but Louisa didn't seem the sort of person I could see her being friends with. Although it was none of my business. The bottom line was it didn't matter what I thought of Louisa. I doubted I would ever see her again.

I changed the subject. "How do you feel?"

"Better."

"Good."

She reached out her hand. "Thank you, Aiden. For everything."

I wrapped mine around her outstretched palm.

"You're welcome."

~

CAMI

AIDEN STAYED AGAIN, after spending the rest of the afternoon and evening. We'd settled on the sofa, watched another movie, and he had rubbed my neck until I fell asleep. I woke a few hours later, thirsty and achy, and I stood carefully so I didn't disturb him. He was asleep on the end of the sofa, his feet kicked up on the coffee table. He looked peaceful, something I was sure was rare for him.

He appeared in the kitchen doorway while I was getting a glass of water, blinking and clearly worried.

"Are you all right?"

"Just a headache."

"You didn't have any pills before you fell asleep." He held out his hand. "I'll get you some, and you can go to bed."

Obediently, I swallowed the pills and lay back down. I fidgeted, trying to get comfortable, and failing.

"What hurts, Sunshine?"

His endearment got me every time. I swallowed, not wanting him to know how it affected me.

"My shoulder. It hurts more than my knee."

"You hit your knee on the stairs. You landed on your shoulder. Full-body impact."

I snorted. "Yes. The weight ratio would be far greater."

He crouched beside the bed. "Don't you start with that bullshit." He ran his hand down my side, resting his palm on my hip. "You're perfect."

I shut my eyes. "Well, there was a lot of perfectness on my shoulder."

To my shock, he snapped off the light, then slid in behind me, caressing my neck and shoulders. "Give the pills a chance to work." His gentle fingers slid along my skin. "Relax, Cami," he crooned. "Just relax." He started a circuit, slow and gentle, pressing and stroking. Never too hard, never too soft. His fingers found the pain, easing away the ache, then moving to the next spot.

I could feel every inch of him behind me, his firm chest close to me, touching my back as he breathed. His legs pressed along my calves, hard muscle to the soft curve of me. His breath was warm on my skin. He gathered my hair away from my neck, kneading at the sore muscles, making me feel better.

"I love your hair."

His voice was low in the dark.

"Oh."

"It's so soft."

I didn't know what to say, so I hummed.

"I hate that you're hurt," he admitted. "I hate that more than anything."

"I'm okay. You've helped me so much." Unable to resist, I reached up and found his hand, threading my fingers with his. "I like having you here."

He stilled, and I was about to release his hand and move away when he did the unexpected. He slid his arm under me, tucking me close to his chest.

"I have to be here, Cami. I need to make sure you're okay," he whispered, so quietly, I knew he didn't want me to hear his confession.

I didn't respond. The moment was too intimate, too overwhelming for us. Something was changing, and I needed to let it take root and grow.

I settled back, the heat of his body helping to dissipate the pain. With a sigh, I fell asleep, wrapped in his arms.

The next day, I only went to school in the afternoon, and I couldn't wait to leave. I wasn't in the right frame of mind to be there; I was still achy and sore, and I couldn't concentrate. I fidgeted at my desk, rotating my neck to stretch it the way Aiden had shown me. I rolled my shoulders and sighed as the action eased the tension I felt. Then I tried again to focus on class. It was a lost cause today.

All I could think about was Aiden and his caring behavior toward me. What it meant—at least, to me.

He checked in with me to see how I was doing during the day and wasn't happy when I told him I was attending my afternoon classes, but I insisted. I should have listened to him.

I was surprised and pleased to find him waiting for me when I left, insisting on driving me home.

"Dee is back tonight?" he asked as he pulled up outside our apartment building.

"Yes."

"Okay, good. You're not alone."

"No."

"All right."

I slid out of the car, unsure what to do or say. He solved my dilemma by joining me on the sidewalk, telling me he would check on me later. He hesitated, then gently pulled me in for a hug and kissed my head.

"Call me if you need me, okay, Sunshine? I'll be right there if you do."

I watched as Aiden got back in the car, wishing I were brave enough to ask him to stay.

I had to remind myself to take baby steps. The ball was in his court.

Watching him drive away was one of the hardest things I had done in a long time.

CHAPTER 9

AIDEN

SATURDAY MORNING, I strolled into the office, feeling at loose ends. I wasn't surprised to see Reid's door open or to hear the constant clicks of his keyboard. I poked my head in, trying not to laugh. He was lying on the floor, a pillow under his head, and his feet propped up on his coffee table. A keyboard rested on his stomach, and a huge monitor on his desk showed some code he was working on. Headphones covered his ears, and his feet moved with a rhythm only he could hear as his fingers flew over the keys. The ground around him was littered with discarded food containers and empty coffee cups.

Maddox would go ballistic if he saw the mess. Everything around him was always in its place. Bentley would have to walk away after telling Reid to clean it up before Sandy saw the chaos. It didn't bother me since I knew he was in his element.

I flicked his light, and he glanced over, pulling off his headphones. "Hey, Aiden. What's up?"

"Just came in to catch up on some things. What are you working on?"

"A program for the condos. It will control all the lighting and plugs. They can do it right from the panel or their phones, if they want to override the main program. Turn on under counter lights in the kitchen or bathrooms, the hall lights, one specific light in the place, all sorts of cool features."

"Awesome."

"Then I'm going to work on the music accessibility feature. Satellite radio in every unit, full access to their own playlists, plus a whole bunch of other features."

"I love it."

He grinned widely. "I think I need to live there. We get, like, a staff discount, right?"

I chuckled. I knew if he asked, Bentley would give him a condo. Bentley would give this kid anything he wanted. After the way he helped find Emmy when she was kidnapped, the sky was the limit.

"I'm sure you'd get some sort of discount if you were serious."

"This place is gonna be epic." He waggled his eyebrows. "I bet some hot cougar would pick me up at the pool and become my love guru. Teach me everything I need to know."

I burst out laughing, remembering his oversharing from his interview. "Okay, kid. Whatever you want. I'll leave that discussion between you and Bent."

"Is it catch-up Saturday with you guys, or what?" he asked, pausing as he pulled on his headphones.

"Why?"

"I saw Bentley earlier, and I swore Maddox looked in, but he was gone so fast I couldn't be sure."

I grinned. If Mad Dog had looked in and saw the shitstorm Reid's office was, he would have hightailed it out of there.

"I guess we're all behind."

"You guys work too hard. You need to live a little."

"Says the one working from the floor and, from the looks of it, who's been doing it all night." I cautioned. "Don't overdo, Reid. We need you around here."

He shook his head, his eyes bright behind his glasses.

"This isn't working, man, this is *fun*." He turned back to his computer.

I walked away, still laughing. We had scored big with him. The kid had suffered enough in his past because of his talent and bad judgment. But he had rebounded, grabbed life and lived it. He was ecstatic with his job and his life—his zest knew no bounds.

I was rather envious of it, if I was being honest.

⌢

BENTLEY WAS AT his desk, concentrating so hard on the screen, he didn't even hear me come in.

"Hey, Bent. What's up?"

He glanced up, startled, and slammed his laptop shut.

"Aiden. Good morning. I wasn't expecting to see you today."

Instantly, I knew something big was happening. Bentley fell back into his formal mode when he stressed over things. I racked my brain, but couldn't think of anything we were working on that would cause him tension. I might need to bring Mad Dog in to help with the situation—whatever it was.

I strolled over and plunked myself into one of his new visitor chairs. I tried to find a comfortable position and failed.

"Have you sat in one of these?"

"Briefly."

"They're uncomfortable as shit, you know that?"

"Yes. People tend to linger, otherwise." He arched his eyebrow at me. "Keeps visitors to a minimum."

I knew he wanted me to leave, and I refused to budge.

"What if it were Emmy visiting?"

He didn't blink. "She could sit on my lap."

I threw back my head in laughter. I loved it when relaxed Bent appeared.

He grinned. "Sandy is sending them back. They are awful. Look great, but terrible to sit on."

"Good." I indicated his laptop. "What are you working on?"

He tensed. "Nothing much."

"Ah."

Internally, I was grinning. *Bullshit.*

"Where's Emmy today?"

"Spending the day with Cami and Dee. She says Cami is feeling better." He paused for effect. "She credits you with that recovery."

I shrugged, though my neck felt warm. "I tried to help. I'm glad it seemed to work. They aren't, ah, doing anything too strenuous, are they?"

He smirked. "Unless you consider the spa day I am treating them to *strenuous*, then no. Emmy's been working hard, and so has Dee. I thought, given the fact that they needed some girl time together, this was a good option."

"Great idea."

He stood. "I need a coffee. The café downstairs is open. Would you like one?"

I pulled my phone from my pocket. "That would be awesome. I'll catch up with emails while you're gone. Grab a few Danish too while you're there. The lemon ones if they have them."

"Anything else?" he asked, the sarcasm thick in his voice.

"No. Unless Emmy sent some scones with you that I can eat while you're gone. I'm starving."

He grumbled as he headed for the door. "Try to survive while I'm gone."

"I think Mad Dog is around. You should grab him a coffee too."

"Only too happy to serve," he called over his shoulder.

As soon as I heard the elevator, I was up. I grabbed his laptop, opening the lid. When the screen came to life, I overrode his password with my security clearance, my eyes widening at the site he had been on before he'd slammed the lid shut when I entered his office.

Bingo.

I reached for my cell phone and texted Mad Dog.

Get your bony ass into Bentley's office. We got a mission, boy.

Seconds later, he hurried in.

"What's up?"

I pointed to the screen.

He leaned down, then whistled. "Oh boy."

"Yep."

"He can't do that *online*."

"He can't do *that* without us." I snorted. "I mean, this is important shit."

"Yep. Wait, where is he?"

"Getting coffee. He was trying to hide it from me."

Maddox sat down, crossing his legs. "Not happening."

I shut the laptop and pushed it back into place. "Nope."

Then we waited to pounce.

⌒

BENTLEY'S FOOTSTEPS FALTERED as he came back into his office. Maddox and I were messing around with our phones, lulling him into a false sense of security.

He slid a tray of coffee onto the desk, along with a box of pastries. Leaning over, I grabbed the box, and snagged a lemon Danish. Maddox handed me a coffee, choosing a cinnamon roll, and we sipped and munched in silence.

Maddox cleared his throat. "What's going on, Bent? Rare to see you in on a Saturday anymore."

"I had a few things to do. Emmy's with the girls." He fixed us with a look over the rim of his cup. "You know—*the* girls."

"I'm aware of the trio, yes," Maddox replied, wiping his mouth.

"I bet you are."

I smirked watching them, until Bentley's eyes landed on me. "Cami probably won't benefit as much at the spa as she did under your personal care, Aiden."

I narrowed my eyes but refused to let him get to me. "Probably not. That's what you do for friends, though. You help them." I arched my eyebrow. "Even if they don't ask for it."

His gaze bounced between Maddox and me, then to his laptop. "Why is my laptop the wrong way around? Dammit, did you open it, Aiden?"

I shrugged. "What would I see if I did?"

"Nothing. I was just browsing."

Maddox rolled his shoulders, leaning back in his seat. "Fuck, these chairs are uncomfortable." He grinned. "Browsing, Bent? Browsing for what, exactly?"

"Do you two fuckers know the words 'violation of privacy'?"

I smirked. "Do you know the words 'head of security'?" I started to laugh. "As if I couldn't find out what you were browsing with a few clicks of my mouse?"

"Leave it."

"No."

Maddox leaned forward, resting his elbows on his thighs. "Really, Bent? Scoping out engagement rings on the internet? Where is your sense of romance? You don't buy a ring like that on the internet."

"I wasn't buying. I was browsing."

"Aha!"

Bentley sat back, running a hand through his hair. "Fine, you got me. Have you seen the jewelry stores? Jesus, they're all over you when you walk in. Let me show you this, can I take that out? I don't even know what fucking size she wears or what kind of ring I want for her!"

"You don't know her ring size?" I asked.

He shook his head. "I tried to sneak the one she wears on her right hand, but she only takes it off when she goes to bed and showers. She would notice." He pulled a piece of paper from his pocket. "I traced the inside, thinking that would help."

I pushed his laptop to Maddox. "Go to jewelryguide.com."

"Okay. Done."

I looked over Maddox's shoulder, tapping the screen. "Print this."

"You're a fucking genius."

"What are you doing?" Bentley asked.

I stood to go and pick up the printed page. "Saving the day. Gimme some scissors."

A few minutes later, after cutting and bending, I looked up. "She takes a four."

"How did you do that?"

"There's a size guide."

"How did you know about that?" Bentley demanded.

"Sandy used it one day to figure out a ring size for her granddaughter. You know me—this stuff sticks."

"Great. One problem solved."

"Bent, you can't choose a ring on the 'net. You need to see what they look like on her hand."

"I want it to be a surprise. I tried hinting and got nowhere. If I let her pick something, she'll be so worried over cost we'll come out with a plain band worth a hundred bucks." He fiddled with his sleeves, the way he did every time he was nervous. "I want to give her something special. Something she'll love. Something that tells the world how loved she is by me."

Maddox and I shared a glance. He spoke quietly.

"You're really doing this, Bent? You haven't lived together very long."

"She's it for me. I'm done. Why should we wait? Because society dictates it? Because people think we're rushing into something? I'm tired of doing what I *should* do. I want to marry her, so I'm fucking *going* to marry her." He thumped on his desk as if to make his point.

Maddox chuckled. "Okay, Bent, just asking."

"I'm just answering. I have never been more certain of anything. I have to figure out how to buy a ring without screwing it up though."

"You do tend to go overboard," I mused.

"I do not."

"Laptop for her birthday right after you met her?" Maddox laughed. "That ring a bell?"

"Whatever. I didn't give it to her right away."

"No, you bought her two outrageously priced shawls and a leather messenger bag instead—and handed her the laptop less than a week later. Such restraint."

"Bite me."

"You first."

I held up my hand. "Knock it off. We need to get back to the issue at hand. I have an idea."

"What?" Bentley asked, suspicious.

"I know a place."

"A place?"

"Yeah. A place. You trust me?"

"Do I have a choice?"

"Not really."

"Then I suppose the answer is yes."

Maddox grinned widely. "Yes! Road trip."

BENTLEY LOOKED AROUND, shaking his head, muttering to himself. "Explain why we are here."

"See all these diamond rings? The loose rocks? They're fake. All the empty settings? You can try them on and see what diamonds look good in them, and then decide on a style and diamond size."

"I don't want to buy some piece of shit ring."

"You don't have to, Bent. You can get ideas, then have it made to your specifications wherever you want. But this is a great place to narrow it down."

"Should I ask how you know all that?"

I snorted. "Bent, do you ever watch TV like a normal person?

I've seen all their commercials. *'Ollies, try before you buy!'* is their slogan. They'll make you a ring right here. Or you can take your idea elsewhere, which is probably the better option." I leaned close. "We'll keep that part to ourselves."

He scoped the room. "All of these men have women with them to try the damn ring on, Aiden. I doubt Emmy's size four will even fit on your baby finger. Any of our baby fingers. How is that gonna help me?"

"First, we'll find some styles you like, then figure that out."

Maddox leaned close. "Holy shit, there are a lot of women trying on rings. Who knew getting engaged was that popular?"

I looked around, noticing a few of the women by themselves eyeing us. Some of their gazes were frank, taking in the three of us standing stock-still and looking like idiots.

"We need to move or we're gonna get picked off," I mumbled. "We're causing a distraction."

"The hormone level in here is through the roof. *Jesus.* Diamonds, gold, and women. It's frightening," Maddox muttered. "Maybe the internet isn't such a bad thing after all."

A shriek behind us made us all jump. One woman had her arms flung around her man's neck, squealing in happiness. Other women were glancing her way, their looks ranging from amused to downright jealous.

"Christ," Bentley mumbled. "It's like feeding time at the zoo. One of them gets the meat, and the others all want it."

Maddox's eyes were wide behind his glasses. "The sound starts a frenzy." He swallowed, looking around frantically. "The chaos is . . . *intense.*"

"Yeah, the atmosphere is *so* romantic. Perfect place for me to pick out a ring for my soulmate. Great call, Aiden," Bentley hissed.

"The commercials made it seem more, ah, restrained and civilized," I admitted.

"What a mastermind this Ollie guy is," Maddox mused as another shriek sounded. "It's marketing genius. Get a few of them in here, let them try on all the rings they want, gape over the big rocks. No self-respecting man is going to let some other chump beat him out ring-wise. He wants his girl happy too. The things sell like hotcakes once it gets going. Brilliant idea."

"Brilliant or not, I don't think I can handle this for very long," Bentley admitted. "It's fucking scary."

I groaned, knowing our time was limited. "Follow me."

We moved through the many display cases. Bentley would pick up the occasional ring, slide it on the tip of his baby finger, then set it down. The choices seemed endless. There were people everywhere, voices talking loudly, and more excited shrieks from women who had picked out a ring. It was overwhelming, and I could sense Bentley's frustration. Finally, I gave in and decided we needed some help. Scanning the crowd, I picked out my target.

"Stay here."

I made my way over to some saleswomen standing in the corner. They all looked at me, commission signs flashing in their eyes, anxious for me to pick them. One woman, though, stood out. Mature, small, and delicate, she would work well. She was dressed more casually than the others were and had a different vibe. She didn't seem to care one way or another if I chose her. I walked straight in her direction, ignoring the rest of them.

She met my gaze calmly. "May I help you?"

"My friend is getting married. We need a ring."

"My sincere congratulations."

"His girl takes a size four."

"That's my ring size."

I fist-punched the air. I knew it.

"I don't think we're going to buy the ring here," I told her, being honest. "If that puts you off helping us, I get it."

"Not at all. I don't work here."

"But you were standing by the salesgirls!"

"You were standing by a case of rings, but it didn't make you one of them, now did it?" she retorted with a twinkle in her eye. She leaned closer. "I work elsewhere. I'm a friend of the owner's. He knows I pop in on occasion to scope out the place, and he's good with it since our clientele is different. He drops by my place on occasion as well. In fact, I was speaking with him when you came in."

"So, you can't help me?"

"On the contrary, I think I can help Mr. Ridge find exactly what he needs. Ollie told me to keep an eye on you."

Instantly, I was on alert. "How do you know his name?"

She laughed quietly. "He's rather well-known. We recognized him right away. All three of you actually—you do tend to stand out." She winked. "I think your secret is safe. The girls here are a bit too young to know who he is. Besides, they're interested in commission, not the men buying the rings."

I studied her face. She gazed back, calm and steady. I made a decision and held out my arm. "Shall we?"

She slid her hand around my bicep and squeezed. "I'm all yours."

DARLENE WAS PERFECT. She listened to Bentley describe Emmy, then she showed him a few settings she thought would be appropriate. When he talked carat size, mentioning six or seven carats, she shook her head. "Larger is not better, Bentley. Quality is of the utmost importance."

"I can do both."

"The way you describe her, your Emmy wouldn't be comfortable with a large ring." She selected a large diamond, inserting it into a setting and sliding it on her finger. "Do you see?"

"It looks like a skating rink on your hand," Maddox observed. "Showy."

"Exactly." She chose another one, smaller but still eye-catching "Now, this. Beautiful. Elegant."

"I like that," Bentley admitted.

"It's a radiant cut. Very special and looks lovely on small hands.

The cut will reflect the brilliance of a perfect diamond. It will set it apart from others, which I believe is what you are looking for. For her hand, three carats would be perfect." She gave him a wink. "The right jeweler can procure the perfect stone for you."

I tapped the glass. "What about that one?"

"Ah." She slid it from the case and onto her hand. "You have a good eye. It's an Asscher cut. Very rare. Another lovely choice, but better suited to a longer finger and a slighter larger hand. This one should be a minimum of three carats to show the artistry of the cuts. Four is ideal in my opinion. Otherwise, it gets a little flashy."

For some reason, I stored that piece of information away.

"I like the other one better," Maddox stated. "What about you, Bent?"

"Yes." He picked up the ring, studying it.

"You could have your designer customize it. Make it perfect for your girl." She tapped the band. "Perhaps some pavé work. The center diamond raised slightly to help set it off, but not too high. Add a unique feature to it," she explained. "Perhaps a perfect sapphire on the underside to reflect the color of your eyes. A private love note from you. I bet she would love that."

"I need to find a designer."

She reached into her pocket and slid a card his way. "You just did."

Bentley gaped at her. "You don't work here?"

"Nope. Your friend commandeered my expertise. Don't worry. Ollie is fine with it."

Maddox started to laugh. Even Bentley grinned. Darlene smiled and pushed her card toward Bentley. "Come and see me if you want. I specialize in high-end diamonds and custom work. I would love to design a ring for your girl. I can tell she's very special. Or if you go elsewhere, make sure you check their credentials well. This is a lifelong investment."

"You have credentials?"

"Yes, I do. The jeweler I work for is very reputable."

"But you come here to . . ." Maddox asked, confused.

"I enjoy coming in here and getting ideas of what women like. I often encourage sales for them." She smirked. "Not everyone can afford the type of ring you are looking to purchase. This is a great spot for the average couple."

"So you just hang around?"

"The atmosphere is . . ." She waved her hand, as if looking for a word.

"Horrendous," Maddox muttered.

She grinned. "I was going to say electrifying." She chuckled. "You made my day, I must say."

Looking at her watch, she grimaced. "I have to get going. You have my card, Bentley, if you are interested." She glanced at the three of us. "Bring your brothers with you if you come see me. They're very funny."

"We're not related," Bentley told her.

"I never said you were. Family isn't always blood, young man." She beamed at us. "I hope to see you again." She slipped into the crowd with a small wave at us over her shoulder.

Maddox picked up her card and whistled. "I know this jeweler. I bought a set of cuff links there last year. Very high-end. I think you might have scored here, Bent. She seems to know her stuff."

Bentley took the card and slid it into his pocket. "I think we're done."

"Yeah?" I asked.

"You can check her credentials, and then I'll go see her."

Maddox sighed in gratitude. "So the frenzy torture is over?"

"Yes, I've had enough, and I think I've found what I'm looking for."

I clapped my hands together. "Sounds good. You guys up for pizza and wings? I'm hungry."

They both laughed and moved away.

I stopped and looked at the ring that had caught my eye.

Why, I wondered, did Cami's long, elegant fingers come to mind?

I found my phone in my hand, about to snap a picture, when I stopped, unsure why I was acting so ridiculous. I slid my phone back into my pocket. Still staring at the ring, I felt a strange yearning in my chest.

"Hey, Aiden, you coming?" Maddox called.

I straightened my shoulders and turned away, hurrying to join them, leaving the ring, and the peculiar thoughts, behind me.

CHAPTER 10

CAMI

AIDEN CHECKED ON me all weekend. He made sure Dee had come home and I wasn't alone. He texted me at random moments, telling me what he was doing or relating some joke. We spoke on the phone, albeit briefly, but I still was able to hear his voice. I even called him to tell him about a funny show on TV Saturday night, and he didn't hang up right away, instead switching it on and laughing while watching it with me for a short time. It was as if we were together in the room, and he seemed to enjoy the time we shared.

He told me he had a great day and spent time with Bentley and Maddox, but other than laughing over something about a men's version of visiting the zoo, he refused to say anything else. He was glad I had taken the day off from my job and asked if I'd enjoyed my spa day. I was honest when I informed him his hands were definitely more soothing. His low laugh gave me goose bumps. I tried not to read too much into things, but he was the one reaching out this time.

He made my weekend brighter with his unexpected actions.

Then this afternoon he texted at lunchtime.

> *Emmy is coming for her lesson. I think we should postpone you joining her until next week. I don't want to push it.*

I replied quickly, feeling disappointed.

> *I feel okay. I could take it easy.*

His response made me smile.

> *No. You need a bit more time. I'll make sure you catch up this weekend. Tonight, we'll have tacos after we're done. Maddox is going to pick up you and Dee and meet us there.*

I wanted to hug myself. He wanted to see me on the weekend, and I would see him tonight. He was making sure I would be there.

I texted back.

> *OK*

"Hi."

I looked up at Louisa, not prepared for the sight, even though Aiden had told me she had dyed her hair. It was dark—even darker than mine was, but the purple highlights were already fading. The color made her look sallow.

"Hey."

She sat down, pulling out a notepad. "I made you notes."

"Aiden told me you dropped by. Thank you."

She sniffed. "You could have called to say so."

I ignored her snide tone. I knew she did it to cover up her insecurities. "I wanted to say thanks in person." I reached into my bag and pulled out three new notebooks, the front covers sprinkled with images of flowers. I had found them on the weekend and thought they were pretty. I slid them across the table.

"I got you these."

She looked shocked, then pulled them toward her. "Why?"

"Because you were nice to me. You even came to see me. I'm sorry I was sleeping."

"It's fine. Aiden and I had a nice chat. He is very friendly."

I frowned, feeling confused. "He thought he made you uncomfortable."

"Just the opposite. He made sure I was relaxed. I told him he should wake you, but he seemed fine to talk and let you sleep. He is such a charmer. Such a way with words. He admired my hair," she added, patting the brown strands.

"You changed it."

"You like it? I was going for a different look."

"Different how?"

She tossed her head. "Just different for me. It was a whim."

"I liked your hair before you changed it." The soft color had suited her. Now it looked harsh and unnatural.

She smirked, her expression almost calculating. "Why? You don't like it because Aiden noticed it? He made a point of trying to get my contact information, you know. I think maybe he wanted my number." She winked at me. "He did say you were just friends."

Suddenly, I was annoyed. I managed to bite my tongue and not inform her that Aiden had thought she was odd. I had no doubt he wanted her last name to run a check on her. Nothing more. What Aiden and I were, or were not, was none of her business. I stood, gathering my things.

"I have class. I'll see you later."

She caught my hand. "Don't be mad. I was just teasing. He was nice, though." She tapped the top of her new notebooks. "Thank you for these. It's the nicest thing anyone has ever done for me."

That caught me by surprise. "They're just notebooks."

She shook her head. "They're much more." She stood and hurried away.

I sat back down, feeling unsettled. Aiden was right.

She was odd.

Then I decided I didn't care about Louisa.

I would see Aiden tonight.

That was all that mattered.

⌒

I DRANK TWO margaritas at dinner. Aiden had ordered a mountain of food, the table almost groaning with the vast variety of dishes. The three men seemed to be sharing private jokes, all of them relaxed. Aiden sat beside me and made sure I had food on my plate, adding extra salsa to the side without my asking. He asked me quietly about my shoulder, and I assured him it was feeling better.

"You're limping a little."

"My knee still aches, but it's getting better."

"Did you use that soft knee brace I left you?"

"Yes. It helps."

His hand found mine under the table and squeezed. "Good."

I didn't know if I imagined how gradually he pulled his hand away, his fingers dragging over my palm as if reluctant to break the connection. He smiled and turned back to Maddox, asking about mismatched socks. Maddox punched him in the arm, and they laughed. Bentley shook his head, whispering something to Emmy, who laughed and kissed his cheek.

After we were done, Maddox stood. "I'm in the mood for bowling."

Bentley groaned. "Seriously?"

Emmy grinned and high-fived Maddox. "Yes!"

Aiden looked my way, a silent question in his raised eyebrow. I felt a quiet thrill at his worry, but I squeezed his knee in agreement. I didn't want the night to end yet.

Aiden stood, flexed his muscles and pointed to Maddox. "You're going down, son."

We arrived at the bowling alley, the smack talk loud and boisterous. Even Dee joined in, making Maddox laugh loudly at her antics. Everyone was relaxed and happy. Emmy and I grabbed a beer for each of us, and the games commenced. Strikes, spares, and gutter balls alike were all greeted with cheers. Emmy and I each had another beer, while the rest of them had water. The games were tied one each when Aiden lined up for his last frame, which would decide who would win or lose the night. I admired his back as he lifted the ball, his biceps flexing, and the muscles across his back tightening. His form was perfect as he stepped forward, the ball racing down the center for a perfect strike. He threw up his hands, spinning on his heels, shouting his victory. His excitement was infectious. So happy.

Plus, I'd had too much to drink.

It happened in an instant. He was celebrating, and without a thought, I was on my feet, rushing toward him. All my common sense disappeared. I wanted to be close to him, drawn in by his effervescent mood. I flung my arms around his neck, yanking his mouth to mine.

For one blissful, perfect moment, he kissed me back. Hard. Then he tensed, grabbing my arms and pushing me back, his hands holding me away from him. Our eyes met—his shocked and angry, mine pleading and apologetic. Behind us, the stunned silence from our friends was loud.

I tried in desperation to play it off. I knew I had crossed the line and broken our silent rule. No PDA—ever.

I held up my arms. "Spoils to the winner!"

He shook his head. I saw him withdraw, the warmth and ease of earlier disappearing.

"Aiden," I whispered. "I'm—"

He brushed past me, pausing only to grab his jacket. He didn't even stop to get his shoes, storming up the stairs. I met Emmy's eyes, and hers filled with sympathy. Maddox and Bentley looked at the floor, their shoulders slouched. Dee held her hands to her chest, her gaze worried.

I hurried past them, rushing after Aiden. He was in the parking lot, leaning on his car, his breathing heavy.

"Why?" I asked. "It was just a kiss. You could have laughed and brushed it off, made light of the whole thing."

He met my gaze, his eyes tormented. "It was more than that, and you know it." He tugged on his hair, the action rough. "We're not together, Cami. We're *not* a couple."

It was my turn to tug on my hair, his words cutting me. "I can't keep up with you, Aiden. You act as though you care. You look after me. You're sweet and funny. Warm. All the texts and calls this weekend? I thought things had changed. At least, a little. Then as soon as I cross some arbitrary line, respond to your actions, you shut me down."

He stepped forward, towering over me. "There is *nothing* to shut down. You knew the rules, and you broke them. It's simple. I helped you because you were hurt, nothing more. The same way I helped Emmy."

"I mean no more to you than Emmy does? You feel nothing more?"

He sucked in a fast breath. "Aside from the physical? No. I told you that already. There isn't anymore, Cami. There never will be."

My heart broke. In that moment in the bowling alley, I had known. I was in love with Aiden Callaghan. Totally, utterly in love. He was everything I wanted in my life. I wanted to witness his joy and help him when the world became too much to handle. I wanted to be his everything because he had become mine.

I stared up into his eyes. They stared back, dispassionate and empty. It hit me like a freight train. It was all me. I had read more into it than there was between us.

I had started it, and now I had to end it.

"I can't do this anymore. I can't play by your rules."

His eye twitched and his jaw clenched, but he only lifted one shoulder, not saying anything.

"I'll act like an adult and make sure our friends aren't caught in the middle. Can you do the same?"

"Yes."

I stepped back, knowing if I didn't leave, I would break. I had lost enough tonight. I wanted to leave with a little pride intact. "Take care of yourself, Aiden."

His voice was tight. "You too, Cami. See you around."

I turned and walked away.

I HEARD OUR apartment door open, and Dee burst into my room. She tossed my shoes and purse on the floor.

"Dammit, Cami! I've been worried sick. You never came back, your phone was in your purse, and I had no idea where you were! We've all been looking for you."

I knew without asking *all* didn't include Aiden.

"Sorry," I whispered. "I couldn't come back into the bowling alley. I just couldn't."

She sat down on the edge of my bed. "Cami-bear," she murmured, using my old childhood name.

I dashed away the tears on my cheeks. "I'm okay. Sorry I worried you."

"Aiden never came back either."

I shrugged, that news hardly a surprise.

"We thought you had gone off together to work this out, but Maddox texted him to say your jacket was with us, and Aiden told him you weren't with him. He said he saw you get in a cab."

"One was outside the bowling alley. I had twenty bucks and my key in my pocket from earlier."

Her phone buzzed, and she tapped at the screen. "Okay, I've let Maddox know. He'll tell Emmy and Bentley."

She stood and crossed to my dresser, pulling out my favorite fuzzy pajamas. "You get into these. I'll be right back."

Too tired to fight, I did as she instructed. When she came back, she was wearing her matching set and carrying two mugs of steaming tea. "Drink."

I sipped the liquid. "Is there liquor in here?"

"A shot of brandy. It will help you sleep."

I tugged at the edges of my blanket. "Not sure I can."

She sipped her tea. "Is it over?" she asked.

I met her gaze. Sympathy, warmth, and understanding met my tormented eyes. "It never began," I whispered.

She covered my hand. "He cares. I know he cares."

"Not enough. He told me that."

"I'm furious with him. Everyone is."

"No," I pleaded. "You can't be. He was honest. He told me there could be nothing but sex between us. I was the one who pushed. I was the one who wanted more." I shut my eyes as the pain hit me again. "I was the one who fell in love."

"Cami!" She gasped. "No, baby sister, no."

I let the tears fall. "Yes. He's been kind, helpful, and caring. We have amazing chemistry together, but that's all it is. He doesn't feel the same, and what I did tonight and his reaction proved it."

"Why did you?" she asked. "Why did you kiss him in front of everyone?"

I shrugged. "I had too much to drink. He was in such a great mood, and I thought something had shifted in our relationship. I didn't think," I admitted. "I reacted. He was so happy, and I wanted to be part of that happiness. I wanted to be close to him."

"Maddox told me he struggles with trust and emotion."

"He hides his pain behind jokes. I thought I had started to see the real Aiden when he looked after me. I thought he had started to really care."

She wiped the tears off my cheek. "Maybe that's what scared him."

"Maybe. But he shut down again, and I can't keep doing this. It breaks my heart, and he isn't going to change. He made that very clear. Whatever he's struggling with is too big for me to fight."

"What are you going to do? He's Bentley's best friend, and Emmy is yours. You're bound to see him."

"I know. I'm going to be the bigger person. I won't make anyone choose. He's really an amazing guy, and I enjoy his company. I'll be friendly and pleasant. I won't get too close."

She brushed my hair back from my face, holding my cheeks in her hand. "I know you, my baby sister. I know how hard you love. How strongly you feel. Can you really do that?"

"I have to. Emmy is my best friend, and I can't lose her."

"I'd like to have a serious conversation with Aiden."

I wrapped my hands around her wrists. "No. You can't be mad at him. You have to promise me you won't treat him any differently. He's damaged, Dee. Something hurt him so much he can't love anyone the way I need him to love me. But I think it hurts him too."

"Not as much as you're hurting. I hate to see you hurt." She sighed. "I was worried this would happen. I knew you were going to fall in love with him."

I smiled through my tears. My sister always knew. She had looked after me for as long as I could remember. She had worried about me, taught me how to be a better person, and always put me first. She was loving and protective. This time, though, she couldn't protect me. I had done this to myself.

"I'll be okay."

"I have to go away next week, and then I'll be gone again for the court dates. I have no idea how long this case might drag on. I don't want to leave you like this, Cami."

"I'll be fine. I'm a big girl." I scrubbed my face, wiping away the tears. "Tomorrow is a new day, right?"

She kissed my forehead, leaned against the headboard, and tugged a pillow on to her lap. She patted her knee, and I laid my head down, sighing as she stroked my hair the way she had done for many years when I needed comfort. When she began to sing, I let go, the tears soaking the pillow. I cried out my sorrow, her gentle voice a balm to my aching heart.

It lulled me into sleep, into dreams filled with warm eyes, and a voice that whispered my name.

Sunshine.

CHAPTER 11

CAMI

FRUSTRATED, I DUMPED out the contents of my drawer, searching for my cuff. I was certain it had been on my dresser, but I couldn't find it anywhere. I had worn it last week when . . .

I sat down heavily, thinking of the last time I saw it. The day at the bowling alley. I had no recollection of taking it off when I got home, but I didn't have many memories of anything after the parking lot and walking away from Aiden.

I must have lost it. I rubbed my weary eyes. I seemed to be losing everything these days. I misplaced notes, lost assignments, and had a difficult time concentrating in class. I looked for items, both at home and school, frustrated by their loss, simply to discover them later that day or the next morning in spots I had sworn I'd checked a dozen times. I had lost my knapsack, only to have Louisa find it in the hall where I had stopped to read something on the bulletin board. I hadn't even noticed I put it down. Twice, I had left my locker open, even though

I swore I had snapped the lock shut. Add in the fact that last night when I got home, after I changed, I had come into the living room and noticed I hadn't shut the front door behind me. It stood ajar, the light from the hallway spilling into the room. If Dee had been there, she would have read me the riot act. She was meticulous about our safety and locking the door.

Now, it seemed, I had lost my cuff. It wasn't expensive, but it meant a lot to me. Emmy had made it for me, the three bands of leather tooled with crystals of my favorite colors, and I wore it often. I would have to tell her it was gone. Tears threatened, and I wiped them away angrily. I rarely cried, yet it happened too often these days, and over the stupidest things.

In the kitchen, I filled my mug, glancing at my phone. It was Tuesday, which meant lessons with Aiden. Emmy was shocked when I told her I planned to go with her. I had told her the same thing I'd told Dee. What happened between Aiden and me was between us, and they weren't allowed to be angry with him or treat him any differently. I refused to drag them into my mess. I texted Aiden and told him I wanted to continue, if he was okay with the idea, and his reply had been short.

No problem.

The truth was, I dreaded going, but I was doing it to prove a point. I liked the way Aiden taught us, and I needed to show I was okay—even if it was a lie.

The heavy skies and rain hitting the windows matched my mood. Dee entered the kitchen, rolling her suitcase behind her.

"Hi, Cami-bear." She smiled. "What were you doing in your room? Digging for buried treasure?"

I poured us each a coffee, shaking my head. "Looking for something."

"What now?"

"My leather wraparound Emmy made me."

"Did you find it?"

"No."

She shook her head. "Huh. You are having a total shit time these days. I hate it."

I lifted my eyebrows in surprise. My sister didn't often swear. With a grin, I patted her hand. "It'll get better." I scowled at her suitcase. "How long will you be gone this time?"

"A couple of weeks, I think. Court dates start next week. Depends on what happens. We're trying hard to get this group to settle out of court. It's going to drag on for ages, otherwise." She huffed. "The only people who will make money will be the lawyers. It's a shame."

"I'll miss you."

"Me too, kiddo."

"What time is your flight?"

"Not until noon. Maddox is going to drive me."

I leaned my arms on the table. "What is going on with you two? And don't tell me 'nothing.'"

She shrugged and sipped her coffee. "We have an understanding."

"Which is?"

She picked a small piece of lint from her blouse. "You know how I feel about romantic love, Cami. I have no room for that in my life, nor am I interested in the chaos it brings. Maddox feels the same. We have a great time together, and neither of us is interested in pursuing anything more."

"So, what, you're together?"

She met my gaze steadily. "No. There is no 'together.'"

"This sounds familiar to me, Dee-Dee."

She grinned at the use of my childhood name for her. "No, there is a big difference, Cami. You believe in love. You want it. In fact, sometimes I think you want it so much, you see it in places where it is not."

"Like Aiden?"

"I think maybe your heart overrode your head on that one, yes."

"You don't want to love someone?"

"I've seen first-hand the devastation caused in the name of love.

Growing up, I witnessed it. Mom was so wrapped up in Dad that when he left, nothing else mattered. She stopped living. I saw it at school with crushes and breakups. I see it daily at the office in the family law department. This case I'm on now, they're destroying each other over money. People who claimed to love each other. It's not for me, no. I will never put my heart out like that." She paused and gave me a pointed look. "Maddox and I understand each other on a different level from most people. We're both fine with the status quo. We like each other, enjoy the time we spend together on occasion, and that is about it."

"And the sex?" I asked boldly.

She didn't flinch. "Amazing. He's a very passionate lover."

"That satisfies you?"

"I know it's hard for you to understand, but yes. We're different, Cami. You feel things with your heart and soul. You dive in with both feet. You're . . . unconditional."

I dropped my eyes to the table, tracing the stained wood. "Do you think I'm like Mom? She was always overboard with everything."

She covered my hand. "No, Cami-bear. You're not. Mom was mentally ill. She couldn't help herself. The manic episodes, the forgetfulness, all of that was because she was unwell. If she took her meds, then she was fine, but the problem was she'd stop taking them." She took a sip of coffee. "I know you were young, but she and Dad fought all the time about her meds. I think it was what eventually drove him away."

I asked a question that had burned inside me for years. "Why didn't he take us with him?"

"I don't know. I think he needed to walk away and leave everything, even us, behind. He sent Mom money, even when he remarried. But he moved away and wanted nothing to do with us. The money stopped a few years after she died. I never found out why, or even bothered to try. I think he decided his obligation was done." She looked sad. "For years, I hated him. Now, I think he was just a man who made a mistake. He protected himself the only way he knew how, and perhaps he wasn't as cold and unfeeling as I thought."

She lifted my chin. "You have a huge heart, Cami, and such capacity for love. But you aren't unstable like Mom. Although I'm different from you, I'm not the unfeeling person Dad was either. Why they didn't love us the way they should have will forever be a mystery, but we've done all right, haven't we? We have each other and a decent life. We're both smart and kind. At least, neither of us is in jail," she added with a wink.

I wanted to tell her my fears—all the odd things happening to me lately, like forgetfulness, misplacing things, not remembering to lock the door. But I couldn't. She was going away for work and already stressed over the task she faced. I'd talk to her when she came home.

I forced a smile. "At least there's that."

She wiped away a tear and stood. "Wow. Intense conversation for this early in the day. I'm going to grab a shower, and I'll tidy the place before I go. It's a bit of a mess. I'll call you tonight, okay?"

I hugged her hard. She smelled like home and love to me.

"I love you, Dee-Dee."

She hugged harder. "Back at you, Cami-bear."

⌒

"YOU NEVER TOLD me that!" Louisa snapped, slamming her book shut.

I shook my head. "I'm sorry?"

"You never told me your hair wasn't permanent. I didn't know you used some sort of product!"

"You never asked."

She tugged on her hair, the purple streaks now a faded shade of mauve. The dark color had begun to fade as well, but I refrained from telling her I preferred it lighter. "That's why it doesn't look like yours!"

"I wasn't aware you were trying to look like me. I thought you did it on a whim, just for a change," I challenged.

She tossed her head, ignoring my words. "What is the product you use?"

"I'll have to look at the name. I order it online."

"Send it to me."

"Please."

"What?"

I drew in a slow breath, trying to find my patience. "If you ask someone for something, be polite and say please."

Instantly, her shoulders slumped. "Sorry. Please send it to me."

Mollified, I agreed.

The snarky, demanding tone returned to her voice. "Today, when you get home."

I rolled my eyes. "When I think about it, I will send it to you."

She grabbed her books with a huff. "I'll do it myself. I can find it fast."

She hurried away, almost mowing Emmy down in her rush.

I leaned my head in my hands, exhausted. Louisa was like a hurricane at times, the way she blew up and stormed off. It was hard to keep up with her emotions.

Emmy sat down. "Someone is in a mood."

I picked up my coffee. "She always is, it seems."

"You okay? You look tired."

"I'm fine. I was up early. Dee leaves today, so we had coffee before I came to school this morning."

"Ah." She opened her sandwich, taking a bite. "Are you sure about tonight?"

"Yes. Aiden is a great teacher."

"It won't be awkward for you?"

"Aiden and I cleared the air," I lied. "We're both good."

She pursed her lips. "Cami—"

I interrupted her. "Leave it, okay, Emmy. I need you to leave it and let me handle it."

She stared at me over her water bottle. "Okay, but I'm here."

I squeezed her hand. "I know."

"At least you found your umbrella. Although maybe you need

your hearing checked."

I scowled. "What?"

"I saw you this morning, walking across the street with your umbrella. I called to you, but you never turned around."

"Um . . . I never found my umbrella, Emmy. Someone else must have found it and is using it." I sighed. "I wish you had seen who it was, so I could ask for it back."

She looked puzzled. "I swore it was you. The coat looked like yours, and they even had on purple wellies, like the ones you wear. The scarf I saw blowing behind them looked like your pretty iris one too."

I paused, confused. "I lost my scarf—I thought I told you. Plus, I couldn't find my wellies this morning. I had to wear old black duck boots until I got to school." I swallowed, suddenly feeling strange. "Are you sure it was my umbrella?"

Emmy's brow furrowed in concentration. "I thought so, but maybe it was only similar. It's just yours was so distinctive with the irises on it. But I could have been mistaken, I guess. I saw the coat and hair, the wellies and scarf that looked like yours, and I thought the umbrella was the same."

"Lots of girls have brown hair and wear those wellies," I stated, needing her to agree with me. The conversation was starting to upset me and made me feel unsettled.

"That's true. They are popular. I've seen lots of girls wear black raincoats with pretty scarves. I was probably mistaken." She winked. "And it makes sense why they didn't respond to your name being called."

Relief filled me. "Yes." I paused, worrying my lip. "Emmy, can I ask you something?"

"Of course. Anything."

"What you do you know about manic-depressive disorder?"

"Nothing, really. Why?"

I traced my finger over the table. "My mom suffered with it."

"I know."

"It often hits women in their twenties." I hesitated, worrying my lip.

"And?"

I rubbed my face. "I seem to be losing things and forgetting things a lot. My mom did that." I met her eyes. "The disease can be genetic."

Her eyes grew round in understanding. "Cami—is that what is bothering you? You think you're like your mom?"

"I'm worried, yes."

"Have you spoken to Dee?"

"A little—she's stressed over this case and leaving. I didn't want to get into it too much with her. She tells me I'm not like my mom. But I can't stop thinking about it."

She leaned forward, rubbing my arm. "I think you've had a lot to handle lately. I know how my kidnapping upset you. You're dealing with school, work, being hurt, and Dee gone so much." She drew in a long breath. "Plus Aiden."

Aiden.

Just hearing his name made my chest ache.

"Everyone goes through bad times, Cami. I think you're overthinking this, and you're making too much about a few lost items. But if you're that worried, then I'll go to the doctor with you and help you make sure everything is okay."

"You would?"

"Of course. You're my best friend." She squeezed my hand. "Anything."

I sighed in relief. "You're probably right. I have a lot on my mind. I'm sure it'll get better. But I may take you up on that offer if it doesn't."

"Okay. You can talk to me too, you know. Even about Aiden. I'm here for you."

I hugged her, glanced at my phone, and stood. "Okay, I have to get going. Meet you at Aiden's later?"

"Okay. What time?"

"I'll be there by eight. I'm going to meet with my group after school, then head over. You can start and I'll catch up later."

"Okay."

⌒

"NO, CAMI, PAY attention. Like this."

Aiden was patient. His movements were slow and deliberate as he showed me the correct stance. He had even touched me, adjusting my arms and shoulders. But his touch had been all wrong, and his voice was cool, as if addressing a stranger.

Everything felt wrong, and I knew I wasn't going to be able to do another lesson.

From the moment I arrived, I had wanted to cry. He wasn't Aiden. He was remote, removed, and only spoke when necessary. His smile was polite, even friendly, but his eyes were blank. He'd totally shut himself off from me. He inquired about my shoulder and knee, nodding when I assured him I was fine.

"Don't strain yourself," he cautioned, turning back to Emmy to finish what I had interrupted when I arrived. It was the only thing he said that indicated he cared about me at all.

I tried not to react. I did as he asked, going through the motions. I asked questions, listened to his instructions, and smiled to try to ease the tension. I cracked a couple of jokes and teased Bentley. Emmy and I sparred, letting Aiden instruct us as we moved and jabbed.

Finally, it was over. I could tell Bentley bought my act. I was sure I had fooled Emmy too. They both looked relieved there had been no emotional outburst or visible tension. Aiden and I acted as though nothing was different.

We were good at keeping our real emotions hidden.

As I was packing up, Bentley spoke.

"Emmy and I will drive you home, Cami. It's late, and I know Dee is away. I don't want you on the subway."

I waited, a small part of me hoping Aiden would find an excuse for me to stay. Or insist on driving me himself. However, he remained silent, his back turned away from me as he picked up the mats we'd been using.

"Thanks, I appreciate that."

"Are you hungry?" Emmy asked. "We could get something to eat on the way home. I mean usually, we . . ." Her voice trailed off and she grimaced, realizing what she was about to say.

Aiden's shoulders stiffened. I waved my hand. "No, I'm good. We ordered pizza earlier while we were working on the project." I hadn't eaten, and Louisa had been a no-show, but it had been a productive session.

"You sure?"

"Yes. I'm not hungry. But if you guys want to stop somewhere, I'm okay with that."

"I think we'll have something at home, right, Emmy?" Bentley spoke, smoothing over the moment. "It's a bit late for fast food."

"Yes, you're right."

We left immediately, me following Bentley and Emmy. I grabbed my bag and knapsack and called thanks to Aiden, hurrying out the door before he finished piling up the mats. I couldn't bear to see his indifference as he said goodbye. In the car, I chatted as if nothing was wrong. Emmy and I made plans for the rest of the week, and I waved to them as I slipped through the main door of the apartment building.

Once in my apartment, I shut the door and let myself go. I slid down the back of the hard door, exhausted, and emotionally drained. It had taken everything in me to appear unaffected tonight. To prove to my friends I was okay and Aiden and I were nothing different from what we had ever been.

Finally, I stood and flicked on the light. The living room was organized, and when I went into the kitchen for a drink of water, I saw Dee had straightened it up as well. I peeked in her room, to see it was neat and tidy, but I was shocked when I walked into my room.

It was spotless. I looked around, flabbergasted. I wasn't sure it had ever been this clean. The bottles on my dresser were lined up with almost military precision, and everything was in its place. Books piled according to size. My jewelry arranged. The clothes I had draped across the back of the chair gone and hung in my closet or put away in drawers.

She'd made up my bed so meticulously, it was like a magazine picture. Pillows plumped, the duvet smooth. I didn't want to mess it up by using it.

I was puzzled, wondering why Dee had spent so much time in my room. We didn't touch each other's bedrooms even when cleaning since that was our personal space. She must have sensed my mood earlier and wanted to do something nice for me. I would have to make sure the rest of the apartment looked as good when she came home.

The only thing out of place was a coffee cup on my nightstand. I picked up it and carried it to the kitchen. As I placed it in the sink, I noticed the lipstick stain on it. It was bright pink, a color I had never seen Dee wear. She usually wore a soft berry color. Obviously, something else new I had missed.

I picked up my coat and opened the closet to hang it up. Right at the front sat my purple wellies. Either I had missed them this morning, or Dee had found them in my room and placed them where I would see them.

Now, if only I could find my umbrella.

With a sigh, I dug out my laptop and sat on the sofa, determined to work for a while then head to bed. I only hoped I could sleep.

IN THE MORNING, I woke, cramped and stiff. I had finally fallen asleep on the sofa about three. Sitting up, I rubbed my eyes, checking the time. It was after eight, so I jumped into the shower and rushed to get ready. It was raining again, and I grabbed the umbrella I had bought to replace mine. It was plain black and matched my mood. On the walk to school, I saw I missed a text from Dee telling me she had arrived, was already overwhelmed with work, and she hoped I was okay. Her last line made me grin.

Hope you liked your surprise! *wink*

I chuckled, knowing she would know how shocked I had been by the clean room. I let her know I was fine, then added:

My room is so clean, I almost didn't recognize it.

A few moments later my phone buzzed, and I saw she had responded.

LOL

I was about to reply when it happened. A car went by, far too fast for this weather and too close to the side of the road, speeding through the puddle and drenching me. I stood stock-still, gasping as the icy water soaked through my clothes. The wind caught my umbrella, tearing it from my hands, and it flew away, over a construction fence, tumbling far out of my reach. I looked down at my clothes. I was soaked through, my phone wet, and with the rain pouring down, I knew I looked like a drowned rat. Thankfully, my wellies kept my feet dry and my knapsack was waterproof. I trudged to school, leaving a trail of water behind me in the hall. At my locker, it took me three tries to open the lock. I had given up on the other one, convinced it was malfunctioning since I often found it open, and bought a new one. I changed the combination and kept forgetting it. Finally, the door swung open, and I heaved a long exhale of air.

"You're dripping."

I turned to Louisa, not in the mood for her this morning. "Thanks for pointing that out. I hadn't noticed."

She glowered at me. "Why didn't you bring an umbrella?"

"I did. It blew away, and a car drove past and splashed me."

"Oh." She scratched her chin. "Want to go for coffee?"

"*No,*" I stated crossly.

"I thought it would warm you up, that's all."

"I don't have time," I snapped, slamming my locker door shut. "Damn it."

"What?"

"I thought I had a pair of sneakers in there. I must have taken them home. I'll have to traipse around in my wellies all day, making squeaky noises on the floor. Just great." I huffed.

"You could borrow mine. You're a seven and a half, right?"

"Um, yes."

"I have a pair of sweat pants in my locker too. Not very fashionable, but at least you'd be warm and dry."

Instantly, I felt bad for snapping at her. Dry pants and sneakers sounded better than rubber boots and damp clothes. "That's nice of you. Thank you." I met her eyes. "I'm sorry. I'm having a bad morning."

She shook her head. "No, I get it. Stay here, and I'll be right back. Class was canceled, so we can do coffee. It'll be great!"

She hurried away, and I looked at my phone. Sure enough, there was a text saying just that. It must have come during my puddle shower. Now, I had no excuse for not having coffee with Louisa.

Except, even though she was being kind, I really didn't want to.

"WE SHOULD HANG out this weekend. Your sister is away for a while, right?"

I was perplexed. "How did you know that?"

"You said something last week."

"Oh. Yeah, she is."

"What about Saturday? We could watch some movies and have dinner?"

"It's inventory time, so I work on Saturday morning. I have plans after, sorry."

"Well, Sunday is good too. I could come spend the day, and we can study and everything."

I passed a hand over my head, too tired to deal with her right now. "Not this weekend, Louisa."

Her expression darkened. "Why not?"

"I have things to do."

"Like what?"

"Stuff. Errands, groceries, some designs I have to work on."

"I'll go with you. It'll be fun."

I drew in a deep breath and counted to ten.

"Louisa, I appreciate the offer, but not this weekend."

Her lips thinned, and her brow furrowed. She curled her fists on the table and glared at me.

"I suppose your plans on Saturday include Emmy."

"Yes."

"Why her? Why not me?"

"Emmy is my best friend," I said, trying to hold in my temper. "I already had plans with her, and I'm not breaking them."

"She wasn't around to help you this morning. I know she gets a ride every day in some fancy car. If she's such a great friend, why doesn't she give you a lift?"

Before I could respond, she kept going.

"She's too busy with her rich boyfriend for you these days. Since Aiden isn't your boyfriend, she's ignoring you now. You need to move on. Find a real friend."

I saw red.

"Emmy *is* a real friend. My *best* friend. You know nothing about her, our relationship, or my relationship with Aiden. For your information, she offers me a ride anytime I want one, but I like to walk. If she knew I needed her this morning, she'd have been there in a second, so don't sit there and judge her based on some silly idea in your head."

"I'm just saying—"

I interrupted her. "I know exactly what you were saying. Stop bad-mouthing Emmy. If you think that it will make you look like a better person in my eyes, you're wrong."

"I'm a much better friend. We have so much more in common than you two do. You and I are so similar, and we've become so close.

You buy me gifts and everything!"

I gaped at her. I was so done with the conversation. I leaned forward, trying to keep my voice level.

"We are schoolmates. That is *it*, Louisa. Not best friends. We're barely even acquaintances. You know nothing about me, and I know nothing about you." I stood. "Frankly, that's exactly how I want it to be. I bought you notebooks to say thanks and replace the one you felt I ruined. That was all it was. Not a gift. I'll wash and return your clothes to you tomorrow."

"Where are you going?" She grabbed my arm. "We're having coffee!"

She looked frantic and angry. I shook off her tight grip. "No, we're done. Leave me alone, Louisa. Just leave me alone."

I turned and hurried away. But something told me I hadn't heard the end of Louisa or the conversation.

CHAPTER 12

CAMI

I MANAGED TO avoid Louisa all day, but our argument kept filtering through my head. Aiden had been correct—she was weird. How could she have come up with the idea we were so close? I had tried to be nice, but aside from school and the project group we were both in, I had nothing to do with her outside of class.

I pulled on my damp jacket and reached for my wellies beside the lockers. They had racks where we could put our boots to dry on rainy and snowy days so our lockers didn't get wet. I slid them on and shut the locker. I was walking across the campus when I saw the colors ahead of me. I stopped, focused on the person moving away, and the item that caught my attention.

My umbrella. There, across the grass common area, was the girl carrying my umbrella. Emmy had been right. Someone had found it and was using it. Like me, she wore a set of purple wellies, and her jacket was dark like mine, which was why Emmy had mistaken her for me the other day.

I rushed across the grass, yelling. "Hey! Miss! You, with the pretty umbrella!"

She ignored me, her footsteps speeding up.

"Wait! I just want to talk to you! Please!"

I raced through a large puddle and stopped in surprise as my feet became wet. Stepping out of the water quickly, I lifted one foot, then the other, unable to stop my gasp of disbelief when I realized both boots had a long tear along the seam. I must have caught them somewhere in my haste.

I looked up to see my umbrella disappearing around the corner. Ignoring the water sloshing in my boots, I chased after the girl. Except, when I rounded the corner, she was gone. There were a few people milling around, most of them sharing an umbrella, but my pretty one was nowhere to be seen. I huffed a sigh, frustrated. Why hadn't she stopped? I only wanted to talk to her. I'd even buy her a new umbrella.

I turned to retrace my steps when a flutter of color caught my eye. I bent down and picked up a sopping piece of material from a puddle alongside the building. Wet and dirty, I still recognized it.

My scarf.

IN MY APARTMENT, I stared at the scarf I had lost, racking my brain, trying to figure out the mystery. The most logical explanation was I had used the scarf and umbrella the same day, lost them together, and the girl had found and kept them. Nothing else made sense.

I examined my boots, surprised to see how exact the tears were in both boots—right along the seam at the bottom. They weren't old enough for the seams to have given out, and I was certain the punctures would be more like jagged tears if that were the case.

What had caused them then?

I rubbed my eyes, weary. What was going on with me? I wished Dee were here to talk to. I knew I could call Emmy and talk it through more, but I didn't want to bother her. My eyes strayed to my phone. I wondered if I called Aiden if he would listen to me—or even pick up the phone if he saw my number. I knew he would help me sort it out. He would talk me through it, his queries intelligent and thoughtful, as he helped me recall when I had last seen my umbrella and scarf. Confirm I had been wearing my cuff last week. He could probably even explain the tears in my boots and the failed lock at school. I'd feel so much better.

But I couldn't pick up the phone. If he didn't answer or refused to help me, I wasn't sure I could handle the rejection.

Instead, I stood and headed to the bathroom. A bubble bath, a glass of wine, and some soft music would help make the awful day better.

It was all I had.

I MADE IT to Friday without running into Louisa. She was at the table when I arrived for our project meeting, but she refused to acknowledge me. I slid a bag her way. "Thank you for loaning these to me."

She picked up the bag and turned her back to me. She didn't speak the entire time and left before I was out of my chair. I knew she wanted more—an apology and an invitation to "hang" together on the weekend, but I offered neither. I refused to be friends with someone who bad-mouthed Emmy.

I was dead tired. I spent the night on the sofa again, and I hadn't slept well at all, constantly woken by my dreams. When I'd arrived home the night before, the door was ajar again, and I couldn't be sure I had locked it behind me when I had left in the morning. My super came in with me and checked out the place, assuring me no one was there. But all night, I thought I heard footsteps and the door opening. I sensed someone there, but when I sat up, I was alone. I was being paranoid over a mistake of forgetting to lock the door. I said nothing to Dee when we texted, not wanting to upset her. This morning, I double-checked the lock and made sure I shut the door tight behind me.

I dragged myself home, grateful to find the door still shut. Inside, I pulled off my coat and dumped my knapsack on the table. I glanced around the kitchen, knowing I should eat something, but my appetite had been off. I hadn't cooked since Dee left, snacking on crackers and peanut butter sandwiches. I hadn't even made coffee.

I pulled open the fridge door, frowning at the container on the shelf. Inside was Dee's homemade mushroom soup. One of my personal favorites. She must have made it for me before she left. A smile tugged on my lips. She'd had a busy morning before she left for Calgary.

Placing some in a bowl, then the microwave, I headed to my room. Closer to the door, I hesitated, confused. The scent of my perfume was heavy in the air. I flicked on the light, glanced around, but there was nothing to see. On my dresser, the bottle stood off to the side, the top off. I picked up the bottle, feeling a prickle down my neck. Had I used it this morning? How much of it had I used if I could still smell it so strongly? I searched the top of the dresser wondering if I had spilled some onto the wood. It was very potent, and I used it sparingly.

Mystified, I turned, my gaze sweeping my room. Nothing was out of place, nothing moved. I yanked open my closet door and pulled on the string to turn on the small bulb. It was empty, except for my clothes. Yet, I shivered. Something felt off.

I forced myself to laugh. I was being silly. I doubted a burglar had come in, used my perfume, and left. I must have dribbled some this morning.

I changed my clothes, went back to the kitchen, and took my soup from the microwave. Deciding I needed to relax, I watched a mindless comedy movie on TV, texted Emmy to confirm tomorrow afternoon after work, and left Dee a voice mail, thanking her for the soup. I tried to make my voice sound as chipper as possible.

"Loved my surprises! You spoil me. I'll talk to you Sunday!"

I fell asleep on the sofa, grateful when I woke early Saturday morning. As I was getting ready for work, my phone buzzed with a text from Emmy.

> *Miserable day. Want to hang here when you get off work? Bentley is gone for the afternoon.*

I smiled and replied.

> *Perfect. I am going in early for inventory so will be off by noon.*

She sent back a smiley face.

Dee had also responded to my text saying she was already exhausted and overworked, but she promised to call the next day.

I treated myself to an Uber after work and headed to Bentley's. Emmy was waiting, and we spent the afternoon just being us. We made cookies in the lavish kitchen, swam in the pool, watched movies in the theater room, and stuffed ourselves with popcorn. I told her about seeing the girl with the umbrella and the fact that she'd been wearing my scarf.

"You must have left them someplace together, and she found them."

"I wish she had stopped. I'm not mad, but I would like it back. I'd buy her another umbrella."

Emmy laughed. "Not as pretty."

"No."

She patted my hand. "We'll go to the craft fair again and get you another one. At least you have your scarf back."

"I tore my wellies, and I need new ones."

"Oh, you too? One of mine ripped right down one seam last week. Bentley thought it was a defect since it was such a perfect tear. He bought me a new pair." She laughed. "With wooly liners to keep my feet as warm as possible."

My chest hurt a little at her words. Bentley loved and cared for her as if she was his entire world. He constantly looked for ways to spoil or cater to her. I was surprised he hadn't bought her four pairs in different colors, the same way he purchased shawls for her. I had to admit, I wanted that—not the presents, but the love. The fierce protectiveness and the adoration in the way he looked at her. I wanted it from one person—the one person who insisted that he was incapable of giving it to me.

I blinked away the sudden moisture in my eyes and forced a smile. "I'll find a new pair."

"We can go shopping next week."

"Sounds good."

I glanced toward the window. "I wonder if it will ever stop raining."

"I know. It's depressing."

I was in full agreement. I was already feeling down, and the weather didn't help.

"Why don't you stay the night and go home tomorrow after brunch?"

"I don't want to intrude."

"You won't be. Bentley loves it when you're here."

"Ah, will anyone else . . ."

She shook her head as my voice trailed off. "No. I wouldn't do that to you." She cocked her head. "You may have fooled Bentley—even Aiden—the other night. But I know how tough that was for you."

"Oh."

"Are you okay, Cami? What can I do?"

"Nothing. I told you I was a big girl. Aiden and I didn't work." I huffed out a sigh. "I wanted more than he did. He laid out the rules, I agreed to them, then I broke them."

She regarded me in silence, then hugged me. "He's a fucking idiot."

"No," I whispered. "He's lost."

"He hurt you."

"I don't think he wanted to."

"I could talk to him," she offered. "Or get Bentley to try . . ."

"No. Leave it. He made his decision, and that is it. I don't want you talking to him, or Bentley risking his friendship." I sighed in exasperation. "I know it's hard, Emmy, but you have to let it go. I have to let it go. Promise me you won't say anything."

"Okay."

"Don't try setting us up or planning things where we have to interact. I know we'll bump into each other at times, and that's fine, but don't push it. Don't talk to him about me. Promise me."

"You're not coming back to his lessons, are you?"

"No."

"You enjoyed them."

"They offer some self-defense classes at the gym. I might sign up for those."

"I'll go with you."

"You'll hurt Aiden's feelings."

She thought it over. "I can do both. I'll see him on Tuesdays and go with you whenever the other classes start."

"Yeah?"

"Yes. You're my best friend."

I hugged her. "Thank you."

I STAYED THE night. When Bentley got home, he was in an odd mood, almost giddy. It was rare for me to see him that animated, and I enjoyed his humor. Watching him and Emmy together was bittersweet. Their love shone brightly, and it hurt to see the way he doted on her, even though I was thrilled for her. She deserved to be happy.

We ordered pizza for dinner; he made us a pitcher of martinis and left us in the movie theater with a pile of chick flicks. I was relaxed, the tension of the past weeks easing off. It felt good to sit back and unwind. I slept well in the big bed in the guest room, safe and secure. After brunch, Bentley drove me home, still in a great mood. I was grateful he didn't push me about Aiden, but he did surprise me by hugging me hard after he opened my door and helped me out of the car. I had to admit, his old-fashioned manners were a nice change.

"I'm here for you, Cami. Anything you need, you only have to ask."

"Thanks, Bentley."

"I mean it."

I hugged him again. "I know."

I paused outside the apartment, feeling some of my tension return. I hadn't said anything to Emmy. My fears and worries seemed almost ridiculous when I stepped back and thought about it. It had been a rough few weeks, and some things had gone badly. I'd misplaced a couple of items. Forgotten some things. It happened. Once I settled back down, life would return to normal.

I *wasn't* my mother. Even Dee said so.

Inside my apartment, I looked around, but everything was in its place. I hung up my coat and took my bag to my room, setting it on the chair. I grabbed a bottle of water from the kitchen and sat down to work on the assignment we'd been given on Friday. I liked to get them done as soon as possible, unlike some of my classmates who put them off until the last minute.

I worked away, stopping when Dee called.

"How's it going?"

I grinned into the phone. "Living the dream."

She chuckled. "Did you eat all your soup?"

"No, I'll finish it tonight. I spent the day with Emmy yesterday after work."

"Have fun?"

"Yes. We watched movies, ate popcorn, just hung out."

"Was . . . ?" Her voice trailed off.

"No. Just Emmy and me."

"Okay."

"How is it there?"

She sighed. "Awful. The case starts tomorrow, and my phone will be on silent most of the time. I'll check in when I can." I heard a voice behind her, and she told them she would be right there.

"I have to go. They just brought in dinner, and we're going to eat and work."

"Okay."

"Love you."

"Right back at you."

She hung up, and I realized I hadn't thanked her for cleaning my room. I sent off a quick text.

My room looks awesome. The bed is like a magazine spread.

Hours later, I woke up, blinking and confused. Once again, I had fallen asleep on the sofa. My phone lay on the floor, and I realized I must have knocked it off the arm of the sofa. Dee had returned my text, and I read it as I walked down the hall to my room.

LOL. Did my absence inspire you to clean your room? Lord knows, I would never enter the inner sanctum and disturb your system. You'll have to send me a picture. I can't remember the last time you even made your bed. I need proof!

I stared at the screen, confused.

Dee hadn't cleaned my room?

Standing in the doorway, I flicked on my light, my confusion morphing into terror.

I hadn't slept in my bed since Dee left. I kept falling asleep on the sofa. Hours earlier, it had been pristine and smooth.

Now, on the wrinkled duvet, was the imprint of a body where someone had sat, clearly outlined.

Someone had been in the apartment, with me, while I slept.

I panicked as my eyes darted frantically around the room, expecting to see an intruder, except the room was empty. Still, they had been in the apartment, moving around freely, touching my things, sitting on my bed in my room. They might still be there.

I thought of all the strange occurrences lately. Everything I had blamed on my exhaustion and state of mind.

Except, it wasn't me. Someone else was doing it all to me.

My heart rate was so loud and fast, it echoed in my head.

I turned and ran.

⌢

EMMY SAT CLOSE, rubbing my shoulders through the blanket she had draped over me. I had run out of my apartment, grabbing only my jacket, purse, and shoes, barely stopping to put them on in my fear. Once I got to the main road, I hailed a cab and went to Bentley's place. I called on the way, frantic and incoherent. Bentley met the cab outside, and Emmy took me inside the house while he dealt with the driver.

They sat with me, and I told them everything. The missing items, the times I found my door open, my locker, all of it. How I had been worried that it was me—that I was becoming like my mother—and the horrible realization that someone had been in my apartment, probably more than once. When I told them about realizing that, and the fact that someone could even still be there, Bentley shook his head and Emmy grasped my hand.

"You should have called the police," Bentley admonished.

"I-I didn't think. I just panicked and had to get out of there."

"I understand. I'm sure they're gone now." He gentled his voice. "Finish your story."

They listened, Bentley asking me questions on occasion.

"Have you called Dee?"

"No, it's the middle of the night there. I feel bad enough about showing up here. I didn't know where else to go."

My first instinct had been to go to Aiden, but I wasn't sure of my welcome there.

"You did the right thing. We still need to call the police, though," Bentley stated.

"What can they do now?"

"They'll check for similar cases, make a list of your missing items, sweep your apartment. You'll need the locks changed as well." He ran a hand through his hair. "Aiden would know the best steps to take."

"Please, Bentley, no. Don't involve Aiden. I can't-I can't . . ." I swallowed around the lump in my throat.

He leaned forward, holding my hands. "He would want to help, Cami."

"I'm sure this is nothing. I mean, if they were going to hurt me, they could have, several times. In fact, maybe next time, they'll clean the whole place," I joked, desperate to stop him picking up his phone and calling Aiden.

"This isn't a laughing matter. This is a scary situation," he reproached me. "There is no one I trust more than Aiden. No one who would know the right steps to take and make sure everything was handled properly better than he would."

"No," I pleaded. "I'll call the police, and I'll have the locks changed. Maybe I can stay here for a couple of days and get some sleep. I don't want him involved." I grasped Bentley's hand. "Promise me you won't tell him."

He stood, looking down at me. "I can't promise you that, Cami. Your safety is on the line, and you came to me for help. Changing the locks and ignoring this is not the answer. There is something disturbing going on, and I won't allow you to let your personal pride get in the way." He patted the top of my head as though I were a child. "You mean too much to Emmy, and to me. Let me handle this the best way I know how, and trust that I won't let anything happen to you, or allow Aiden to upset you. However, if anyone can get to the bottom of this quickly, he can."

I looked at Emmy, who grasped my hand. She was pale and worried, beseeching me with her eyes to listen to Bentley.

"Okay," I whispered, hating the fact but knowing he was right.

"Good girl," he praised. "I'm going to shower and figure out the next step. You go up to your room and try to get some rest. You look as if you might fall down at any moment. Emmy, baby, you go with her. You're both safe here. I'll be back in a little while, and we'll talk, okay?"

I suddenly felt exhausted.

"Thank you, Bentley."

He leaned down and brushed a kiss to my forehead. "You're part of my family now, Cami. No thanks are needed."

CHAPTER 13

AIDEN

I STARED AT the document in front of me, unable to focus. I didn't even bother to try to decipher the words today. Turning in my chair, I looked outside into the city. It had been raining for days, the skies heavy and oppressive.

Much like my mood.

I turned back around, using my finger to push the pages around the top of my desk. Up, down, right, left. Aimless. Groaning, I shoved them hard, not caring that the pages scattered to the floor. I let my head fall back, shutting my eyes.

I was exhausted. Night after night of restless, broken sleep. Nightmares, rampant thoughts, the burning image of Cami's pain-filled eyes as she walked away from me in the parking lot. Her stubborn bravery in showing up for the self-defense lesson, her body rigid with tension while she attempted to act nonchalant so no one would be uncomfortable, even though she had suffered the most.

Because of my issues. My behavior.

I sighed, lifting my head. Bentley was in my office doorway, talking on the phone. He glanced at me, brow furrowed, as he dropped his eyes.

"Okay, Freddy. Good idea. Yes, let her sleep." He listened for a moment. "Aw, baby, that's very thoughtful of you. Frank will be there when you're ready."

Our eyes met again, and with another frown, he turned on his heel and went down the hall. I heard Maddox's door shut, and with a shrug, I leaned back, shutting my eyes again. The same odd, disconnected feeling I had been experiencing lately swept over me. For the first time ever, I didn't care what Bentley wanted or needed from me. I couldn't give a shit about the document I was supposed to read and discuss with him or the fact that he was having a private conversation with Maddox. Normally, I would have jumped up and gone to see what was going on, but I couldn't find it in me to care.

I swung my chair around, staring aimlessly out the window. I didn't seem to care about anything these days. Everything was too much—and not enough. I felt as if I had lost something, yet I had no idea what it could be.

"*Liar,*" whispered the voice in my head. "*You know exactly what you lost.*"

I refused to listen.

"Aiden."

I turned my chair, surprised to see both Bentley and Maddox in front of me. My office door was now shut. Annoyance seeped into my lethargic brain.

"If the two of you are here on some sort of intervention, you can show yourselves back out."

Bentley shook his head and leaned on my desk.

"Stop the pity party and shut up."

I raised my eyebrow, but stayed silent.

"I need to talk to you about something important. But I need you to stay calm and focused."

"I couldn't be calmer if I tried," I mocked him, reclining back in my chair.

He slammed his hand on my desk. "I need head-of-my-security Aiden right now, not the half dead idiot you've been acting like the past few days. Get your head out of your fucking ass, and listen to me. I have a situation, and the only person who can help is you."

His voice and words caught my attention. I sat straighter. "What's going on?"

Maddox moved, standing beside me, not fooling me for one second with his laid-back attitude. He leaned against the wall, dropping his hand to my shoulder with a squeeze. "Calm, Aiden."

I met Bentley's gaze. "Tell me."

"It's Cami."

Instantly, it was all gone. The lethargy, the disconnect—vanished. Every nerve in my body lit up, and I stood abruptly, sending my chair flying back. "What?"

"She's in trouble. I think she might be in danger."

I leaned on the desk, my hands curled into fists. I met his serious gaze.

"Tell me everything. Don't leave out a single fucking detail. Not one."

⌒

I WALKED UP the steps at Bentley's, anxious and twitching. Emmy met me, looking tired and stressed.

"Hey. Is she asleep?"

"Finally. I spoke to Dee, and she suggested a Gravol. She said they always knocked her out. It worked."

"How is Dee?"

"Upset. Concerned. She wanted to fly home right away, but I told her we'd look after Cami and call her later."

"Good idea."

"Is Frank downstairs?"

"Yes, he's waiting for you." I smiled at her. "You don't have go to Al's to get donuts."

"Al's fritters are Cami's favorite. I thought she'd like one when she wakes up." She wrung her hands. "I want to do something, and that's all I can think of. He made some special for her."

"They're awesome, and I'm sure she'll like them." I patted her shoulder. "You *are* doing something, Emmy. You're here for her, and now she's safe."

She stepped forward, her voice low and concerned. "You'll make sure she stays that way, right?"

"Absolutely."

"Okay. I'll be back in an hour."

"We'll be here."

I watched her hurry away, and I climbed the steps to the bedrooms. I knew where I was headed. She was here so often, Bentley referred to it as "Cami's room." The door was open, and I went inside cautiously. The blinds were down, but there was a small lamp on in the corner. Cami had her body curled up on the bed, facing the door, one hand tucked under her cheek as she slumbered. I could see she had been weeping, the evidence of dried tears on her face. Her hair was a mass of dark waves spread out on the pillow.

She wasn't a tiny woman like Emmy, who made me feel like a giant when I stood next to her. Cami stood about 5'7", which was more than average for a woman, though she still was a foot shorter than I was. She was lush and curvy and kept herself in great shape. She seemed to hold herself taller, refusing to back down from anything or anybody. With her forward personality, she always seemed strong and capable. Yet, at the moment, curled up and tucked under a blanket, she looked small and vulnerable. Defenseless.

I crouched beside the bed, scrutinizing her closely. Even as she slept, I could see her fear. It was in the way her hand clutched the blanket, the slight frown on her face, and how she huddled into herself. Unable to resist, I reached out and wrapped a long strand of hair around my finger. Today, her hair was untouched, the strands a dark chestnut against my skin. Carefully, I stroked her head, needing to offer her some sort of comfort. After a few moments, her eyes blinked open, her gaze unfocused.

"Aiden?"

"I'm here, Sunshine."

Tears filled her eyes. "I'm sorry they bothered you. I didn't want Bentley to involve you."

"Shh," I crooned. "He did the right thing. I won't let anything happen to you. I promise." Her hand reached for mine, and I entwined our fingers. "Everything is going to be okay."

"Emmy phoned Dee." She sighed. "She's really upset."

"I'll call her later."

"She's mad I didn't tell her what was happening."

"Why didn't you tell her? Or Emmy?"

She sat up, wrapping her arms around herself, her fingers constantly clasping and unclasping. "I thought it was me, Aiden. I thought I was forgetting things—moving items and losing things." She met my confused gaze. "My mom did that a lot. When she was depressed or began having one of her manic episodes, she couldn't concentrate. I-I was afraid I was starting to show signs of being like her."

She was very agitated and upset; I had to do something. I sat beside her, wrapping my arm around her shoulders. Her head fell to my chest, fitting naturally in the spot below my chin.

"And?" I prompted gently.

"I haven't been myself the past while, and all I could think about was my mom. It started for her in her twenties. What if I was becoming a manic-depressive like her? How would Dee handle it? What would that mean to my life?" she confessed. "Then at other times, it seemed silly. People forget. Everyone goes through bad times." She plucked at the edge of the blanket. "I guess I didn't want to say it out loud because it scared the hell out of me. I hoped it would blow over."

"I wish you had said something. Even to me."

"I wanted to. This week after the umbrella incident, I wanted to call you, but . . ."

I pulled her closer. "I'm sorry you didn't feel you could."

She tilted her head back. "What happens now?"

I smoothed her hair away from her face. "I've already been to your place with a detective friend I know at the police department. We looked around, but we couldn't see anything out of place. No one was there. He dusted for prints, so your place is covered in black powder. I'm going back later to meet my locksmith guy to have the locks changed. There is zero security around there, by the way. No cameras, no intercom, and how long has the front door lock been broken?"

She shrugged with a sad smile. "Most of the time we've lived there. They fix it, and a few days later, it's broken again."

I huffed. That was going to change if she was going to keep living there.

"I want to look at your locker. Bent said things have gone missing from there too?"

"Yes."

Rushed footsteps brought me to my feet. Emmy hurried into the room, her color high.

"What's wrong?"

"Louisa," she gasped out.

"What about her?" Cami asked.

"I just saw her at Al's. She was sitting in the corner and looked . . . strange, so I went over to talk to her."

"What did she say?"

Emmy shook her head. "It wasn't what she said, Cami. She seemed agitated, and she kept pushing her hair back. I didn't notice at first, but then I saw it."

Cami leaned forward. "Saw what?"

"She was wearing your leather cuff, Cami. The one I gave you that you thought you lost."

"What?" Cami asked, shocked, sitting back against the headboard.

"Did you ask her about it?" I demanded.

"No. I didn't want to spook her. I told her I had to go, and as I turned, I saw something else. Your umbrella was on the chair beside her."

She stepped closer, her gaze fixed on Cami. "It's her. She's the one taking your things and doing this to you."

⁓

"KERSHAW IS THE last name, Reid." I spelled out the name. "I think she's Cami's age. I don't have much other information until I talk to the school, not that I expect them to give me much."

Reid chuckled. "Don't waste your time. I'll be into their system and have all the information before you can even get there to see them."

"I only want info on her. Don't be poking around in the private files." I caught Cami's eye and sent her a wink, desperate to make her smile. "Unless you can dig into Cami's grades and give her A-plusses all around."

He laughed, and Cami lifted her lips in a half smile that didn't reach her eyes. She was incredibly disturbed, thinking Louisa had been in her apartment, taking her things, and touching her personal items. She had confirmed Louisa had been in her apartment as a guest, but only a couple of times with her group from school. I reminded her that was all she needed to grab one of the spare keys Cami kept by the door.

"Just her information, especially address and phone. Snag her parents' information too, if it's in there. Any family stuff." I turned my back, lowering my voice. "This is your priority, you understand?"

Reid's voice was serious when he responded. "I know, Aiden. I'll work on this now and get back to you as soon as I have something. I know how important this is to you."

"Be careful."

He snorted. "Not an issue."

I hung up and turned back to Cami. She sat at the dining room table, a blanket draped over her shoulders. Bentley and Maddox had shown up, and Bentley sat beside Emmy, his arm around her. Maddox was across from Cami, urging her to eat something. Striding over, I pulled out the chair beside her and poured a cup of coffee. I reached into the bag for a fritter, tearing it in half. I handed it to her, arching my eyebrow at her in silence.

She took it from me, and I didn't fail to notice the slight tremor to her fingers. I tugged her chair closer to me, knowing I made her feel safe. It was the least I could do. I waited until she nibbled at the sweet dough, then I addressed everyone.

"I'm going to Cami's to have the locks changed. Reid will find out what he can about this Louisa girl. Then we'll make a plan."

Cami swallowed a bite. "I'm going with you."

I knew she needed some clothes, so I agreed. "Fine."

"I'll stay once you're done." Cami didn't look up as she spoke.

Everyone appeared startled at her announcement, but they remained silent.

"The fuck you will," I hissed. "You're not staying alone in that apartment."

"Once you change the locks, it'll be fine. I'm not going to inconvenience Bentley and Emmy anymore."

"You aren't an inconvenience," Bentley interjected. "You're welcome to stay here as long as needed. Aiden is right. You shouldn't be alone."

She shook her head, stubborn and proud. "I won't let her mess up my life. I have classes and a job to go to. I'll be careful where I go and what I do. If she wanted to hurt me, she's had lots of opportunity. It's obvious she wants my attention."

"Is that your professional opinion?" I snapped.

"If she can't get into my apartment, she'll approach me at school or someplace. She's not going to harm me."

"You don't know that. We have no idea what's going on with her."

"Well, if you are worried about it, then it's even more imperative I go home. I won't put Emmy or Bentley in danger."

"They aren't her target. *You* are."

"She dislikes Emmy. I'm not risking it."

"It's not your decision to make."

"Yes, it is."

I stood, tugged her from her chair, and led her to the kitchen. She scowled at me, her green eyes a myriad of emotions. The strongest of which was fear.

"You are *not* staying on your own."

"Then I'll tell Dee to come home."

"That's a totally stupid idea. Bring her home, so both of you are in danger."

She swallowed and licked her lips. I tried not to notice the way her tongue ran along the edge of her plump mouth.

"I'll be fine on my own."

"Not happening."

"If she approaches me, I'll yell or something."

I crouched at the knees, bringing us to eye level. Restrained anger made my voice rough. "She won't get that chance. You'll be escorted wherever you need to go. Frank can drive you."

She rolled her eyes. "*Frank* is not at your disposal, Aiden. I am not Emmy. He drives her places because she is part of Bentley's life. A part of his world. I'm just the friend. I won't ask that of him, so forget it. Change the locks. Add a camera if you want, and I won't open the door unless I know who is there."

Our gazes locked, and I knew she wasn't going to back down. However, I still saw the fear in her eyes and felt the tremors in her body. She was serious about making sure no one else was hurt because of her and determined to follow through with her crazy idea. In her mind, she didn't want to bother anyone or cause any trouble. She really thought she would go home, and everyone would go about their lives and forget about her situation because the lock had been changed and she'd be on alert.

Not on my fucking watch.

I crossed my arms. "Fine. You're coming home with me. I'll

protect you."

Her eyes widened. "Absolutely not."

I stepped closer until we were almost touching. She refused to back down, glaring up at me. Her bravado and fierceness made me want to yank her into my arms and hold her until she broke down. "You can come to your apartment with me, pack some clothes, then you're coming back to my place. You're staying with me."

She started to shake her head, and I wrapped my hand around the back of her neck, stopping her.

"Until this is done, you are stuck with me, Camilla Wilson. End of discussion. Do you understand?"

Her eyes widened at the use of her full name. I knew she disliked it, thinking it too formal, but it got her attention. I thought it was pretty, but I kept that to myself. I continued to speak.

"Your sister and best friend have asked me to take care of you, and I promised them I would. I don't fucking break my promises, so stop fighting me. We're doing this my way."

"I'm not sitting around your loft and letting my life float by."

"You don't have to. You can keep doing everything you do now, except I'll be around. Until we find Louisa and figure out what the hell is going on, that is how it's going to be."

"What about your job? I'm sure Bentley isn't going to be happy."

"I'm a fucking VP, Sunshine. I haven't taken a day of vacation in three years. I think I'm due."

I watched her give in. Relief flooded her body, her eyes became damp, and her shoulders sagged. I knew I was making the right decision. No one would protect her the way I could.

"Okay," Cami acquiesced. "But quit with the Camilla. It's Cami."

"I like Sunshine," I insisted. "But piss me off again, and it's Camilla. Really piss me off, and you'll be Camilla Marie."

"You wouldn't."

"Try me."

"Whatever, Aiden Joseph Callaghan," she muttered, petulant. "Bossy man."

"Boss of you right now," I responded.

She ignored me.

We returned to the dining room, and Cami headed for the stairs. "I'm going to go have a shower."

Emmy stood. "I'll find you something to wear home."

They left, and we sat silently for a minute.

"So I need some personal time."

"We heard," Maddox drawled. "I think it's closer to four years since you took some time off, if I remember correctly."

"You could have just as easily convinced her to stay here with us," Bentley mused. "Or we could have given Simon and Joe the task of watching over her. They'd be a good choice."

"I'm not having *them* watch over her. That's my job," I snapped.

They exchanged a look.

Bentley cocked his head. "Can you handle that?"

I focused my gaze outside. "I have no fucking clue, but I know I have to do this for her."

Maddox chuckled as he lifted his mug. "This should be illuminating."

Bentley snorted. "In many ways."

I didn't respond.

They were right.

~

CAMI WAS SILENT on the drive to her place, her head bowed and her eyes shut as I maneuvered us through the heavy traffic. She could have been asleep, except for the constant movement of her fingers playing with the edge of a scarf around her neck.

We pulled up by her building, and I parked the car. There was no mistaking the nervous tremor going through her. "Hey," I called quietly. "I'll be right there with you, Sunshine. No one is gonna get close."

She nodded, still not speaking.

I left her in the car and rounded the back, my gaze scanning the area, alert. I opened her door, held out my hand, and tugged her from the seat. I kept her close until we got to her door. We entered the apartment, and she hesitated, unsure what to do. I asked to see her boots and studied the soles. As I suspected, they weren't torn.

"These were cut with a knife. A sharp one. Emmy's looked exactly like these."

"Do you think Louisa cut hers too?"

I shrugged. "Easy enough to do. The boots are on racks in the hall. Someone might have interrupted her while she was cutting Emmy's. She sliced both of yours, though."

"I don't understand why."

"I think she's jealous of Emmy and mad at you. Her actions are like an angry, petulant child. She lashes out. The day I met her, I thought she was all over the place emotionally." I sighed and rubbed my forehead. "I wish I had paid more attention."

I set down the boots. "Sit down while I do a walk-through."

"Couldn't I come with you?"

Her voice sounded so stressed, I held out my hand. She gripped it tightly. Each room looked undisturbed and she began to relax. She grimaced at the occasional glimpse of the fingerprint powder on various surfaces. In her room, she shook her head. "He went crazy in here."

"We were able to isolate you and Dee for the most part. In here, though, he got a lot of prints."

"Now that we know it's her, do we need fingerprints?"

"We might. There could be a trial, Cami. We would need to place her here. Beyond the fact that she'd been here before."

She looked horrified. "I don't want a trial. I think maybe she's mentally unstable, but not a criminal."

"We'll cross that bridge when we come to it."

There was a knock at the door. "That will be the locksmith. Pack some clothes, and I'll help him."

"Okay."

CHAPTER 14

AIDEN

THE LOCKSMITH WAS fast, and Cami had watched him work from the sofa after she packed a bag. I made sure to have a lock on the handle and a heavy-duty deadbolt installed, each with their own key. Once he was done and gone, I gave Cami a new set of keys, hung a set for Dee beside the door, and pocketed the third set. I wanted to talk to her super about a new front door lock, an industrial one, not easily broken, but I decided to wait a couple of days. I didn't want to leave Cami alone in the apartment while I did that.

We left the apartment, the door shut firmly behind us, the locks engaged. We stopped to get some groceries since I wasn't sure what I had on hand in the kitchen.

"Do you like to cook?" I asked.

She shrugged. "Dee is better than I am, but I can make a few good things. Emmy taught me."

"Oh, yeah? Like?"

"Pancakes," she stated. "I make great pancakes."

"I love pancakes. I can make bacon. I use the convection oven. It's crispy, just the way I like it."

She smiled. "Breakfast for dinner?"

"Perfect."

It felt strange to have her in my space, yet not unpleasant. We worked well as a team, moving around the rarely used kitchen.

"You're very different from Bentley, aren't you?" she observed as she mixed up the batter, looking around the large space.

I laughed and slid the pan of bacon into the oven. "As we discussed before, Bentley is used to the finer things in life. I like it simpler." My loft was spacious and open, the ceilings soaring to twenty feet with huge windows. Overhead beams and floors made of wide oak timbers gave it a rugged look. The only walls were for the bathroom and massive bedroom, and they were all unadorned. The rest of the space was open-concept, a living and entertainment area on one side, the long kitchen with a polished concrete counter that separated the area, and my workout corner. Unpretentious and uncluttered, just the way I liked it. I didn't need a dining room, an office, or a lot of furniture. I had learned to like high thread-count sheets and thick towels, but otherwise, I kept things simple. I glanced at Cami. "Too sparse for your taste?"

"No, it suits you." She tested the griddle I'd insisted on buying at the store. "I like it," she added. Unable to resist, I wrapped my arm around her waist for a quick hug.

"Good. Because you're stuck here with me until I say otherwise."

She turned away, but I saw the flush on her cheeks.

She was right. She made awesome pancakes, and I ate eight, along with a plate of bacon. I had been afraid I wouldn't be able to get her to eat, but the longer she was in my company, the more she began to relax. She ate the two pancakes I slid onto her plate and a couple slices of bacon. At least it was something.

She was quiet most of the night, and I'd heard her crying when she spoke with Dee. As they talked, I kept myself busy working out to give her some privacy. When she was done, she looked exhausted. I decided we both needed an early night and grabbed some extra pillows and blankets, telling her to take the bed.

Cami passed a weary hand over her face. "I'm not taking your bed, Aiden. I'm fine on the sofa. Don't give me the 'I promised your sister to look after you,' thing again either. Dee would agree with me. I fit way better on the sofa than you do."

"I've slept on that sofa many nights. It's perfectly comfortable," I insisted. I was worried she was going to pass out right in front of me; she looked pale and drained. I needed her to stop arguing and to accept the care I wanted to give her.

She smiled and took the bedding I had in my arms. "Good. If it's that comfortable, then I'll sleep well."

"Jesus, you are frustrating."

"Hello, pot," she muttered.

I chuckled since she had me there. We were both stubborn.

I was about to argue with her, then changed my mind. She was stressed enough.

"Why don't you have a bath?" I knew she loved to soak in the tub. "Mine is big with jets, and I've never used it."

"Not a bath guy?"

"No. It was here when I bought the place. Part of the design."

"I'd like that."

I headed to the bathroom, started the water going, and grabbed some towels. "I don't have any stuff—girlie stuff—for the tub," I told her.

"It's fine. A nice soak will be great. The jets should feel good."

I turned on the small radio, letting the music fill the room. I caught sight of her in the mirror, the slight haze on the glass making her look even sexier than usual. I headed to the door fast before I did or said anything I regretted.

"Call me if you need me."

"Okay."

I left her, pulled the door shut, and went to call Reid.

"Hey," he answered. "I just emailed you everything I found. I got her address, cell number, even her shoe size if you want, which I might add, is not the same as Cami wears. There's no incidents listed on her school records. Her grades are average. She misses a lot of days, though. I did some digging, and there are some blank spots in her history. In fact, quite a few of them. I'm going to do some more searching tonight."

"Her family?"

"Divorced. Bounced between her parents. Looks like the father pays all the bills."

"No siblings?"

"She had an older sister named Jessie. She died five years ago."

"How?"

"She drowned."

"Hmmm."

"Think that's relevant?"

"It could be."

"Okay, I'll keep digging. My dinner is here."

"What's on the menu? Pizza? Sushi? Thai?"

"I got a bucket of wings and some cold beers with my name on them. And on the TV? Dude, I'm spoiled for choice. Baseball, hockey, basketball. All that and permission to do some hacking? It's a fucking banner night in Reid Matthews's world."

"Okay, my man. Let me know what you find. No matter what time it is."

"Will do."

I hung up with a grin. The kid always made me smile.

I entered the kitchen, grabbed a bottle of open wine, and poured a glass. At the door to the bathroom, I knocked, waiting for Cami to tell me to come in.

"I brought you a glass of wine," I explained as I went in, freezing in place.

The room was steamy and smelled of my soap. Cami was sitting in the tub, her knees drawn up to her chest, the swells of her breasts visible. Her skin glistened with moisture. She had her hair tied up on the top of her head, long pieces escaping and hanging down her neck. The small group of freckles at the base of her neck was a beacon, and I kept staring at them.

She held out her hand for the glass. "Thank you."

"Yeah," I sputtered, unsure why my brain no longer worked. "No problem. I, uh, thought you'd like it while you were in the tub."

"I would," she agreed.

"Okay."

"May I have it?"

I looked down, seeing I was still holding the glass. "Right. Sorry." I stepped forward, handing her the glass, trying not to stare but finding it impossible. She was a siren. My pants felt uncomfortably tight, and I realized why my brain wasn't working. All the blood was pooled in my cock. Regardless of what else was happening, the bottom line was I wanted her. Despite everything I said, how I acted, there was no denying that fact.

"Aiden?" she asked, her brow furrowed. "Why are you looking at me like that?"

I wanted to drag her from the tub. Fuck her on the floor, then carry her to my bed and do it all over again. Help her forget today and the stress of the recent events.

But I couldn't take advantage of her that way.

"Nothing. Sorry I interrupted. You're taking my bed by the way. I'm not arguing about it anymore." I backed away, shutting the door behind me with a little more energy than necessary. I had to force myself to pull my hand off the doorknob and walk away, my dick screaming at me to turn around.

How was I going to handle this for the next few days?

"*Illuminating*," Maddox had said.

Fucking right.

⌒

AFTER CAMI WAS settled in my room, I had a shower. A cold one. I dragged on some sweats and towel-dried my hair. As I went past my bedroom, I looked in to make sure she was all right. Cami was leaning against the headboard, her knees drawn up the way they had been in the tub. Her Kindle was open, but she wasn't reading.

"Okay, Sunshine?"

She offered me a wan smile, but I could see something was wrong. I entered the room and sat on the edge of the bed. "What's wrong?"

"I feel . . . odd."

"It's nerves." I rubbed her leg. "You're perfectly safe here."

"I know. It's just . . ."

"I know. It's been quite the day." Wanting to distract her, I pointed to her Kindle, recognizing the cover that was on the screen. "I just bought that book on audio. Is it any good?"

"I haven't started it yet." Her face brightened. "I could read it out loud for you. I know you like that."

"You remembered that?"

Her fingers traced the Kindle, her voice soft in the room when she replied. "I remember everything you tell me."

That strange and overwhelming feeling hit me again. Why did it feel so right sitting there? She was perfect in my bed, and the thought of being with her, listening to her lovely voice as she read to me, was too much to resist.

"Yeah. I'd like that."

It worked. Her sunshine smile broke through, lighting her face and making her eyes happy for the first time all day. She scooted over and pulled a cushion to her lap, patting it in a silent invitation.

Knowing I was playing with fire, I lay down, resting my head on her lap. She began to read, and I shut my eyes in satisfaction. I was correct. She had the perfect voice for reading—not too fast or loud, but a flawless level and tone. I found myself smiling when she tried to deepen her voice for the male parts and chuckled aloud when she added in a sound effect. As she read, we both relaxed. I felt the tension ease from her body, and when she gently began to run her fingers through my hair as she read, I was a goner.

I had missed her easy affection—and her touch. Aside from the occasional backslapping hug from Bentley or Maddox and the motherly ones Sandy dispensed, I was never touched. I didn't like it, yet when it came to Cami, those rules flew out the window. Her touch was different. Why or how, I didn't know, but it simply was.

With a groan, I wrapped my arm around her legs and settled closer. What it meant, or how I would deal with it, I would figure out later. For now, I was too content to worry about it.

Hours later, I woke, confused. The bedside light was still on, but the faint rays of dawn were spilling through the windows. I looked down in confusion. I had fallen asleep on Cami's lap, but somehow in the night, we had moved and twisted. She had draped herself across my chest, and her warm breath drifted over my skin. My arm was around her, holding her close, and my hand was fisted in her long hair. I had slept through the night—no nightmares disturbed me, as if her being with me was a sort of talisman. She had slept as well, and I wondered if my closeness helped.

Unable to resist, I ran my hand over her head. Her eyes opened, green pools of light, groggy and blinking as she woke.

"Hi." I grinned, feeling more rested than I had in weeks.

"Hi." She quirked her eyebrow. "I guess we both fell asleep."

"I guess so."

"Are you mad?"

I stroked her cheek. "No. I slept well. That's a rare thing for me."

"I didn't think I would sleep at all, so it's good for me too."

I tweaked her nose. "Good. We need to get up and figure out the day."

She sat up and stretched, the action causing her tank top to lift. I could see her nipples through the thin material, as well as the smooth skin along her stomach. I tried to ignore the way my dick stirred at the sight of her sensuous beauty.

I slid out of bed, turning my back and subtly adjusting myself. I inhaled deeply and casually picked up the towel on the floor, holding it in front of me as I turned around.

"I'll take you to school and check out your locker. I'm going to talk to the director and see if I can locate Louisa."

"You're not planning to sit in during my classes, are you?"

"No. But I'll be close."

"You're a lot less likely to blend in than Joe or Simon was for Emmy."

I leaned down, my face level with hers. "That's the point, Sunshine. I am not trying to blend in. Louisa isn't getting near you ever again."

She swallowed. "All right," she responded, her voice breathy.

"Okay. Now get ready."

I had to leave the room before I gave in to my desire. I wanted to push her back on the bed, make her forget school, forget Louisa, and have her screaming my name in that breathy voice.

However, it wasn't happening. It wouldn't be fair to her to lead her on or to take advantage of her when she was vulnerable. She would hate me even more later.

I gripped the edge of the sink, staring into the mirror, wishing things were different.

Knowing I was too weak to change them.

CHAPTER 15

AIDEN

THE NEXT FEW days were tense. Louisa never showed up for classes. She wasn't at her apartment, and her cell phone number went straight to voice mail. I had Cami leave her a message, asking to speak to her, hoping she would return the call so we could trace her location. However, she never called back, which frustrated me. It was as though she had disappeared. I checked Cami's place, but the door remained locked, and no one had seen Louisa.

The school was cooperative, allowing me to hang around while Cami was in her classes. I spent a lot of time in the cafeteria, passing the hours with my computer. I was in constant contact with Bentley and Maddox and worked on the items they forwarded to me. I checked on Cami often. She tried to ignore the whispers and stories she heard, but I knew she found it taxing and hated the attention my presence brought. Emmy stayed close, which helped, but I remained closer.

Cami was exhausted when we returned to my place every night, and we fell into a pattern. After an easy dinner, she would have a bath, speak with Dee, then she would read to me. Inevitably, I would fall asleep, waking up in the morning with her draped over my chest, me holding her close. We would stay connected for a short time, then separate and begin another day.

Friday morning dawned bright and sunny. Cami lay on my chest, silent but awake. I twirled a piece of her hair in my fingers.

"I spoke with Louisa's parents yesterday."

Cami rolled her head to face me. I felt the tension creep into her body at just the mention of Louisa's name.

"Oh?"

"Her mother hasn't seen her daughter in two years. Apparently, Louisa witnessed her sister's death, and she has never gotten over it. Her mother says she changed from a happy, normal girl to being emotional, prone to outbursts, and secrecy. Everything had to be perfect and in its place. She had a system for everything, and when it didn't work, she became 'unhinged.'" I studied the curl I had wrapped around my finger. "Her mother informed me it had become too much to handle, and she washed her hands of Louisa. She sounded rather blasé to me. I don't think she'd be mother of the year in anyone's books."

"What about her father?" Cami wondered.

"He says there have been some past episodes where Louisa became unhealthily attached to people. There have been a few incidents. She fixated on a guy in her class, telling people he was her boyfriend and showing up everyplace he went. He threatened a restraining order before she backed off. She freaked out another student by changing her appearance and emulating everything she did. She followed her around, telling people they were best friends, and showed up at her house more than once, insisting she'd been invited. Louisa's father stepped in and took her out of school and had her admitted to a hospital." I released the curl, watching it drape across Cami's skin. "He told me she was released and has been better. Still, he admits he only talks to her on occasion, and he couldn't recall the last time he paid a bill for her therapist. He said the last phone call from her was over a month ago." I huffed. "Again, not parent of the year."

"Why wasn't that in her records?"

I sighed, scrubbing my face. "Her father paid off the school and the kids to keep it all quiet. He wanted her to start with a clean slate, so he moved her here, and being the idiot it sounds like he is, left her on her own." I captured another curl, needing to touch her. "I'm afraid neither of them cares a great deal. He tosses money at the situation, and her mother ignores it. I told her father what she'd been doing, and he didn't seem shocked or particularly interested."

"So she's all alone and sick."

"Mentally unstable, yes. Her father told me she adored her sister, literally worshiped the ground she walked on. They were only a year apart in age, and people thought they were twins. Louisa copied everything her sister, Jessie, did. It appears after her death, Louisa has transferred that . . . *need* to other people."

"But she's never, ah, hurt someone?" she whispered, fear in her voice.

I ran my hand down her arm in comfort. "No, not that her father admitted. She gets obsessed and can't let go easily. I have Reid digging a bit more because her father was too light on details."

"She needs help."

"Yes, she does."

"If she is just lonely, maybe I should go home. She might come see me, and I could convince her to get help."

"No," I stated firmly. "That isn't happening."

"Aren't you tired of me being in your space already?"

"No," I said, quiet and reflective. "I like having you here. I find your company very soothing."

Her cheeks pinked. "Really?"

"Yeah." I ran my knuckles down her cheek, an idea coming to me. "You only have one class today, right?"

"Yes."

"Wanna blow it off and play hooky with me?"

Her eyes lit up, and she nodded.

"Okay, Sunshine, up and at it. Be sure to bring your knapsack."

THE WIND WHIPPED past us as we hurled down the highway. Cami had been excited when I pulled up in front of Jay's garage and she realized what we were doing.

"We're going on your bike?"

"Yep."

"I don't have anything—like a helmet!"

I laughed, pulling her out of the car. "Jay is loaning me some protective gear for you. We're covered."

She ran her hands over the bike, then winked at me. "This is hot."

"It's a Ducati Monster."

She was nervous getting on, but that dissipated quickly once we'd been traveling for a while.

I loved how she felt on my bike, her chest pressed to my back and her hands wrapped tight around my waist. She was excited when we pulled up to a winery, one of the two I planned to visit that day.

"You remembered!"

I tweaked her nose, happy to see how thrilled she was. Her tangled hair fell around her face, her cheeks flushed from the wind, and her eyes sparkled. She was stunning.

"You bet. I booked us a wine tasting and lunch here, then another tasting later." I winked. "Of course, you'll be tasting. I'll be driving."

Lunch was great. They offered a tour with a picnic, and since it was such a beautiful day, I had taken that option. We sat at a table in the sun, eating the gourmet lunch, and she sipped the wines that accompanied the meal. I tried a small taste of one I liked the sound of, and Cami seemed to enjoy. After lunch, we went inside, and I ordered a case of wine to have delivered since I couldn't carry it on the bike. We put one bottle in Cami's knapsack.

Cami wandered over, talking to another woman as I paid, and

when I was done, I joined her. I slid up behind her, wrapping my arms around her waist and pulling her back to me. "What are you doing?"

"I'm entering a contest. It's a trip to Vegas for four people, and the draw is in a couple of weeks. Wouldn't that be fun?"

I hummed. I'd never been to Vegas or had any inclination to go, but it made her happy to enter, so I agreed.

We left and went to the other winery. It was smaller, and the owner was behind the long bar, offering tastings. Cami was fascinated, and he seemed taken with her, answering her questions and giving her several samples. One vintage she particularly liked, so I bought two bottles, adding them to her knapsack. He gave us information on the ice wine festival in the winter, and after she had a sample of their specialty, she assured him we would be back.

"We need to get Bentley and Emmy here. She loves ice wines."

"Sure," I agreed. "We'll figure something out."

We walked around the vineyard, enjoying the sun.

"Thank you for today, Aiden," she said, not looking at me. "It was an unexpectedly good day."

I slipped my arm around her and tucked her to my side. As if drawn by an invisible thread, I couldn't stop touching her. All day, I'd held her hand, kissed her temple, drew her close. And when I looked down at her, she was grinning.

"I'm glad. I wanted you to smile. I love it when you smile." I blew out a breath. "I especially love it when you smile at me."

She beamed, making the light around us seem dim by comparison. Without thought, I turned and tugged her closer, never breaking her gaze. Her breathing picked up as we stared. There was nothing around us. No vineyard and sunlight. No voices from other people as they strolled through the neatly laid-out rows.

Only her. Only us.

"I can't give you what you want," I murmured. "But I've missed you."

"I'll take what you have to give."

My lips were on hers instantly. I lifted her, holding her tight to my chest as I devoured her mouth. It was passionate and intense. Full of yearning and need. Her tongue slid along mine sensuously, filling my senses with her taste. I felt every one of her curves aligning with my body, forming around my hardness perfectly. The desire I had pushed down and tried to ignore exploded. I gripped her hard, molding my hands around the swells of her ass, letting her feel how much I wanted her. I groaned low in my chest, dragging my mouth to her ear. "I need to take you home, Sunshine."

"Here," she pleaded. "Don't make me wait."

My cock was in total agreement with her. Frantically, I looked around, finding a small shed a few rows over. Still holding her, I headed in that direction, rounding the corner to the back of the building. It was shaded and secluded, away from everyone.

"You have to be quiet."

"You need to be fast."

"Not an issue, baby. Trust me."

Minutes later, I'd buried myself inside her. She cried out softly, her head falling back on the rough wood wall. I was out of control, pounding into her, chasing my release, and desperate for hers.

"Give me your mouth."

She lifted her face, and I captured her lips, kissing her hard, frantic, and controlling. The worry I had been feeling, the odd contentment of having her with me every day without acting on my feelings, was too much. I gripped her hips, sinking as deep as I could go, almost growling in my need. She stiffened, her fingers digging into my shoulder, tightening around me.

"Yeah, baby, like that," I praised her. "Just like that. Come for me." I buried my face into her neck, my lips by her ear. "Come all over me. *Right now.*"

She whimpered and shuddered, her body taut as she rode out her orgasm. I drove into her again, my balls tightening and pleasure spiking through my spine. Her name broke from my lips as I came, and my body stilled with the strength of my orgasm.

We stayed connected until we both stopped shaking. Gradually,

I lowered her to the ground and helped her pull up her jeans, before yanking mine back into place. I slipped my fingers under her chin, making her meet my gaze.

"Okay, Sunshine?"

Her eyes glowed, her smile wide. "I am."

"I still need to get you home."

"I'm good with that."

We walked to the bike hand in hand, grinning. I made sure her helmet was on correctly, she was seated properly, and then I swung my leg over the bike. She wrapped her arms around my waist, leaning into my back with a sigh.

"Hold tight," I instructed, covering her hands with mine for a brief moment. "Don't let go."

She increased her grip in reply.

I ignored the small voice in my head.

"Ever."

CHAPTER 16

AIDEN

I LEANED BACK in the tub, enjoying the feel of the warm water lapping at my skin. Or maybe it was the feel of Cami reclining into my chest, the way her hands drifted up and down my calves. Either way, the bathtub was more pleasurable than I had expected. The rain had returned, and we spent Saturday in the loft watching movies. Cami did some schoolwork, while I slowly made my way through some documents Bentley had sent over from the office. When she had stood, stretching, I had suggested a bath, and she agreed as long as I joined her.

I was good with that.

My phone rang, and I stiffened when I saw who was calling.

"Aiden Callaghan."

"Mr. Callaghan, it's Calvin Hob from the School of Design."

"Yes, what can I do for you?"

"I wanted you to know we had a call from Miss Kershaw's mother informing us she was withdrawing from the program and would not be returning."

"When did she call?"

"Today, as a matter of fact. I was in my office, catching up on some work, and picked up the phone."

"Are you sure it was her?"

He sounded surprised. "She identified herself as Louisa's mother. I have no reason to suspect it was anyone else."

"Did she say why Louisa was leaving?"

"She said it was for personal reasons, and that her ex-husband would be in contact shortly about the remaining tuition." He cleared his throat. "There are no refunds on unused portions, but I will take that up with him."

I rolled my eyes. "Did you see the number the call came from?"

He sighed. "No. It showed a transfer from the main line. I can inquire on Monday if they can look it up."

"I would appreciate that. Thank you."

Cami turned, meeting my gaze as I disconnected the call. "I heard the uncertainty in your voice. You don't believe it?"

I shrugged. "I don't know. It would explain why no one has seen or heard from her. Maybe she went home to her mother."

"That would be good—she needs someone to care for her. And I could go home, put this behind me, and get back to my life." She eased away from me, crawling out of the tub and reaching for a towel. She slid it around her body and tucked it closed.

For some reason, her actions and words rankled. As if she was closing me off from both her and her life. I shook my head over the stupid notion.

"Let's not jump ahead of ourselves. I'll call her parents again and check it out, okay?"

"Okay."

Her phone buzzed, and she picked it up, reading the screen. "Emmy is inviting us for brunch tomorrow. She says Bentley is making coddled eggs."

"Oh man, I love those. He only makes them on special occasions. He never makes enough, though."

"I could make pancakes so you don't go hungry."

I stood, the water coursing down my body. Her gaze was intense as I stepped out onto the mat beside her. My cock stirred at her leer. With a grin, I tugged at the top of the towel that was hiding her curves from me. "I'm hungry *now*, Sunshine. I need you to feed me."

⌒

I HUNG UP the phone, frustrated. I hadn't been able to reach either of Louisa's parents. Her mother's voice mail box was full, and her father hadn't returned my messages.

Something felt off. If it was true that Louisa had left and gone to her mother's, it was good news, although I still felt she needed to answer for what she had done to Cami. But it seemed too convenient. Reid had obtained the files on the missing spans of time, and there had been four cases of her odd behavior of fixating on another person. All four times she had to be stopped. She had never ended it voluntarily.

I paced around the room. I knew there was a possibility that, after my calls, one or both of her parents had come to town and taken her away. In fact, I hoped that had happened, but until I spoke with one of them and confirmed it, we still had to be careful.

Cami came into the room and stopped as soon as she saw my agitation. "Are you okay?"

"Yeah, I'm fine."

"Did you–did you talk to them?"

"No, I can't get ahold of either of them."

"Oh." She worried her lip.

"Sunshine."

She looked up.

"Nothing changes. You're with me until we confirm. You're safe, okay?"

She pushed her hair away from her face. "I spoke with Dee.

Things are still up in the air about when she'll be home. She told me to listen to you."

I smirked. "I always liked your sister. Smart woman."

She rolled her eyes. "Are you ready to go to Bentley's?"

I clapped my hands. "Yep. Coddled eggs, here I come."

BENTLEY WAS IN fine form when we arrived. With a grin that stretched from ear-to-ear, he sat back on the sofa in his massive living room, his feet kicked up on the coffee table. I had never seen him that relaxed. Delicious aromas filled the house, making my mouth water. I sipped the Bloody Mary Bent handed me and cocked my head.

"What's up?"

He smirked. "What makes you think something is up?"

"The fact that you look like the cat that swallowed the canary. Plus, you're making coddled eggs. I hope you made a lot, by the way."

"You can have Maddox's share."

Maddox was sick with a wicked cold, so he decided not to come and infect us.

"He is missing out."

A squeal from the kitchen interrupted us, and I was on my feet in an instant, relaxing when I realized it was a happy sound. I glanced at the table, taking in the flowers, then realized there were flowers everywhere.

"You did it, didn't you?"

Cami came barreling into the room, heading straight for Bentley. She flung her arms around his neck, laughing and crying at the same time. "Congratulations!"

He patted her back awkwardly, but he couldn't contain his smile. Emmy appeared, smiling and blushing. Lots of hugs and backslaps were exchanged, and Cami exclaimed in rapture over the ring.

It was perfect on Emmy's hand, just as Darlene had described. The diamond was brilliant in the bright light of the room, and Emmy obviously loved it.

"Darlene did an amazing job."

"It's more than I ever expected," Emmy said with a sigh.

"Gorgeous," Cami gushed. "It's one of the most beautiful rings I have ever seen."

Bentley kissed Emmy's head. "It was for the most beautiful woman in the world. It had to be."

Emmy rolled her eyes and slapped his chest. "Rigid. Stop it."

"Just speaking the truth, Freddy."

She pretended to be annoyed, but like Bentley, her joy was evident. She tugged Cami's hand. "Come on. We need to finish brunch."

They disappeared into the kitchen, and we sat down.

"How'd you pop the question?" I asked.

Bentley laughed. "I had planned a whole thing. Dinner, champagne, violins, the whole works. Then I realized she would hate the whole idea. So I took her for a drive and had a florist come in and decorate the sunroom with flowers while we were out. When we got home, I surprised her. She was so overwhelmed with the flowers, it took her a moment to realize I was on one knee." He chuckled. "Then she lunged so fast she knocked me right on my ass—and said yes."

I raised my glass. "Congrats, Bent."

He tilted his chin. "You're my best man, right?"

"Absolutely."

"Maddox is my second-in-command."

I chuckled and reached for my phone. "We need to call and tell him."

I put it on video, and Maddox answered after a few rings. His hair was mussed, his eyes heavy and bleary, his voice rough.

"What? I was sleeping."

"Bentley's been busy."

He scowled in confusion.

"He completed that project we helped him with."

A grin broke out on his face. "Hey, man," he rasped. "Congrats."

Bentley grinned. "Thanks, Mad Dog. You'll stand up for me with

Aiden, right?"

"Wouldn't miss it for the world. I'll take us all out to celebrate once I'm over this cold." He coughed, the sound painful.

"Ouch."

The girls entered and sat down, offering him sympathy over his cold. Emmy told him she would make him some chicken soup and send it over later.

He grinned. "Thanks, Emmy. Congrats on your engagement. Bent is a lucky man."

"I am," Bentley agreed.

Maddox coughed again. "I think I'm out for the next bit. Don't want to spread this around the office."

"No worries," Bentley assured him. "We'll figure it out. Get some rest."

We hung up, and I drained my glass. "He sounds bad."

"Yeah. Not to change the subject, but I need you tomorrow, Aiden."

I huffed out a long breath, glancing at Cami.

She patted my knee. "Aiden, I'll be fine. I'll be at school. You can drop me there, and I'll wait until you come back."

"I'll stick with her," Emmy offered.

"You could just stay at the loft."

"No," she said. "I have a presentation tomorrow. I worked hard on it, and I am not letting her screw that up for me."

Before I could protest, she leaned forward. "Aiden, her mother told the school she is gone. No one has seen her. I think I'll be fine now. I'll go back to school, and soon Dee will be home and things will get back to normal. You need to go back to work." She smiled, although her eyes looked sad. "Bentley needs you. And we need to get back to reality."

I heard her underlying words.

Reality meant she would leave me and go back home. We'd live two separate lives again because that was how it had to be.

Emmy laughed softly, and I looked over at them. Bentley was

nuzzling her cheek and whispering something to her, adoration written all over his expression.

His reality was with her. A life together.

I had done what Cami needed and gotten her through a bad time. My reality was to be alone.

My gaze returned to Bentley. For the first time ever, I felt a flicker of resentment.

CAMI

I FELT AS if the brunch would never end. Everything appeared normal. The food was great, and Aiden amused us with his retelling of the ring-shopping event. Emmy was almost in tears at his droll imitations, and I had to laugh with her. Bentley insisted on champagne, and I drank a few glasses, needing to relax. I was thrilled for their happiness, but I had to admit my heart ached watching them. I wanted that closeness, that absolute knowledge that the person you loved, loved you in return, and they would be there for you no matter what occurred.

I had felt Aiden's emotions shut down. You wouldn't know it unless you knew him the way I did. He did all the right things: smiled and laughed, offered toasts and well wishes. He ate as if he hadn't seen food for a week. Yet, I knew his forced joviality hid his real feelings. His smile never reached his eyes, and his stiff posture belied his laughter. Once again, he was hiding his true self from the people he cared about the most because he didn't know how to deal with what he was feeling. He was slipping away from me, and I wasn't sure how to get him back. Or even if I could.

Bentley leaned back, sipping his coffee. "What if tomorrow Frank picks the girls up for school, and you drive us to the meeting? He can bring them back here after, and you won't have to worry?"

"It's the time in between I worry about." Aiden scowled.

"Want to call in Joe or Simon?"

"No!" I exclaimed. "I'll be surrounded by students. I'll go in, go to class, do my presentation, then head to the cafeteria and wait for Emmy. I don't even have to go outside. I will be *fine*." I met Aiden's gaze. "You can pick me up here after you're done." Hating the vacant look in his eyes, I added, "Or I can even bring my stuff here and stay until Dee comes home."

The room stilled. Aiden sat straighter, his shoulders expanding as he inhaled. "If that's what you want."

I tried to lighten the tension by teasing him. "I thought maybe you were tired of me in your space and I'd give you a break."

"It's your decision," he answered, his voice clipped.

I shrugged, noncommittal, unsure what to add or why I had even said it. It wasn't as if I expected him to stand and declare his feelings for me.

Yet, a small part of me wished he would.

Bentley looked between us, setting down his coffee. "You're always welcome here, Cami. I'll leave that decision between the two of you. Whatever you feel is best is fine with Emmy and me."

I could only nod, not trusting my voice.

"We should take Reid with us tomorrow," Aiden announced out of the blue.

Bentley's brow furrowed in confusion. "Oh?"

"Maddox usually makes notes and asks questions while I concentrate on the conversation. Then we discuss. Reid is a freaking typing whiz. He'd be able to transcribe the entire conversation on his tablet for us. It would come in handy. Since we're meeting about specs and ideas, he would be in his element."

"Does he have something decent to wear? I don't want him walking in looking like we picked him up off the streets."

Aiden shook his head. "I happen to know Sandy insisted he buy a suit. He'll wear it if we tell him to. He'll do a good job."

"Okay. Call him." Bentley laughed. "Sandy will have a great day. None of us there to bother her."

Aiden stood. "Okay. I'll call him when we get home and arrange it." He bent down and kissed Emmy's cheek. "Thanks for brunch, and congrats again."

"Thanks, Tree Trunk."

He shook Bentley's hand. "All the best, bro. I mean it."

Bentley slapped his shoulder. "I know."

⌒

AIDEN WAS QUIET the rest of the day, not mentioning what had occurred at the table. He talked with Reid, walking to the far side of the loft, speaking low so I didn't hear. I wasn't an idiot, so I knew it had something to do with Louisa. He had some other calls and once disappeared into his room, shutting the door. When he emerged, he looked defeated, but he didn't say anything. He was there in the loft with me, yet so far away it might as well have been the other side of the world.

I did some reading and checked my laptop, but I didn't spend a lot of time on it. I did best when I didn't cram for a test or overthink a presentation. I knew my facts; I had it all done and ready to go, and I would do a quick read-through in the morning once I got to school. I wouldn't be able to concentrate now anyway. I was too tangled up in the knots of my own making. I never should have said anything about leaving, and I was too much of a coward to address it with Aiden, fearful of his reply.

Aiden worked out, and I couldn't help but stare as he went through his routine. His muscles rippled and strained under his tight T-shirt as he hoisted weights. His calves bunched and sweat poured down his back as he pounded on the treadmill. I lost count of the number of push-ups he did. When he stopped, I was fascinated watching his Adam's apple bob as he drank in long, heavy swallows.

Our eyes met, and my body heated at his intense gaze. Even across the room, I could feel his pull.

He tugged his T-shirt over his head and wiped his face. "I need to have a shower."

I licked my lips and nodded.

"You done with your schoolwork?"

I could only nod again.

He held out his hand. "Come with me, Sunshine."

Wordlessly, I stood and took his hand, letting him pull me with him. By the shower, he undressed me, his actions swift and certain. His fingers danced over my skin, caressing the spots he knew well. I pulled on the waistband of his shorts, pushing them over his firm ass. His cock jutted out, heavy and long, begging for my touch. I wrapped my hands around it, stroking the silky skin that belied the iron beneath it. His head fell back with a groan, and he yanked me to him, tugging us under the warm water. He crashed his mouth to mine, and I tasted the salt of his sweat and felt the desire race through his body. His kisses were desperate, almost bruising, and he left me breathless and yearning for him. He lifted me, and the cold tile pressed into my back. I gasped as he licked his way down my neck, biting at the juncture. I yanked his hair, moaning at the feel of his blunt tip nudging at my entrance.

How could someone break my heart, yet make me want them with just one look?

It was a power Aiden had over me—and one I was helpless to resist.

"Tell me you want me," he demanded, his hands squeezing my ass. "Tell me."

"Yes," I gasped. "I want you."

He pushed his cock in, teasing. "Tell me to fuck you."

"Fuck me, Aiden. *Please.*"

"Hold tight, Sunshine."

He slammed into me, and I cried out. Over and again, he thrust, his hips driving hard and fast. His mouth covered mine, muffling my noises, swallowing my cries. I clung to his shoulders, pinned between him and the wall, unable to move or stop him. Only to feel—his muscles straining, his tongue sliding on mine, his chest hairs rubbing my sensitive nipples, and his hands gripping me as though his life depended on it. My body tightened, and he dragged his lips to my ear.

"Yeah. That's it baby. Give me what I want. Give it all to me."

I shattered, crying out his name. He never relented, driving into me hard until he climaxed, and he dropped his head to my shoulder with a long groan.

The water poured over us, the air heavy with steam. He withdrew, setting me down on my feet. He cupped my face and kissed me. His mouth was gentle now, and I opened my eyes to meet his tormented gaze. Slowly he lowered his head and kissed me again.

I wasn't sure if it was his tears or mine I could taste.

I SAT IN his bed, waiting, wondering if he would come into the room. I had the Kindle open where we had left off last night, but I wasn't sure he would join me.

After he turned around in the shower and picked up the soap, I had slipped out. I'd dried off, and crawled under the covers, confused and weary.

He entered, toweling off his hair, naked. His body was glorious. There was no other way to describe it. Muscled and heavy. Powerful. Capable of inflicting pain, yet he always touched me with such gentleness it made me feel special.

For a moment, he hesitated, but I lifted his pillow to my lap, and he slid into the bed. Then, instead of laying his head down and facing away the way he did as I read to him, he curled up tight, wrapping his arms around my waist, facing me.

I ran my fingers through his damp hair. The utter dejection on his face broke my heart.

"Talk to me," I whispered.

"There was a message from Louisa's father. He said he and his ex-wife had talked, and she agreed she would come and take Louisa out of school."

"So she's gone."

"It appears so."

I drew in a shuddering breath and forced a smile. "It's over. I can go home."

"I don't want you there alone."

"Dee won't be home for a while."

"Maybe . . ." He swallowed, then continued in a resigned voice. "Maybe it would be best if you did go stay with Emmy until Dee got home."

I felt my heart shatter.

"Cami, I have nothing. I can't—"

"Don't," I said, interrupting him. I knew what he was going to say, and I didn't want to hear it. Once again, I had been fooling myself.

"It's fine, Aiden. I'll take my bag in the morning. It's best that way."

"Yes." He took the Kindle, laid it on the nightstand, and shut off the light. He settled back on my stomach, his arms wrapped around me.

Neither of us spoke. I stared into the darkness, too sad even to cry.

Morning came too soon and was tense, each of us lost to our own heartbreak, and unable to share. As I packed my small bag, I watched him.

He scowled as he dragged on his pants and tucked a dark green shirt into the waistband, his movements jerky.

Desperate to hear his voice, I spoke.

"Are you upset over Bent and Emmy getting married?"

"Don't be ridiculous. Why would I be upset my best friend is getting married? I'm happy for him. Emmy is his perfect match."

"The news seemed to set you off. I was simply wondering."

I wished he would just talk to me. Yell. Anything. Despite what he said, I knew Bentley's engagement had spooked him, reminding him we were getting too close. What I saw as progress, he saw as unacceptable. He had been so good, looking after me, taking time off and spending it with me. We had amazing chemistry, and I loved talking with him, listening to his thought process. He was kind, generous, with a mischievous boyishness about him that made me laugh. However, he was damaged. He couldn't see how much he loved or was loved. Every time the light flickered, he was quick to extinguish it, refusing to admit it was possible. He had so much to give, but he was too afraid to try.

Even for me.

He dragged a hand through his hair. "It was hardly news since I knew it was going to happen soon. I have a lot on my mind. It's not all fun and games, Cami."

"I am aware of that."

"I have this meeting today. Maddox is sick. Bentley is worried about Reid, so I need to make sure he behaves. I'm still worried about you. Bent is nervous over Emmy because of this crazy chick, even though it seems to be over. It's all on me." He grabbed a belt, threading it through his waistband. "Don't turn this into something about us."

"I wasn't doing that."

He turned his back, the tension evident in the set of his shoulders. I felt terrible, knowing how much he was handling. I reached out, placing my hand on his shoulder. He froze, and I stepped behind him, leaning into his back. He didn't move, and I carefully slid my arm around him. With a sigh, he wrapped his hand around mine and spoke quietly.

"I'm sorry, Cami. I can't be what you need, and I know it hurts you."

"You don't have to worry about me, Aiden." I swallowed, tamping down my emotions. "I'll be fine."

"Cami, it's not . . . I can't—"

I closed my eyes, dreading what he was about to say. "No, Aiden. You don't have to say anything." I withdrew my hand. "I have to finish packing."

He didn't turn around.

⌒〜

THE CAR PULLED up, and Aiden took my bag, sliding it into the trunk. Knowing it was the last moment alone with him, I grabbed his hand.

"Thank you, Aiden, for everything." I squeezed his fingers. "We're good, okay?"

His eyes were tormented. Without a word, he pulled me in for a hug, his massive arms caging me in. I felt safe there.

He stood back. "If you need something, call me. Day or night."

"I will."

I slid into the car, meeting Emmy's sad gaze. I shook my head slightly. If she said anything, I was going to burst into tears. Instead, I turned to Reid who was standing outside with Bentley. "You clean up nice."

He preened, tugging at his collar. "I know."

Everyone chuckled, and I pulled the door shut. They all climbed into Aiden's car and drove away. Frank pulled away from the curb smoothly and followed. My eyes stayed on Aiden's car until they disappeared around the corner.

I needed the day to be over.

⌒〜

I FROWNED AS I scanned through the strange files. I didn't understand. Where was my presentation folder? I checked again, cursing under my breath.

"What is it?" Emmy asked.

"My stuff is missing." I yanked out the USB drive, studying it. "Shit."

"What?"

"This is the wrong drive. It's one of Aiden's. I must have left mine at his place." I checked my watch. "Damn it, they'll already be in their meeting."

"Don't you have a key?"

"No," I said despondently. "I left it this morning."

"Oh."

"Do you have another copy?"

"Yes. At home." I stood. "I have to go get it."

"You can't!"

"Why? I can grab a cab and be there in ten minutes, get the drive, and be back long before my class starts."

She looked around, nervous. "But Louisa . . ."

"She's gone," I said impatiently. "One of the girls in our group told me this morning Louisa had even sent her files on the project and told her she was taking a break. It's over. We can all move on."

"Aiden wouldn't like this, Cami."

"He has no say in the matter."

"I'm coming with you."

"No. You have class in a few minutes. I'll be back soon."

"Cami—"

"I don't have time to argue. I'm going." I hurried to my locker and grabbed my coat. I dreaded going back to the apartment, but I had no choice, and I'd only be there for a few minutes. Outside, I hailed a cab and jumped in. Feeling guilty, I called Aiden, and his voice mail picked up. I hesitated, then left him a message, knowing, no matter what, he would be furious I had left the school grounds. Yet, if I didn't tell him, it would make it worse. I forced myself to sound chipper.

"Hey, everything is fine, but I brought the wrong drive, and I have to go home and get another one. I am heading there now and going straight back to the school. Don't worry. I just wanted you to know."

At the apartment, I asked the cab driver to wait. He didn't look happy, but I paid the fare, and he agreed to wait five minutes.

"If you're not back, I am leaving," he snapped rudely.

"I will be," I assured him.

I hurried upstairs, letting myself into the apartment. Silence surrounded me, but I felt uneasy. I hesitated in the doorway, giving myself a pep talk. The door was double-locked. Louisa no longer had a key. The spare set for Dee was still hanging on the hook where Aiden had left them. Everything was okay.

"Get a grip," I murmured.

I rushed down the hall, snapped on the light, and headed to the dresser, locating the drive in the small basket. I huffed out a sigh of relief, just as the scent hit me. Once again, the overpowering fragrance of my perfume was in the air.

I looked in the mirror, gasping in shock at the sight on my bed.

Louisa, wearing one of my hoodies and sweat pants, stared at me. In her hands, she held a knife.

Scattered around her were streaks of bright fabric. My favorite umbrella was in ribbons, cut into shreds and discarded. The bright colors were tangled and unrecognizable, the images destroyed by her blade.

My blood went cold.

CHAPTER 17

CAMI

MYRIAD EMOTIONS AND thoughts flittered through my brain. Fear and dread settled into my chest. A paralyzing lethargy poured over my body, making escape impossible. The fact that I should have listened to Aiden or let Emmy come with me drifted into my mind. Minutes passed as we stared at each other, and with a sinking heart, I realized the cab driver would leave any second, and I would be stuck here, with Louisa.

Alone.

No one would know, until it was too late.

I thought of the self-defense moves Aiden had shown me. They had never included disarming someone with a knife. I swallowed and cleared my dry throat.

"Louisa. We've been looking for you. We've all been worried."

She tilted her head as if unable to comprehend my words. Her voice was robotic. "I've been here."

"This-this whole time?"

"Your sister's closet is very deep. It's a great place to sit and wait behind her clothes. Her soup is good. Even cold."

I wanted to weep. Aiden had looked in Dee's room. So had the police. I hadn't even thought to tell them how far back the closet went, and it wasn't something easily noticed. All you saw were Dee's clothes lined up, neat and in order and undisturbed.

"I thought you went home with your mom."

She laughed, the sound brittle. "Like she cares. She left me a message and said she heard I was misbehaving again. She said I needed to stop it or she would cut off my monthly allowance and put me back in the hospital." She shook her head. "You all are so anxious to get me to go away, so I decided to play your game. I told her I would come on my own, and I even called the school and pretended to be her, and Mr. Hob bought it." She changed her voice. "Of course, I do a wicked imitation of my unfeeling mother." Her eyes glittered. "I knew you had to come home soon."

"What do you want?"

She moved, more ribbons of fabric falling from her lap. She ignored my question. "Take off your coat." She stepped closer. "You aren't leaving."

I hesitated, and she jerked her arm, the knife flashing. "Now."

I dropped my coat to the floor, knowing my phone was in my pocket. It was always on vibrate during the school day, and I felt it buzz against my feet. I wondered if it was Emmy checking on me and if she would call the police when I didn't answer.

"You don't take care of your things, Cami. You don't deserve to have them." She waved her arm. "All your nice things and I had to straighten them for you." She narrowed her eyes. "You didn't even say thank you."

"I-I didn't know it was you. That-that was very kind of you. Thank you."

She shook her head. "You don't appreciate it. You have never appreciated *anything* I did. I even tried to give you a push in the right direction." Her mouth twisted into an evil smile. "Still, you didn't learn."

I gaped at her. "That was you? *You* pushed me down the stairs?"

"Technically, I shoved that Jen girl. She fell into you, so I didn't touch you. In the chaos, no one noticed me." She grimaced. "No one ever notices me."

I felt ill.

"You showed no appreciation for anything. Not the notes, going for coffee, or my friendship. Even loaning you sneakers when your feet were wet or coming all this way to see you." The knife in her hand caught the light as she clenched her fist, the sight terrifying me all over again.

"Did you cut them?" I asked. "My boots?"

"You deserved it," she confirmed. "You were rude."

"You took my umbrella."

"*You* left your umbrella by the lockers. Discarded."

Now I remembered. It had rained, and I left it dripping there so it didn't get my locker wet. The sun was out when school finished, and I had forgotten it. But I hadn't discarded it.

She wrinkled her nose, as if laughing at a private joke. "It was fun sometimes moving things around so you couldn't find them. Making you look for them." She grinned, her lips twisted and evil. "Making you frown for a change."

Despite my terror, she made me angry. "That was a shitty thing to do. Mess with my head like that."

She scowled, not caring. "Just paying you back."

I wanted to scream at her and ask her what she was paying me back for, but I was too scared of her answer.

"My scarf and cuff were here, in my room."

"I liked them. You had spare keys by the door, and I took one." She shrugged as if that was acceptable. She wanted them, so she took them.

"You could have asked if you could borrow them."

"So you could say no again? You kept saying no to me!" Her voice rose with each sentence. "You barely noticed me. You have time for everyone else. Emmy, the project group. Work. Your sister. *Aiden.*" She scoffed. "But me, you ignored, no matter what I did. You didn't even get it when I changed my hair!"

"I'm sorry," I offered, confused and unsure what else to do. "You're right. I was a bad friend. I just get busy, Louisa, and I forget. You know what it's like. Between school and responsibilities, you just forget. I-I didn't mean to ignore you."

She scowled, and I kept talking.

"Why don't I make us coffee now, and we can talk. I-I know about your sister, Jessie, and I'm sorry. We could talk about her if you want?"

Her voice rose even louder. "I don't *want* to talk about her. We were so close, then she left me and I was alone!"

I realized hearing her sister's name upset her, and I quickly tried something else. "Okay," I soothed. "Maybe watch a movie and relax. That would be fun, wouldn't it? Just hang for the day?" I babbled, trying to figure out my next step, my phone buzzing like crazy at my feet. I needed to stall and keep her mind off whatever plan she had. I needed to distract her.

She paused, the knife turning in her hand. The closer she came, the stronger the scent of my perfume grew. She had doused herself in it to cover the stench of her unwashed body. And, no doubt, to smell like me. But it wasn't pleasant on her. Instead, it was sickly sweet and rancid.

"You can have a shower, and I'll get you fresh clothes while the coffee is brewing. I'll change into something comfy too." I edged toward the door, praying she didn't notice.

"How stupid do you think I am?" she asked, her voice suddenly dripping with rage.

"I-I don't think you're stupid at all. I was just offering—"

"You think you're so much better than me. That you're too good to be my friend," she spat, moving between me and the door.

"No," I protested. "That's not true, Louisa."

"Hanging with rich people who pretend they care about you. You think Aiden is going to love you? He likes to *fuck* you, but that's all. I saw the way he looked at me. He'd be just as happy to fuck me. He's not in love with you. You are pathetic. Worse than me."

I knew she was crazy and spouting bullshit. Still, her words struck a nerve.

"I know," I stated. "I know he isn't in love with me." I passed a weary hand over my face. "Tell me what you want, Louisa. Just tell me."

"I want you to like me," she screamed, stepping forward. "I want you to be my friend and care about me!"

I regarded her sadly, her words reminding me of what I wanted from someone else.

"You can't make someone love you, Louisa. I'm sorry."

It happened in slow motion. One moment, she was staring at me, livid and shaking. Her arm lifted, and I knew any second, I would feel the pain of that knife. I prepared to defend myself, trying hard to recall what Aiden had taught me, and fighting against the panic that threatened to engulf me instead.

The next moment, there was the thundering of footsteps, and Aiden appeared, catching us both off guard. Louisa recovered, pointing the knife at him. I gasped, terrified she would strike in his direction and he would be hurt. He moved fast, and in seconds, the knife sailed through the air and Louisa spun away, a crumpled, sobbing heap on the floor across the room.

I met Aiden's horrified gaze. His chest was heaving, his body shaking as he reached out to me.

"I'm okay," I managed to get out.

He wrapped his hands around my arms, pushing me toward the door. "The police are on their way. Go sit in the living room."

My gaze skittered to Louisa. Her body shook with the force of her sobs. Despite everything, I felt a strong, abiding sorrow as I looked at her. Inadvertently or not, I was part of the reason she was in this position.

"Sunshine."

I tore my eyes away from Louisa and looked at him.

"Let me handle this. Go."

Numb, I stumbled away.

~

I SLUMPED INTO the armchair, my shaking legs unable to hold me upright. My mind raced with everything that had occurred recently, and especially today. I dropped my head into my hands, remembering Louisa's garbled words. The way she spat them at me and the fear she instilled as she went on about how hard she had tried to get my attention. How much she wanted to be my friend.

Shame washed over me as I realized I had acted no better toward Aiden than she had with me. I had tried to push him into liking me more, wanting me the way I wanted him. It was time to stop. He was never going to change, and I needed to accept that. To accept him as a great person, someone who was part of Emmy's life and with whom I would have to interact for a long time. I would never do anything that would force her to have to choose between us, so I needed to change my behavior.

I lifted my head, feeling weak and weary. Aiden shook the officers' hands and let them out of the apartment. They had taken Louisa away, and I had given my statement to the police. Aiden shut the door, his hand resting on the wood. His wide shoulders slumped, and I was certain he was as exhausted and emotionally drained as I was feeling.

He sighed and straightened, crossing the room and sitting on the chair opposite me. He kept his voice low and gentle, as if speaking to a frightened animal.

"Are you all right, Cami?"

I wanted to fling myself into his arms and tell him no. To explain how terrified I had felt, more so than I had ever been in my life—right up until the moment he had disarmed Louisa and I knew he wasn't going to be hurt. I couldn't bear the thought of him injured because of me.

Instead, I only nodded. "I'm fine."

"What do you need?"

Inside, I screamed, *"You!"*

However, again, I repeated myself. "I'm fine. Really." I swallowed. "How . . . ?" The word hung in the air.

"Emmy phoned Bentley. She told him you had come here, and I heard your message. I had my phone on vibrate because of the meeting, but I saw your number and checked the message. Bentley had forgotten to turn his off, and when he saw her number, he answered. I was already on my feet when he told me to go. I drove here like a madman. I kept phoning, but you didn't pick up. I knew something was wrong. I called the police, frantic. I beat them here." He shook his head and closed his eyes, his hands shaking. "Seeing her in front of you with a knife is an image I will never get out of my head. I can't even think about what might have happened if I had been a few minutes later . . ." His voice trailed off, and he opened his eyes, his gaze tormented.

"I don't think she would have hurt me."

"You're wrong. She wasn't thinking," he snapped. "Her mind wasn't processing reality anymore, and right and wrong didn't exist. Rage, the grief over her sister, and her hatred had taken over, Cami. She finally snapped."

I didn't want him drowning in any more guilt. He already carried enough around. "Then you got here in time, and you saved me, Aiden. Thank you."

"She was here the whole time. Waiting. I missed it."

"She was smart." I stroked his clenched hands. "Stop blaming yourself. I'm not."

"I would never have forgiven myself. I'm not sure I can forgive myself for what occurred today. I should have listened to my gut."

"You have to let it go. We thought it was over. Her mother lied about her whereabouts because she was too lazy to care or actually do anything. Louisa played everyone. It's on her and her family." I shook my head ruefully. "Some of the responsibility is even on me. Not you."

I stood. "I'm going to take a bath. You can let yourself out, okay?"

He frowned, standing as well. "You really think I'm going to leave you alone after what just happened?"

I drew in much-needed air and curled my hands into fists, seeking strength. "Aiden, I can't express my gratitude enough. For everything you've done for me. But it's over. She's in police custody, and I'm safe. I need a bath to warm up, then I'm going to lie down." A shudder ran down my spine. "I'll nap in Dee's room or here on the sofa." I wasn't sure I would ever sleep in mine again. "Before you go, though, I need to apologize to you."

He narrowed his eyes. "Apologize?"

I swallowed to rid myself of the lump that was forming in my throat. "For my behavior. I know you don't have the same feelings for me as I have for you. I have pushed and forced my way into your life, and you've been amazing. I know you allowed me to hang around because of Emmy and Bentley, and you've been patient with me. You told me right from the start there would never be a relationship beyond friendship between us. Even when we were intimate, I knew how you felt, but I was arrogant enough that I thought you would change your mind. That somehow, you would know I was different, and that I could be what you needed." I brushed my hair off my face. "I kept pushing you—trying to force you to feel something you didn't. Just like Louisa did with me."

He started to speak, and I held up my hand.

"Don't. Please. I get it now. I really do. I promise you it won't happen again. I won't make you uncomfortable, and I won't do anything to embarrass you. Our best friends are getting married. It's inevitable we'll be around each other, but I won't push anymore. I promise. I'll just be Cami—Emmy's slightly weird friend and someone who will be grateful to you for the rest of her life." Leaning up, I pressed my lips to his cheek. "Thank you."

He stood stock-still, a muscle working in his neck, but he said nothing. Desperate to keep my emotions hidden, I went down the hall and quietly shut the bathroom door behind me. I leaned against the wood, covering my mouth with my hand as the tears began to drip down my cheeks. I dashed them away and bent over the tub, pushing down the plug and turning on the tap. I grabbed Dee's citrus bubble bath, needing a different scent than my usual jasmine. I would never again wear that fragrance.

I heard the telltale sound of the door closing firmly at the front of the apartment, and with a quiet sob, I disrobed and slid into the water. Aiden was gone, and I was alone. I laid my head back and let the tears flow. I was so exhausted I couldn't weep. No sounds came out, only tears rolled down my cheeks, hot and heavy. I let them go, knowing I needed to mourn. I had so many regrets, and I was going to relive them every time I saw Aiden. I could only hope the pain would lessen and one day I would be able to smile at him again without my heart breaking.

I startled when the bathroom door opened, and Aiden came into the room.

"What are you doing?" I gasped, wiping my hands across my cheeks.

He shrugged, flipping the lid to the toilet down and sitting on it. He had changed, and he rolled up his sleeves, careful not to look at me. "You didn't give me a chance to reply, so I thought I would come in and take advantage of the fact that you couldn't walk away while I said my piece."

"I thought you left. I heard the door."

"I went to my car and grabbed my bag. I always have a change of clothes with me. I didn't want to smell her on me anymore."

"I'm never wearing that perfume again," I admitted.

He bent forward, resting his elbows on his thighs, and shook his head. "No, Cami. I love your scent. That perfume didn't smell like you at all when she wore it. It was overpowering and sweet. Frankly, on her, it made me nauseous. On you, it's light and airy. I like it. Your scent calms me like nothing else does. Don't let her take that from us."

I had no idea how to reply to his statement.

"Oh."

"As for what you said earlier, I think I'm the one who owes you an apology."

"I doubt that."

His unique eyes burned into me. "You have been offering me the gift of your love—without an agenda or any chance of it being reciprocated—and all I have done is treat you badly."

"You haven't treated me badly—just the opposite. It's not a gift if you don't want it. I know that now."

He raked his hands through his hair roughly and huffed out a curse.

"It *is* a gift. One I wanted so much but was too afraid to take." He kept on talking, not giving me a chance to reply. "Today, when I realized what was happening, the danger you were in, I kept praying." He snorted. "I never pray—I've never believed in any of that shit. But I did. I prayed and begged that you'd be safe—that you wouldn't be hurt, or even worse." His eyes drifted shut, then snapped open, once again pinning me with his gaze. "I promised, I *swore*, if I got there in time, if you were safe, I would tell you."

"Tell me what?" I breathed, terrified, yet enthralled with his words.

"Tell you everything. How I feel about you. Why I pushed you away. Why I so desperately want you, even though I don't deserve to have you."

"You want me?"

He lunged, moving so fast that before I knew what was happening, he was on top of me in the tub, his heavy torso pushing me into the porcelain. His mouth claimed mine as he buried his hand into my hair and yanked me tight, holding me close. His kiss was possessive, deep, and carnal. He moaned low, the sound reverberating in the room.

I whimpered, unsure where his actions came from, afraid to believe they meant what I hoped they did, and still so in love with him, I wasn't sure it mattered.

He dragged his lips over my cheek, pressing them to my ear. "I feel, Cami. I feel so much, and I'm fucking terrified of what I feel. I need you to help me."

"Tell me what you need."

He kept his voice low, as if ashamed to say it out loud. "Hold me for a minute. Let me feel you against me so I know you're okay."

"She didn't touch me, Aiden. You got here in time."

"Please. I need that."

I wrapped my arms around him, feeling the tremor that went through his massive form. I could feel his lips moving on my skin, but I had no idea what he was saying. He ghosted his hands up and down my back, never settling anywhere, but touching me so reverently, I felt the tears begin to well again. He had never touched me this way before now.

"Please don't," he murmured. "I hate it when you cry. My chest aches."

"I-I don't understand what's happening, and I'm scared to hope that maybe it's something . . ." I sucked in a long gulp of air. "Significant."

"I want it to be."

"But?" I whispered, my heart in my throat.

"I have things I need to tell you."

"Now?"

He drew back, bringing his hand up to cup my face. "Yes, but I think maybe I should wait until you're out of the tub. You're very distracting like this."

"Like this?"

A slow smile spread across his lips, and his expression changed, becoming lighter. "Wet, slippery, naked, and far too tempting."

"You're all wet now too."

"I have another shirt."

"I'll get out. We can talk. I can have a bath when you leave later."

He pressed his lips to mine sweetly. "What if I don't leave?"

"Then you can join me and wash my back."

His mouth was warm as he kissed me one more time. "Okay, deal."

CHAPTER 18

AIDEN

CAMI CURLED UP on the sofa, looking more tranquil than she had been lately. I had stayed with her, making her lie back in the tub and relax for a while. Despite the fact that I was still hard and aching for her, and seeing her naked and wet in the tub only made it worse, I ignored my throbbing cock and talked to her. Nothing heavy or personal—I knew that was going to happen soon enough. I talked about the project we were working on; I shared a few stories of Bent and Mad with her, things to get her to smile. While she was getting dressed, I had called Bentley, let him know everything was okay and promised to have Cami call Emmy later that evening. I sent a fast text to Dee, telling her everything was handled, Cami was safe, and she could relax. I would call her later and explain.

I sat close, needing to feel Cami beside me for our impending conversation. I picked up her hand, studying her long fingers, and stroked the soft skin of her wrist. The passing thought that a diamond bracelet would suit her skittered through my mind, surprising me. I had never bought a woman a gift before—I had never wanted to, until now.

"Talk to me," she whispered, sounding unusually shy.

"Love scares me, Cami."

"Why?"

"The only thing I associate with love is pain. I know I told you I had dyslexia, but there is a lot more to my childhood than simply a disorder I've had to struggle to overcome."

She shifted closer. "Tell me."

"My parents, for lack of a better term, were Henry and Gabby. I stopped calling them Mom and Dad when I was very young. They didn't deserve to be called those names after the way they treated me."

Cami bit her lip, as if she already anticipated what I was going to say.

"Henry was a drunk. A mean one—well, to me, anyway. My older brother and sister he liked well enough, but not me. I was different. If you can believe it, when I was a kid, I was a runt. I was little and scrawny—scared of my own shadow. I was slow to talk, didn't catch on to things quickly, and was backward with everything in life."

"Because of your dyslexia."

"We didn't know about it then. Henry simply didn't like me. He was an impatient man at the best of times, and with me, he had zero tolerance."

"Why?"

I met her confused gaze. "As I found out later in life it was because I wasn't his. Gabby had an affair, and I was the result."

"Oh. That must have been hard. Did your . . . Gabby protect you from him?"

I laughed, the sound harsh in the room. "She hated me. I was a constant reminder of her past. They, my whole family, had straight, sandy-colored hair, brown eyes, and freckles on their faces with red cheeks. Then there was me. Dark, curly hair, mismatched eyes, and no freckles. My skin tone was a little darker—just enough to be different.

I stuck out like a sore thumb."

"Aiden, no mother hates her child, no matter how different they look."

"She did. I was never enough. If he hit me, she walked away. If I did something to displease her, she was the one who hit me." I paused as memories swirled in my head. "I displeased her a lot."

I met her wide gaze. "She liked to use the belt. It hurt the most. Almost as much as her cruel words."

She slipped her hand into mine, holding tight.

"I remember being hungry all the time. I was a runt, like I said, and my brother used to grab my food." I grimaced as memories flooded my mind. "There was never a lot to eat, and when he took my food, I had to go without."

"Were you very poor?"

"No, not poor. Gabby didn't believe in wasting food, so she made just enough for each meal. She served the food from the kitchen, and because I was the smallest, I got the smallest portion. Once Eric grabbed some, I was often left hungry."

"Maybe that was why you were so small."

"Probably."

"That's why you eat more quickly than some people."

"It's a reflex, I think. I try not to, but it happens." I smiled sadly. "I think that's why I'm always hungry to this day."

"I like watching you eat. You enjoy it."

I had to grin. "I do. It's one of the pleasures I can enjoy without guilt. Bentley calls me a garbage disposal."

"He teases you because he cares."

"I know."

She squeezed my hand. "Go on."

"I didn't do well in school. I had trouble getting people to understand me. There were more times I didn't comprehend what was going on than I did. My grades were terrible. I was picked on and bullied, and I got beat up a lot. The dumb runt, you know, is an easy target."

"I assume your parents did nothing to keep it from happening?"

"No. I stopped saying anything since I knew they didn't care. In fact, I think they thought I deserved it. Just like when they hit me." I shrugged. "I know I did."

"No child deserves to be hit."

"You start to feel like you do, though. At home I was punished for my bad grades and failed tests. Criticized for being scrawny and weak. Called stupid and homely. I was picked on by my perfect brother and, for the most part, ignored by my sister. When the beatings would start, she'd leave the room."

"No one at school helped?"

"They just pushed me forward to the next grade. They didn't care either. Schools were overcrowded, so it was easier, I suppose. I was lost most of the time. I had one teacher, Mr. Randall. He was a good guy. He noticed how hard I struggled, and he did some tests with the school. They told my parents they thought I was dyslexic and explained about some treatments to help me cope. But they cost money, and my mother had zero interest in spending it on me. My brother, Eric, was in soccer and was pretty good at it, but it was expensive. My sister, Veronica, liked synchronized swimming. They were important, so my parents made sure they got what they wanted. They refused to 'waste' the money on me."

"But you needed the help!"

I shrugged. "I wasn't important, Cami. I never was to anyone. My entire life."

"You are to me."

My heart sped up at her soft declaration. "I don't deserve it after the way I treated you."

"I disagree."

Unable to stop myself, I leaned forward and brushed her lips with mine. "Thank you."

"I want to hear more."

I wanted to kiss her more and forget the conversation. However, she deserved to hear it all.

"Mr. Randall was great. He went above and beyond what he had to do for a student. He researched my condition and spent hours with me, helping me find ways to learn more easily. He discovered methods and tricks that helped me concentrate. Not everyone responds the same with this learning disability, and some find it manageable, while others struggle. I found ways of zeroing in on words I could understand, and slowly making my way through pages using those words."

"The font thing helps too, right?"

"Yes. Plus, my memory trick, while unusual, is very helpful. I can remember details other people would forget. Once I read something and understand it, it sticks. I can recall passages and quote them." I ran a hand through my hair. "I find listening to documents as I study them helpful. I can associate words easier and remember them. Technology has helped make my life simpler in many ways. Still, I struggle at times."

"It's nothing to be ashamed of."

"I was taught it was. I was made to feel I was something to be ashamed of in every way. No matter how hard I tried, I could never get their approval." I leaned my forearms on my thighs, dropping my head for a moment as memories flew through my head. "I acted out a lot when I was younger. I was desperate for attention, but I didn't know how to get it in a positive way. The affection my parents gave my siblings was denied to me. Instead, all I heard was a constant list of my shortcomings and failures. No matter what I did, I was never as good as they were."

"That would be hard to live with. No wonder you acted out."

"Henry was a wrestler in school. A good one. Once I finally started growing, he insisted I be part of the team. I did it to please him, hoping to finally do something he would be proud of, but I hated it. I hated every second of it."

"Why?"

I shut my eyes, admitting another of my faults. "I hated being touched."

She looked horrified. "You hate it when I touch you?"

"No, not at all—I like your touch." I pushed her hand to my cheek, confessing my need. "I crave your touch." She stroked my skin, once again so gently, I wanted to weep. I leaned back and cleared my throat.

"Growing up, I related touching to pain. No one ever hugged me or gave me pats on the back. They hit me. Punched me. Crowded me into a corner and smacked me with a fist or a belt. Wrestling was like that—the grabbing and shoving. The need to overpower another person to win. It reminded me of everything in my life. I was overpowered constantly. I felt like my world was one big wrestling match, and I was constantly being thrown to the mat." I ran a hand over my face. "I quit the team when I was fifteen, and that caused a huge fight with Henry. In his anger, he told me for the hundredth time all the reasons I was such a loser, why he hated me so much, and that I wasn't his son."

"Oh, Aiden . . ."

"It got ugly. I was bigger, and it wasn't as easy to push me around. Now, I could push back. He became enraged. Screaming in my face. Swearing and saying horrible things. I yelled at him, and somehow, we started wrestling—only it wasn't for sport. I was sure he was going to kill me. I fought back with everything I had, and we bounced around the room, knocking over furniture and breaking things." I swallowed as visions of that awful night replayed in my head. "At one point, he had me locked up, and I shoved back against him. We went flying right through the glass patio doors with me landing on top of him. It broke his hold, and I rolled away, right through all the glass that was around us."

Cami scooted close, gripping my hand harder. Her touch returned me to the moment, and I looked down at her elegant fingers restlessly clutching my skin. I traced her hand and bent down to brush a kiss on her knuckles.

"What happened?"

"I don't recall a lot of that night after that point. A neighbor had called the police. Gabby was screaming. I was bleeding, and Henry was unconscious. The police sent me to the hospital in a different ambulance from him—I got stitched up, and I spent the night. I never went back there again. A social worker came and saw me the next morning and said my parents had basically washed their hands of me. They said I was violent, disruptive, and they were worried not only about their safety, but also that I might hurt my siblings. They swore I attacked Henry without reason."

"That was a lie."

I smiled forlornly at her, tucking a lock of hair behind her ear. "Who was going to believe me, Cami? I never said anything at school. I had no friends. By that point, Mr. Randall had retired, and I had no teacher I confided in. I was just another student with issues. My file was full of times I when I got angry and lashed out at someone. I never hurt them, but I would yell. Now my parents were just confirming what everyone already knew. I was a waste of space and not worthy of love. Not even from my family."

She lifted our clasped hands to her mouth, brushing her lips to my skin. "No, you are," she breathed out. "You so are." She pressed my hand to her cheek, and I was startled at the wetness on her skin.

"Don't cry for me."

"Someone has to. You deserve to have someone who loves you enough to cry for you."

Her words rolled around in my head.

Loves you.

Deserve.

They were foreign to me.

"What happened to you?"

"I went to a shelter. Then I was sent to a few foster homes, but they never worked. They expected a kid who needed discipline, and they acted accordingly. The abuse continued."

"What you needed was to be loved."

"I didn't get that. I didn't know a touch didn't have to hurt until I was older." I met her sad gaze. "Sex was the only way I knew how to connect with someone. Even then, I preferred to do the touching rather than be touched. I could never let anyone in. I didn't know I could want the touch of another person on my skin all the time until I met you. I never felt the need to connect with someone the way I do with you. It scared the ever-loving shit out of me, if I'm being honest."

Our eyes locked, my mismatched irises meeting her beautiful green. Mine pleaded for patience; hers filled with acceptance.

"Go on," she urged.

"I was lucky, though, and I had a social worker who helped me. Lori watched over me as best she could, and she tried to get me placed into the right home." I barked out a laugh. "The trouble is there isn't a huge line of people waiting to take a fifteen-year-old boy with anger problems, as I had been labeled. She stuck with me, though. Made sure I kept up my schoolwork and even got me a part-time job. When I aged out, she found me a little place to go. It wasn't much, just a room with a bed and a chair, but it was mine. I worked hard, saved for school, and got in with a scholarship."

"Where did you work?"

"Her son, Neil, owned a gym and she had gotten me a job working there not long after she became my case worker. I started as a cleaner and worked my way up. Part of my payment was that I could use the equipment. I discovered how much I loved to exercise. I had finally grown into my body, and the physical release was something I needed. It was something I understood. I got along well with her son, and he encouraged me. Neil said I was a natural. Watching the therapists at his gym showed me that touch had the power to heal as well as hurt, and I found it fascinating. I decided to take both business and physical therapy courses—I thought I wanted to run my own clinic. I got accepted at Toronto, and I moved here. Then I met Bentley and Maddox, and I finally I found friends who really cared, a place I could call home and where I was comfortable."

Reflectively, I traced the ink on my arm. "I got this tattoo when I was twenty. Bent and Maddox came with me. I wanted to cover up the scars I had. The ones *they* gave me. I didn't want to look down and see them anymore."

Her voice was drenched in tears. "Aiden . . ."

"When I was young, I would sneak away to the library. Every Wednesday, there was a woman who read out loud. I loved the stories about fierce, strong dragons." I tapped my upper arm. "The dragon reminds me to stay strong."

She touched the clouds etched into my skin and traced her fingers over the red flowers. "What about these?"

"The clouds represent life. They float and change, the darkness balancing the light."

"And the flowers?"

I smiled, feeling strangely nervous about telling her their meaning. "The house the guys and I rented together had a bush in the front of it that bloomed with red flowers every year. Every time I saw it I knew I was home. It was the first time I had ever truly had a home."

"That's beautiful, Aiden."

"I've never told anyone that before now."

"Thank you for telling me," she whispered, the sadness in her eyes apparent. Her obvious emotion at hearing my story shook me.

I had only ever shared it with Bentley and Maddox, and I had never gone into as much detail as I had with Cami. We all knew each other's pasts. It was something that drew us closer—made us brothers instead of simply friends. They had been understanding and empathetic since they had both experienced trauma growing up themselves, but they weren't emotional. We were tight and would do anything for one another, but aside from the odd hug, the constant banter, and the occasional argument, we didn't do the whole emotion thing. It just wasn't us, and we all preferred it that way. I knew Bentley was different with Emmy, and although he refused to discuss it, Maddox showed an alternate side of himself to Dee. For the first time ever in my life, I had opened up fully to someone. It was, I found to my surprise, cathartic. Cami's tender compassion made the pressure I always felt in my chest ease.

"Thank you for listening to me."

"You can talk to me anytime, about anything."

I lifted her hand and kissed the delicate skin of her wrist.

"Do you stay in touch with anyone? Mr. Randall or Lori and Neil?"

"Mr. Randall died before I finished school. He had a massive heart attack after breakfast one day. I went to his funeral and wept at the loss of the first man who had shown me kindness, and who told me I was more than my family let me think I could be."

I had to stop and clear my throat. "Lori retired, and when I became successful, I paid off Neil's gym and helped him make improvements to it. He runs an after-school program now to help more kids like me. I moved him and Lori into a nice house, and I make sure they're okay. They will never need anything for the rest of their lives if I can help it."

"That's amazing."

I shrugged, self-conscious. "It was the least I could do. They changed my life's path. If Lori hadn't seen beyond the reports and helped me, God knows where I would be today."

Cami sighed, her breath shaky. "I'm glad you're here, with me."

The emotion in her eyes was overwhelming. No one had ever looked at me the way Cami did. She made me feel invincible. Strong. And more vulnerable than I had ever been because of the depth of my need for her. And my need for that look.

"You frighten me, Sunshine. You scare the ever-loving shit out of me."

She gasped. "How is that even possible? I'm half your size."

"No, I don't mean physically." I hesitated, then spoke my fear. "Emotionally, you could destroy me."

"You have that power over me as well," she declared quietly. "I don't want to destroy you, Aiden. I want to share your life and be your partner. Help you through the bad days, not cause them." She cradled my hand to her cheek. "I want to be the missing piece to your world."

I pulled her onto my lap fast, surprising her. "Love has always equaled pain for me, Cami. I let down my guard once, and it bit me in the ass. It proved to me that I was right. I wasn't worthy of love."

"Can you tell me?"

I pushed a tendril away from her face, tucking the curl behind her ear. "You really want to know?"

She captured my hand, kissing the palm, and holding it to her cheek. "I want to know everything, Aiden. I want to know you. To understand why you feel the way you do." She sighed. "Then I can show you why you're wrong and that you're so worthy of being loved."

I stared at her for a moment, unable to comprehend her thoughts. She was adamant in her feelings for me. She never wavered.

"I think I need a drink," I confessed.

"You don't have to tell me."

"No, I do. But I need a break, if that makes sense."

"I understand."

In the kitchen, she opened the cupboard and pulled out a bottle of whiskey. "Dee likes this stuff. Will that do?"

"Perfect. What about you?"

"I haven't eaten today, so I'll just have water."

I reached for my phone. "I'm ordering pizza."

"I'm not really hungry," she admitted.

I spoke as I dialed. "You need some food, and frankly, so do I. I need you to eat. Please? For me?" I added, knowing she would agree. The break would help us both.

"Okay."

A short time later, I sat back, replete. Cami had only eaten one slice, nibbling away while I devoured the rest, but at least it was something.

"Is pizza your favorite food?"

"No, but it's fast and easy."

"What is your favorite?"

"Fried chicken. Homemade, not the takeout garbage."

"Dee makes great fried chicken. She'll make it for you."

Her words stirred a memory, making me frown.

"Will you tell me now?"

"Yes." I focused on staying calm, choosing my words carefully without too much detail. I knew she'd have questions, and I didn't want to get too upset, so I chose to tell her the story as briefly as possible.

"My sister, Veronica, showed up a few years ago. She appeared out of the blue, with no warning. She told me she had moved here and saw my name in the paper." I paused, thinking how shocked I had been when I heard my name called and turned to find Veronica standing behind me. "She asked me for coffee. She wanted a chance to apologize."

"Oh."

"I was curious, so I agreed to go with her. She told me Gabby and Henry had both died recently. She said she had no contact with Eric, my brother. Then she told me she was sorry for how everyone had treated me when we were younger. She explained she had always been afraid of our parents and the one time she had tried to stick up for me, she was punished."

"Had she done that?"

I shrugged. "Not that I remembered, but I did know she never joined in the bullying or mistreatment the way my brother did. She always left the room."

I kissed Cami's hand and stood, unable to sit in one place anymore. I prowled around the room, picking up things and studying them. A picture Cami had sketched of a dress. A small piece of metal sculpture. Touching her things, items she loved, calmed me.

"What happened, Aiden?"

"She told me she wanted the chance to be friends. To get to know each other as adults. She seemed sincere. I told her I would think it over, and I left. I talked to Maddox and Bent and told them what happened."

"What did they think?"

"That I should be cautious."

"I take it they were right."

"Things seemed great. I checked her out, and her story matched up with the information I could find. We met for coffee, had dinner. We talked—sometimes about the past, but more about our lives from after I had left until the present. She told me she'd gotten out of a bad relationship and moved here to start over, much as I had done years ago. She met Bent and Mad. They were polite but reserved."

"And?"

"We started to grow closer. She worked from home as an online editor with a magazine company. I'd drop by on occasion with lunch or for coffee. She would pick up my favorite brownie from the bakery down the street from my place, drop by to say hi, and check up on me. She called and sent funny texts. She remembered my favorite dinner growing up was fried chicken, and she made it for me." I met Cami's sympathetic glance. "She did all these things, caring things, which made me think she was real. She slowly got under my skin, and I decided that maybe she had also been a victim and not one of the criminals in my childhood. I forgave her because I felt she had done what she needed to do in order to survive. We had both suffered in different ways."

"That was a brave decision, Aiden."

I sat down beside her and took her hand, playing with her fingers. "A stupid one."

She lifted one shoulder. "I think it takes a brave person to try—be it a relationship, a new career, anything, really. Anything you try that is new and different takes guts, but putting yourself out there emotionally? Very brave."

I stared at her in amazement. *How had I denied how incredible she truly was?*

She squeezed my hand. "Keep going."

"One day, when I stopped by, I could see she had been crying. It took a while to convince her, but she told me her ex had racked up a ton of debt in her name, and she was trying to figure out how to pay it off. She was setting up some appointments with debt consolidators."

Cami's eyebrows rose. "I see."

"I didn't. When I had checked her out, I saw her lousy credit, and I should have checked again—dug more. Used my head and not my heart. I think I was so desperate to believe her, to think I had been wrong, that I turned a blind eye, and I fell for her con. I told her I would help her. I transferred fifty grand into her account that afternoon."

"What happened next?"

"She lost her job and couldn't find another one. She couldn't pay her rent, so she lost her apartment and needed a place to stay."

"So, she moved in with you?"

I snorted. "Yep. Then I hired her as my assistant and paid her myself since she wasn't able to find another job right away."

"All things that show what a caring man you are to others."

"And stupid. She had me right where she wanted me. Gradually, she started taking over. She did it well, in subtle ways that, until it was over, I never noticed. She had control of my house, my accounts, everything. I confided in her daily." I sat down heavily. "I was so eager for her affection. She was my family—the one thing I had always wanted—and she was there. In my head, if I took care of her, she would love me." My head fell to the cushion. "I really thought she did."

Cami stood and paced, and I waited until she spoke.

"What happened?"

"Bent and I were away on a business trip, looking at some property out West. Maddox called me and told me there was something odd going on with my finances. Money was disappearing fast. He told me he was going to freeze all my accounts. I flew home that afternoon, and I caught her. She was packing up to leave. She actually had a suitcase filled with cash, like some bad TV movie. Still, it wasn't the worst part."

Cami crouched in front of me. "What was it?"

"Eric was there—they were in it together. They were arguing when I let myself in. She was telling him how awful it had been pretending to like me, and she was glad it was over. How pretending to give a shit about what was going on in my life was tedious, and I annoyed her. That his idea of getting some money had been harder on her than she expected, and she wanted a bigger cut. He was arguing that she had to ride out this storm, convince me it was a bank error, and get more money. He was angry that she'd gotten tired of the subterfuge and decided to take as much money as possible and get out while I was gone." I huffed out an exhale of air, trying to ease the tightness in my chest that memory brought up. "To say they were shocked to see me standing there, Bentley beside me, listening to their secret confession, would be an understatement."

She rubbed my thighs, making small clicking noises of disapproval in her throat. I looked down at her hands, thinking despite how elegant and long her fingers were, how small they looked on my legs.

"Once they knew they'd been caught, it got ugly. They told me I owed them. Because of what happened that night when I was a teenager, Henry was never able to work again. He drank more and was verbally abusive to them. There was no money for university— there was barely enough to live on. My parents lost the house and had to move in to an apartment. They were ostracized at school—no longer part of the in crowd. Neither had done much with their lives. Years later, they saw my name in the paper, read about my success, and decided I owed them for what they lost."

She stared up at me, aghast. "None of which was your fault. Henry did that to your family. He treated you like shit your whole life. They all did."

"That's not how they saw it. Maddox showed up a few minutes later, and things went from ugly to horrible. There was shouting and threats. And a lot of pushing and shoving between Bent and my brother, who tried to grab the suitcase and run. My sister became hysterical and started screaming." I shook my head. "Then Maddox called the cops. Or, at least, started to. My brother and sister begged me to give them the money. Promised never to return if I did."

"You gave it to them, didn't you?"

I shrugged. "It was twenty-five grand. Compared to what I had already given her, not a lot, and frankly, it barely made a dent in my bottom line. I just wanted them gone. I was reeling from how easily I had fallen for her act and the betrayal. Luckily, Maddox stepped in and made them sign something. And before they were out the door, he had all her cards and the lists of my accounts she had maintained. He had her access denied, the locks changed, and even took her cell phone. She left with the cash, her clothes, and that was all."

"And she destroyed you."

"Do you know what she said to me one day? The words I held on to so desperately?"

She shook her head.

"I care about you, Aiden. I care so much."

Cami's eyes widened. "I said that to you at the lake. The night you got upset."

"It brought back that painful memory so vividly, I shut down. I know I acted like an asshole, something else I need to apologize for, but it hit me like a wrecking ball. It reminded me that I had already learned my lesson. Love wasn't for me. It proved I'm not worthy of that emotion."

She wiggled between my legs, reached up, and cupped my face. "The fact that you forgave her and tried to have a relationship says a lot about the kind of man you are to me, Aiden."

"You mean needy and stupid?"

Her hands tightened. "I mean forgiving and strong. Generous and capable of love—both of giving and receiving." She shook her head. "They were the ones in the wrong, but Aiden, can't you see you're allowing them to win?"

"What are you talking about?"

"You refuse to let me in. You keep up walls and never allow yourself to be truly happy. You've cut yourself off from the chance of real love. Don't let her, *them*, do this to you. Don't believe the awful things they said and did, because what they said is bullshit. They knew how to hurt you, and that was all they wanted."

Tears glimmered in her eyes. "Don't let them keep hurting you. Choose to believe the people who really care about you."

My throat felt thick. "Who should I believe?"

"Bentley," she stated promptly. "Maddox. The two people who love you the most. Know you better than anyone." She drew in a deep breath. "Me. I see the *real* Aiden. I see the hurt you hide and the need you try to disguise. I see *you*."

"How can you think so highly of me after the way I treated you?"

"That's what you do when you love someone, Aiden. You forgive them."

I met her wide, green gaze. There was nothing but honesty in her eyes. For the first time, I allowed myself to see what else her stare reflected.

Love. Real, honest love. Not for my money. Not for anything else, except me.

Cami loved me.

All I had to do was reach out, and the one thing I wanted, I *needed*, all my life could be mine.

I only had to take it.

Reaching down, I lifted under her arms and crushed her to me.

"Mine," I whispered. "All mine."

"Yours," she replied.

I held her tighter.

⌒

WE SAT TOGETHER silently. I enjoyed being able to hold her. After what happened today and the discussion about my childhood, I needed it. I needed her.

"Aiden, can I ask you something?"

I pressed a kiss to her head. "Anything."

"Why can you forgive everyone around you, even your sister, but you can never forgive yourself?"

"I'm sorry?"

She tilted back her head, meeting my confused gaze. "You never give yourself a break. If something goes wrong, you blame yourself. If there's a problem, you always take responsibility. You heap coals on your own head, and you carry too much. What happened in your childhood wasn't your fault. Your sister's actions were hers, not yours." She hesitated. "What happened with Emmy or Greg wasn't because of you either."

I tensed. "What are you talking about?"

"I think you're still blaming yourself for the situation." She cupped my face. "I heard you, Aiden. At night, when you slept here. The nights I spent with you. Your nightmares. You carry too much pain and blame inside you. You need to let it go."

I met her gaze. There was no judgment. She looked worried, sad, and unsure. No doubt, she was concerned about my reaction to her words. I thought about what she said.

"I don't know how," I admitted in a low voice. "I was blamed for everything all my life. I don't know how to be any other way. It's almost easier to take the blame for things at times."

"You could talk to someone. A professional to help you."

I huffed a laugh. "You sound like Bentley."

"Who is a very smart man and loves you like a brother. You and Maddox are family to him. Do you think he would ever suggest you do something that would hurt you?"

That stopped me. She was right. Aside from the occasional words spoken in anger, or disagreement, neither Bentley nor Maddox had ever done anything to hurt me deliberately. Since I met them, they had protected me the way I protected them.

"He only wants to help you," she added.

"I know. He's right. I wasn't ready, though."

"But you are now?"

"Do you think I should talk to someone?"

"What I think doesn't matter. *You* have to want to talk to someone."

"I think maybe I do. I know Bent and Emmy think the world of this Chloe person."

"She has helped Emmy. Bentley finds her helpful as well."

I leaned my forehead to hers. "I want to try. Not only for me. I want to be able to show you how I feel, Cami. To be what you need. I'm ready for that, but I do need some help. Would you . . . would you come with me?"

She slid her arms around my neck, holding me tight.

"Yes. Whatever you need, I'm here for you."

CHAPTER 19

CAMI

"I WANT TO take you home to my place," Aiden murmured against my head. "I don't want you here. Not until Dee comes home." He sighed, his breath ruffling my hair. "Not even then."

I tilted my head up to study his weary face. "This is where I live."

"Maybe we can find you a new place. The building we own where Maddox lives has some nice two-bedroom units."

"I doubt we can afford the rent."

He smirked. "I think we can arrange something."

"Aiden," I scolded gently. "I don't need you to do that. I'm not with you for your money or what you can give me."

His eyes were soft, and he slid his fingers over my cheek. "Are you with me, Cami? Even after all I've put you through?"

"Yes."

"Let me take you home. I can't relax here, and I think you'd feel better too. Please."

He was right. I was on edge, and the thought of going into my bedroom down the hall made me anxious.

"Okay."

⌒

AIDEN STAYED CLOSE all night. While I talked to Emmy, and later Dee, on the phone, he was beside me, constantly touching my shoulder or arm, wrapping his hand around mine and kissing the knuckles. My heart soared every time he touched me. He huffed a little when I assured Emmy I would be at school the next day; although he gave up the fight quickly when I explained why.

"I need to see my teacher and the director to explain why I wasn't there for my presentation. I have to get a make-up date." I sighed. "I hope they give me one."

"I'll go with you."

"You're not going to beat anyone up, are you?"

"No. What happened, though, is not the normal 'the dog ate my homework' excuse. I want to make sure they understand and you get the chance."

I tapped my chin. "You know, I think you BAM boys are a bad influence."

"BAM boys?" he asked with a chuckle. "Do explain."

"Emmy gets involved with Bentley and misses her presentation because she's kidnapped. I get involved with you, and some madwoman comes after me and I miss mine," I teased with a grin. "The common denominator seems to be BAM boys."

"Maybe the common denominator is you girls. Seems to me both of you are trouble."

"A little."

He wrapped his hand around my neck, tugging me to his mouth. "A lot. I'm still going with you tomorrow, by the way."

"Okay."

He brushed his mouth over mine. "You're still tense." He rubbed my shoulders. "You're safe now, you know that, right?"

"I know." I shut my eyes with a sigh. "I need a little time, Aiden. The past few weeks have messed with my head. I was convinced I was going crazy or developing the same symptoms as my mother."

"You're not."

"My head knows that now. I just need the rest of my body to catch up."

"Okay, here's the plan. I'm going to run you a bath, bring you some wine, and then we're going to bed."

"Then I can read to you?"

"I want you to relax."

"Reading to you does relax me. I want to. Please?"

His eyes were warm, his mouth even more so. "Yes."

I watched him walk away and heard the water come on in the bathroom. I was tired, but my body was tense. My mind wouldn't shut off either. Yet, not for the reasons Aiden probably thought. Louisa had scared me, and it was going to take some time to recover from everything that had occurred in the last while, but it was his confession, the things he told me about his life and upbringing that had my head spinning. The fact that he did care, and he wanted to try to be *more* with me. The look on his face when I said the word love to him . . . he was incredulous, incapable of believing himself worthy of being loved. Unable to comprehend that he could love someone.

Yet, with every gesture, every brush of his fingers on my skin, every endearment, he proved himself to be more than capable. The fierceness of his protection, the need to look after me, it all showed his feelings.

He came down the hall, extending his hand. "Come on, Sunshine, the water is ready."

I reached for his hand, letting him tug me down to the bathroom.

I only hoped that one day he could say the words.

ONCE AGAIN, AIDEN had his body curled around me, his head facing me and his eyes gazing at my face. I glanced down from my Kindle with a smile. "You're supposed to be relaxing, not staring."

He tucked himself closer, his head burrowed into my stomach. "I like looking at you." He sighed as I ran my fingers through his hair. "I like being close to you. To be able to touch you."

"You can touch me anytime."

"I'm not good at this, Cami. I have never been part of a couple."

"Ever?"

"No. I'm going to mess it up."

I shut the Kindle and gazed down at him. "So will I. No one is perfect, Aiden. We'll learn together. All I ask is that you don't shut me out. Talk to me. Share what you're feeling and let me help you."

"You help me without even knowing it."

I ruffled his hair, then smoothed it away from his forehead.

He played with a wrinkle in the T-shirt I was wearing. One of his that was too long, too big, and perfect. A frown creased his face, pulling down his lips, and his eyes grew tormented. "Today," he whispered, "I-I thought I would be too late. That I would never have the chance to tell you how I felt and what I really wanted."

"It didn't happen," I soothed him. "I'm right here."

He pushed up on his hands, kissing me. It wasn't his usual, controlling, passionate kiss. His mouth and tongue moved languidly with mine. He wound his hand into my hair, caressing my scalp, his touch tender. He tugged me down, hovering over me, his mouth never leaving mine. Endless minutes passed as we kissed. Never rough, never forceful, but passionate, claiming, and soulful.

"I want you, Sunshine."

"Yes," I pleaded. "Yes, Aiden."

He swept the T-shirt over my head, gazing down at me. "You are so beautiful. I've never told you how beautiful you are."

"Show me."

He kissed my cheek, his lips soft. He started at my mouth and slid down, every inch of my body touched with slow, sensuous drags of his lips. He whispered thoughts into my skin, his voice reverent, gentle.

"These freckles drive me wild." He traced them with his tongue, light and teasing. "Like a tiny patch of stardust on your skin.

"Your breasts are perfect for my hands, Sunshine." He licked and tugged on my nipples, making me groan. "The way your nipples swell for me, little buds just for me."

His mouth ghosted along my forearms, kissing the thin skin on the inside of my wrist and pressing his lips to my palm. "Your hands touch me with such tenderness." His awed and shy gaze met mine. "I had only ever known harsh touches until you."

"Aiden," I breathed out, cupping his face, tugging him to my mouth for another kiss.

He swirled his tongue down my torso, his fingers dancing on my skin. He kissed the arch of my foot, teased the back of my knee, and slid his tongue up my thighs. He didn't rush, and I let him do what he wanted. He would stop and lean forward, capturing my mouth with his and kissing me, then with a grin, go back to the body part he was worshiping. Because I realized . . . That was exactly what he was doing.

He stopped at the top of my right thigh where I had a beauty mark. Lazily, he traced it with the tip of his tongue, making me shiver.

"You like that, Cami? You like my tongue there?"

I gripped the sheet, fisting it tightly in my hand. "Yes."

He slipped his hands higher, pushing my legs apart. "Is it because you know, once I've been there, where I'm going next?" His hot breath drifted over me. "What I'm going to do to you next?"

He had me so turned on; I couldn't take it.

"Please, Aiden—"

"Shh, baby. I'm gonna take care of you."

He dipped his head and found me wet and ready, aching for him. He groaned, his mouth and fingers working in tandem. I cried out with the force of my need, but he refused to hurry. Gradually, he built a rhythm, until I shattered, my cries of his name echoing in the room.

Then, for the first time, Aiden made love to me. He showed me with his body what he wasn't able to say out loud. Pulling me up on his thighs, he filled me inch by inch, claiming the last part of me. He moved leisurely, his hips curling in tight circles, his mouth covering mine. He wrapped his arms around me, holding me close, our bodies fused together so tight we moved as one, never apart. We rocked, our eyes locked on each other, desire and need overriding all else.

"Cami," he moaned. "I need you. All of you. Oh God, baby . . ."

I wrapped my arms around his neck, clutching on tight. Tears spilled from my eyes at his need, the way he whispered my name, his breathless words of adoration.

I felt the tremors of my orgasm begin. I held him harder, surrendering to his body. Giving him everything he needed. Letting him have everything.

His arms became vises. He buried his face in my neck and stilled. A long, low groan escaped his mouth. He jerked, his cock kicking up inside me, triggering my release. I sobbed his name, my orgasm washing over me the same way he had loved me. Long, slow, peaking, and ebbing like the tide.

I collapsed into his chest, spent.

He lowered me to the bed, keeping me close, refusing to release me.

"Sleep, Sunshine. Know I'm here, and you're safe. I've got you."

I flexed my arms, sated, sleepy, and content.

"I have you too."

I felt his smile.

"I know."

~

MR. HOB AND my favorite teacher, Madame Franklin, were aghast when they learned what had occurred. I was grateful Aiden was with me. I began to talk and became overwhelmed, my voice shaking, and I knew I was going to cry. Aiden picked up my hand and took over when I faltered. He used words I never would have, which made the story seem scarier. Words like perpetrator, terrorized, stalker, and victim, all peppered his statements.

"What is the next step?" Mr. Hob asked.

Aiden frowned in displeasure. "It's in the hands of the police. Louisa's parents have been contacted. She is in a locked medical facility."

"I don't want to press charges," I murmured.

Aiden huffed, already knowing my thoughts.

Madame Franklin looked puzzled. "Why ever not, child?"

"I think she needs help, not jail."

Aiden spoke. "I explained to Cami it may not be her decision, but we will see what the police decide."

"And from us?" Mr. Hob inquired. "What do you need?"

"A chance to do my presentation," I requested. "I know, usually, once you miss it, you are deducted marks."

"Of course. No marks will be deducted. The circumstances are rather . . . unique."

Aiden smirked. "A fact I pointed out last evening."

We stood, and Aiden shook their hands.

Madame Franklin hugged me. "Come and see me after class, Cami. We will pick a new date."

"Thank you."

I walked Aiden out to his car. He held my hand within his, strong and firm.

"I'll be here to pick you up later."

"Okay."

At his car, he bent and kissed me. Sweet and soft. He lingered, his hand resting on my neck, his fingers tracing circles on the skin, holding me close. With a satisfied smile, he stepped back. "Have a good day."

I couldn't help beaming at him.

He grinned back widely. "There's my smile."

Laughing, I turned and began to walk away, when he called, "Hey, Sunshine?"

I spun around, waiting. He didn't say anything, but he shuffled his feet and dragged a hand through his hair. I hurried back to him, laying my hand on his arm.

"Aiden?"

He met my eyes, anxious and worried.

"What is it?"

His expression tugged at my heart. Bashful, fearful, yet determined. He cupped my face with both hands and leaned close.

He spoke three small words. Three words that seeped into my heart, stitched the worn edges, and mended the cracked and beaten shell.

"I love you."

CHAPTER 20

AIDEN

I SAT AT my desk, unable to concentrate. I knew I would never forget the look on Cami's face when I finally got the balls to tell her what I felt.

The words hung in the air between us. For some reason, I couldn't let her walk away without saying them. Without letting her know how much she meant to me. As they sank in and her expression changed from confusion to understanding, euphoric was the only word I could think of. Never mind sunshine; she transformed into a fucking sunbeam as she clutched my wrists and tears spilled down her cheeks. I had braced myself for the panic, the denial that uttering the words would bring, but there was none. Instead, there was only a strong, abiding feeling of it being right.

We were right.

She was what I needed in my life, and I was done denying it.

Denying her.

Laughing, I swung her around in my arms, then cupped her face again, dropping light kisses all over her cheeks, eyes, nose, and finally, kissing her hard, pouring all the love I felt into that kiss. Though I was not one for public displays, even the catcalls directed our way couldn't stop me.

I set her back on her feet, meeting her glowing eyes. "I love you, Sunshine."

"I love you right back."

"I know." *I exhaled hard.* "It's the greatest thing in the whole fucking world."

My phone beeped, and I shook my head. "That will be Bent. You need to get to class."

"You'll be here later?"

I pulled her in for one last hug. "I'll always be here, Sunshine. You're stuck with me now."

She winked and turned to walk away. "I think I can handle you," *she threw over her shoulder.*

I had to laugh. If anyone could, it was Cami.

I lifted my phone to my ear. "I'm on my way, Bent. Hold your horses."

He chuckled. "Just letting you know Maddox showed up. He's better, but he looks like hell. We're meeting over lunch."

"Okay."

"Everything go all right?"

I glanced toward Cami's disappearing figure. From across the parking lot, she turned and waved, then hurried into the building. I already missed her.

I climbed into the car, shaking my head over how pussy-whipped I had become overnight. I grinned, though, because I didn't really care.

"Yeah. Everything's good. See you soon."

I hadn't seen anyone except Sandy, who handed me some files and offered a cup of coffee, which I gratefully accepted. When she brought it in, she slid a plate onto my desk with two of my favorite lemon Danish pastries on it.

"Special occasion?"

She grinned. "I think it must be. Cami called and asked if I would get these for you."

I looked down, and the horrible feeling I was about to blush in front of Sandy filled my head.

"What else did she say?"

"Nothing. I was pleased to hear she was doing well considering what she went through yesterday. I'm not blind, Aiden. I have never seen you look this . . . happy." She patted my shoulder. "Just remember, you deserve to be."

With a wink, she sashayed out of my office, leaving me to my thoughts.

A few minutes later, Bentley strolled in, promptly sitting in front of my desk. I finished swallowing my treat and grinned at him. "Sorry, all gone."

"Big surprise."

Maddox walked in, looking terrible. His nose was red, and he looked tired. He sat down heavily, regarding me seriously. "Are you all right?" he rasped out.

"Better than you."

He waved his hand. "I'm okay. Cami? She okay? Dee was freaking on the phone last night."

I exchanged a glance with Bentley. I wondered how often the two of them spoke while she was gone.

"I spoke with Dee this morning. Cami is fine. She's strong." I rubbed a hand over my chin. "Although I'm not sure she will ever want to live in that apartment again. She couldn't go into her bedroom to get some clothing. I had to do it for her."

"Dee said the same thing."

I glanced at Bentley. "I was thinking of the two-bedroom units in the building Maddox lives in. We keep a couple of them for out-of-town business guests. We rarely use them. Do we really need two?"

He didn't hesitate. "No. We could let them have one."

Both Maddox and I spoke at the same time. "They won't accept it for free."

He chuckled. "Of course not. They're as stubborn as Emmy. We'll charge them what they pay now. It sits empty anyway, so really, they're helping us."

Maddox cleared his throat and popped in a lozenge. "That would work."

"You want to talk to Dee about it?"

"Sure." He coughed. "You'll, ah, handle Cami?"

I chuckled. "I'm not sure anyone can *handle* Cami." I became serious. "I don't think she'll object. If she never went back there, she would be okay with it."

"Is she okay?"

"She will be." I sucked in a deep breath. "Bent, could you, ah, give me that number again? For Chloe?"

"For Cami?"

"For both of us."

He dug into his pocket, bringing out his phone. "Absolutely." He stopped. "You'll really go and see her, Aiden?"

"Yes."

"Cami's staying with you again?"

I dropped my eyes. "Yeah."

"For how long?"

I lifted my gaze. "For fucking ever if that's what she wants."

"Holy shit," Maddox muttered, repeating the words I had said to Bentley on Sunday. "You did it, didn't you?"

"I love her," I said simply.

He sat back, shaking his head. "Jesus, I get sick and miss a couple of days, and look what happens. Bentley gets engaged, you declare your love." He grinned. "Thank God I came back before Reid stepped up to the plate."

We all started to laugh.

Maddox leaned forward, his hand extended. "Congrats, Tree Trunk. You deserve it."

I shook his hand and met Bentley's gaze.

"So the engulfing happened." He grinned.

"Yeah." I grinned. "It did."

Bentley stood and rounded the desk, waiting.

"What?"

"I'm proud of you, Aiden. For taking care of Cami, admitting your feelings, and for facing your fears. I know none of it was easy." He held out his hand. I stood, shocked, when instead of a handshake, he pulled me in for a hug.

"I'm proud of you," he repeated in my ear.

His words were simple but profound, and they meant everything to me.

He stepped back and slapped my shoulder.

Maddox looked between us. "I am not hugging you. Even if I didn't have a cold, I am not doing that shit."

"Whatever, Mad Dog. You're just jealous Bent got in first." I held out my arms. "Come on, you know you want to." I pounded my chest. "You want a little piece of Aiden loving too."

"Fuck you."

I started to laugh, and they joined in. Of the three of us, Maddox was the least fond of PDA. Bentley sat down and sent me Chloe's number.

"Let's get down to business so Maddox can go home. The last thing I need is to catch his cold."

Sandy entered, a hand on her hip. "You know, if the three of you behaved like normal businessmen, I wouldn't have to walk around the office trying to find you. You don't have to sit around a desk having your little powwows. I set up the boardroom with your lunch." She fixed a stern eye at Maddox. "I got you chicken soup. Eat it."

"Thanks, Sandy."

"You love it, woman." I grinned at her. "Keeps you on your toes."

"Whatever. Do you need anything else?"

"Can you dig out the files on the apartments we keep on Westside?"

"Yes, and 1740 is the nicer of the two. Better view and a great layout."

"Okay. That one, then."

"All right."

We all exchanged a glance when she left. "She's scary good."

Bentley chuckled and stood. "Yep. And she is all ours."

Maddox followed Bentley, and I was behind him. At my doorway, he stopped and turned sharply, grabbing me in a fast, hard hug.

"Way to go, Tree Trunk. I'm proud too."

Then he hurried away.

DEE CAME HOME a few days later, an unexpected end coming to the case she had been working on. One female member of the family had exploded outside the courtroom, refusing to have any part of the proceedings. She had told the various family members exactly what she thought of their greediness, and somehow managed to do what no one else had done—open up the lines of communication. They settled the disputes themselves, splitting everything in a peaceful manner and bringing the tumultuous situation to a close.

We picked Dee up at the airport, with Maddox tagging along. The emotional reunion between the two sisters was touching. Dee enveloped Cami in her arms, rocking her like a child, tears running down her face. Cami's shoulders shook with sobs. The stress of the past weeks showed in Dee's fatigued posture and unusual emotion. She was always stoic and calm.

I felt Maddox tense when he saw her, and I heard his muttered curse. I cast a glance his way and saw the raw emotion on his face, before it smoothed out and he adopted his usual neutral expression.

There was definitely more going on between them than either was admitting.

We stood to the side, giving the girls privacy. I had done the same thing when Emmy came to see Cami. She had been emotional, hugging Cami hard, and crying. Even Bentley's hug had been longer than usual, his formal façade disappearing as he spoke to her quietly, expressing how worried they had been. It had done my heart good to see the way people loved my girl. It made me grateful I was able to love her openly now and give her what she needed.

When they finally broke apart, Dee approached me, her voice quavering.

"I can't begin—"

"You don't have to."

She flung her arms around me, and I hugged her in return.

She stepped back, wiping her eyes, and turned to Maddox. Cami and I discreetly moved away to get Dee's luggage. I glanced over my shoulder. He had her engulfed in his arms, and he was stroking her hair while talking to her. There was no doubt it was a private moment.

Once we collected Dee's luggage, we drove them home. I watched Cami carefully, not surprised to see her tense up when we entered the apartment. I had agreed to leave them alone for the night and let Cami talk to Dee about the place in Maddox's building. They needed the time together, but I hated the thought of her in a place that frightened her. Sandy had arranged a cleaner, and Cami's room was fresh and back to its normal state. Thoughtfully, Sandy had purchased new bedding as well, so all traces of Louisa were gone, but I wasn't convinced it was enough.

Leaving Cami was difficult, and that was a new experience for me. "Call me later, all right, Sunshine?" I urged. "Anytime." I bent my head lower, my voice quiet so only she could hear my words. "I'll come get you if you need me to." I paused, brushing my lips over her ear. "I love you."

She smiled up at me, her eyes bright. "I love you too."

"I mean it."

"I know."

Maddox dragged me away and kept me company. We worked out, ordered pizza, and sat back with some cold beer. The entire time, I thought of Cami. I had never known anyone to take over my thoughts the way she did. Since I admitted my feelings for her, it seemed a completely new side of my mind and heart had opened up, and she occupied every square inch. For the first time, I understood Bentley's devotion to Emmy.

"Aiden."

"Sorry, what?" I asked Maddox, twisting open the cap on another beer.

"I asked how it went with the lawyers and police."

I took a long pull on the bottle, the icy liquid soothing the burn of the hot peppers Maddox had included in the pizza toppings. I wiped my mouth with a napkin, tossing it into the empty box.

"Rather than having to go to court and dealing with the expense of a trial, a deal was made. All parties agreed, so it was done quickly."

"One you're not happy about, I take it."

I shrugged. "Louisa is being confined to a long-term mental rehab facility in Alberta. She'll get counseling and treatment. She isn't going to be free for a long time. When she does, she will not be allowed anywhere near Cami. Louisa's parents, well, her father at least, is finally stepping up and admitting his daughter needs help." I shook my head in disgust. "Cami was her biggest advocate. She didn't want Louisa to go to jail. She wanted her to get help."

"You wanted her to go to jail?"

"I'd lock her up and throw away the fucking key, but Cami says that wouldn't do anyone any good. I suppose she's right." I picked at the label on my bottle. "She has a huge capacity for forgiveness."

"That is a good thing considering . . ."

I chuckled dryly. "I'm well aware I have benefitted from that forgiveness."

"You're a lucky man."

"I know." I let my head fall back to the cushion. "I love her, Maddox. She's changed me so much without even trying. It's as if she's brought the world into focus."

"And she's the center of that focus?"

I stared at him. "Exactly."

Our eyes met and he looked away with a nod. His expression told me without words there would be no more discussion on the matter tonight.

I reached for the remote. "Netflix?"

He reached for a beer. "Yeah. We need to chill."

I threw the remote at him as he laughed.

⁓

DEE AND CAMI walked around the condo, peeking in cupboards and talking quietly. They both looked exhausted.

Cami had texted me early in the morning, saying her sister had agreed to see the condo, and Dee wanted to speak to me in private.

I wasn't sure that was a good thing. I was certain she had a few choice words for me, but I knew I deserved them.

I wanted to sweep Cami into my arms and just hold her when I saw her. Take her back to the loft and make love to her until she forgot everything except being with me. Hold her while she slept. I held myself back from doing that, though—at least for now.

Dee entered the larger of the two bedrooms and Cami brushed past me in the hall. I pulled her close briefly, then stepped into the room as she returned to the kitchen. Dee was by the windows, staring at the city below.

"This is a nice condo," Dee murmured. "Beautiful view."

"I agree."

She turned, meeting my eyes. "I find it hard to believe the rent is the same as what we pay now."

"It's a business thing."

She crossed her arms. "Business, as in you taking care of my sister business, Aiden?"

I mimicked her actions. "Business, as in the place is available, it's safe, and it's free of memories for Cami, so yes."

She studied me for a minute, then began to talk.

"When our mom died, it was just Cami and me. I had to work, go to school, and look after her. She was just a kid, you know?"

"So were you, really. You were young to take on so much responsibility."

She shrugged. "I hadn't been a kid for a long time, and there was no choice. Our father wasn't going to help look after her. She only had me. Cami was always good, though. She never complained and always tried to help. She had a paper route, collected bottles, all sorts of things when she was young. When she got older, she babysat, tutored other kids, waitressed, anything she could to help contribute. When she left school, she got a full-time job waitressing. We didn't have the money for tuition, and she didn't know yet what she wanted to do with her life."

I waited, knowing she was going somewhere with this conversation.

"She quit waitressing and got a job as a PA because the money was better. I started with the law firm, although it was the lowest of the low jobs." She chuckled. "You have to start somewhere. Cami hated the PA job almost as much as she hated waitressing. Her boss was an idiot and liked his fruit cut up for him daily. Cami was better than that. She had finally figured out she wanted to follow her passion and become a fashion designer and where she wanted to go to get her education. She has such talent."

"I agree. She does."

"She hated her job, but she stuck with it and saved for her tuition. She refused to let me help her. I was paying my student loans and trying to make ends meet for us. She worked as a PA and found the job at Glad Rags where she's still working. She saved and paid her own way."

"Like Emmy."

"Yes."

"That's one of the reasons they're so close. They're similar in many ways."

She hummed in agreement. "Once she went to school, the only thing she let me do was pay our rent. She contributes every month toward the bills and looks after herself financially."

"Why are you telling me this, Dee?"

She sighed and passed a hand over her face. "She didn't sleep all night. Even though her room is clean, she will never be able to go back in there and rest. She could barely stand getting her clothes out of the closet."

"I'm not surprised."

"She came into my room to sleep, but neither of us could rest. Knowing that woman had been hiding in *my* closet, knowing what she'd done to Cami. I could almost feel her in there with us, *feel* her hatred—even though I know she's miles away and can't hurt us." She shook her head. "I couldn't sleep either."

"Then, please, accept this place."

"Cami has always been independent, refused to let me help her, even when I started making more money. But she'll accept this from you."

I studied her. "Will you?"

"Why are you doing this?" She waved her hand. "Why are you *all* doing this?"

I stepped forward, holding out my hands beseechingly. "Dee, I know you haven't been happy with me, with my actions. I can't take back my behavior. I wish I could." I dragged a hand through my hair. "I pushed Cami away even when I wanted her close. I fought her. I fought what I felt, but I'm done fighting. I love her. I can't deny it, and I'm tired of trying to every day. I need to make sure she's okay. The place you're living *isn't* okay anymore. She is never going to be comfortable there again. No matter what we do to change the way it looks, she is never going to feel safe." I swallowed heavily. "I thought I was going to lose her. I swore if she was okay I'd never to let her go. I'd take care of her."

"You saved her."

"She saved me right back." I swept my arm around the room. "We, all of us, want you to have this because it's something we can do to help. Bentley and Maddox both are onboard with this idea. It's not charity or a handout. It's family helping one another."

"Family?"

"You're Cami's sister. I love her, which means you're part of my family. You already were because of Emmy, but it's more . . . personal now. I need to take care of her *and* you. If you let me."

"You really want to do this for us?"

"Yes."

"She loves with everything in her, Aiden. A little piece of her breaks when she gets let down. You'll be good to her?"

"Always. I love her, Dee. I never thought I could love, but she's proven me wrong. She's everything I've needed and never allowed myself to hope for in my life. She's my Sunshine."

Her eyes shone with unshed tears. "Good."

"She'll never want for anything. Including love. I promise." I grabbed her hand. "Let me do this. For both of you."

"Okay."

With a grin, I hugged her hard. "Let's go tell her, then head to brunch. Emmy wants to see you, and Cami's gonna make pancakes again."

"All right, let's go."

It was a fun brunch around Bentley's table. All six of us laughing and relaxed, the way things used to be when we were together. Dee exclaimed over Emmy's ring, hugged Bentley, and I noticed, stayed close to Maddox. Emmy cooked a feast, and I ate at least five of Cami's pancakes. She added blueberries this time, and I informed her I needed them just that way from now on.

Her phone rang, and she glanced at the number with a frown. Excusing herself from the table, she answered as she walked away. I watched her, constantly on alert now when it came to her. However, her stance was relaxed, and she began to smile widely and talk quickly.

Returning to the table, she was almost vibrating with excitement.

"What's up, Sunshine?"

She grasped my knee. "I won!"

"Excuse me?"

"That trip to Las Vegas! I won!" She turned to Dee and Emmy. "I call girls' weekend in Vegas!"

There were a lot of high fives and fist bumps as Cami explained how she had won the trip. I tried to look happy, but I didn't really feel it. The thought of the three of them going to Vegas on their own wasn't sitting well with me, yet I was pretty sure I had no say in the matter, given they were adults. Glancing at Bentley, I could tell from the rigid set of his jaw he was thinking along the same lines as me. Even Maddox looked slightly put out.

"Isn't it a trip for four?" I asked, remembering the day at the winery.

Cami looked confused. "Yes. Did you want the fourth? I suppose since you took me to the winery, you should have first dibs on it."

"No, I was just wondering."

The girls rose and started carrying dishes to the kitchen, discussing the trip animatedly. We, on the other hand, sat and stared at one another.

"I don't like this," I muttered.

Bentley snorted. "Me either."

Maddox filled his coffee cup with a smirk. "I don't think you have much choice."

I drummed my fingers on the table. Cami's phone beeped, and I looked at the screen, which had a text with information. "Includes coach airfare for four, accommodations, transfers to and from the airport, and five hundred dollars spending money," I read.

"Which hotel?"

"The Travelodge."

Bentley got out his phone, checking the hotel. His frown deepened. "I don't fucking think so."

"Coach." I snorted. "Packed in like sardines."

"Probably a cheap van service to the hotel."

"I bet the spending money is gambling chips," Maddox piped up, a grin on his face.

"I don't like this," I repeated.

"What should we do?" Bentley asked.

I thought about it. "Up the ante."

"Now you're talking." Maddox smirked, egging us on.

"I like it. How?" Bentley asked.

"I think, boys, we're going to Vegas. BAM style."

"What does that consist of?" Maddox chuckled. "Do tell."

"Brace yourself. We are about to misuse company funds, Mad Dog. I've decided I want to expand our horizons and have a look at some property in Vegas."

Bentley chuckled, and Maddox's shoulders shook with suppressed laughter. "Is that a fact?"

"Yep. We're renting a private plane and flying all of us there. We'll do a few land inspections while the girls hit a spa or something."

"Not sure this is gonna fly with Revenue Canada as a business trip."

I shrugged. "Then bill me. You figure it out, whatever way works. But it's happening. Suites at Bellagio. Whatever side trips the girls want. An entire weekend of whatever they desire. They want Vegas? They fucking get Vegas."

"As long as you're with them," Maddox added.

"You're coming with, Mad Dog. Your girl is on board for this weekend too."

He didn't argue, although he mumbled something more about the company funds. I ignored him. We could look at some land while we were there. He could figure it out. He was great at figuring things out.

Bentley grinned. "BAM style, indeed."

The girls returned from the kitchen, still chatting and excited.

"Who's going to tell them?" I mumbled.

"You are," Bentley and Maddox stated in unison.

I flexed my shoulders.

"Right."

⌒

THE ROOM FELL silent, my words not met with the enthusiasm I had hoped. All three girls stared at me incredulously.

"You three are certifiable, do you know that?" Cami said, aghast.

Emmy turned to Bentley. "This smacks of you, Rigid."

Dee smirked. "You came up with all this in five minutes?"

I thought fast. "We were discussing the fact that only one of us got to accompany you. It seemed fair to broaden the plans to include everyone."

Cami arched her eyebrow. "Perhaps we weren't going to take any of you. We thought of asking Sandy to come with us to say thanks for all the things she has done for us."

I met Bentley's frantic gaze. We hadn't factored in that decision. "She's busy," I objected.

"We haven't picked a date."

"She's busy every weekend. Husband, grandkids, you know. She hates flying," Bentley interjected.

Emmy crossed her arms. "Strange. She was telling me last week of all the traveling she wants to do once she dumps your demanding ass."

He grimaced. "She called my ass demanding?"

"You're missing the point here, Rigid."

"Which is?"

"*Girls'* weekend."

"You can have a girls' weekend. We won't bother you."

Cami shook her head. "You're going to fly all that way and just sit in a hotel room?"

We were losing the argument, and I needed to figure out how to convince them. "Actually, we are going to do a little business while we're there. We were talking about it just the other day."

Cami snorted. "Of course you were. How convenient."

"I know. Very fortuitous."

Emmy coughed *bullshit* into her hand, but I noticed she was grinning. I locked eyes with Cami. "We've all been going through shit, Cami. A weekend away would be great. You want to go to Vegas, we'll go. However, we're taking you."

"But I won a trip. It will go to waste."

"No, you can call them back and say you can't go and let them redraw. Someone else can go."

"Why do I have a feeling even if I say no, every time I turn around in Vegas, I'll see you skulking around a corner?"

I snorted. "I won't be skulking, Sunshine. I'll be right behind you. You can bet your sweet ass on that fact."

"Why is this so important to you?"

I played dirty. I bent closer, my voice low. "I thought I lost you. I'm not ready for you to be out of my sight yet. Please."

Her expression softened, her green eyes misty. She was faltering. "Aiden . . ."

"You know, I've never been on a private plane," Dee mused, meeting my eyes with a subtle wink.

"It's awesome," I assured her, returning her gesture.

"I hear the Bellagio is spectacular," Bentley said. "Completely amazing."

"Oh," Emmy breathed out. "That's where we'd stay?"

"Best suite in the house, Freddy."

I interjected, "They have notoriously big limos to pick us up and drive us anywhere too."

Cami pursed her lips. "I want to go to the Grand Canyon."

"Yep. They can take us."

"With champagne?"

"Bottles of it."

The girls all looked at each other.

Then Maddox added the icing on the cake. "I have a friend who can get us awesome tickets for the Michael Jackson tribute show. Probably backstage passes."

And just like that, the game was over.

Blackjack.

CHAPTER 21

AIDEN

SANDY STEPPED INTO the boardroom, one arm filled with files. In her other hand was a large carafe of coffee. She set down the coffee, pushing it toward Maddox. He grinned at her with a wink.

"Thanks, Momma Bear."

She rolled her eyes, then slapped down the files onto the wooden surface.

"All right, boys. Listen." She handed us each a different colored folder. "Your itinerary for your stalking expedition."

"It's a weekend away," Bentley objected.

"It's the three of you going overboard."

"Aiden's idea." Maddox smirked as he poured himself a mug of coffee. "I'm just along for the ride and to make sure no more company funds are abused."

She ignored him. "Plane is booked. Four suites at Bellagio."

"Four?" I asked.

"Emmy and Bentley. You and Cami. One for Maddox, one for Dee."

I looked at Maddox with a frown. "Really?"

He met my gaze steadily. "Really."

I shrugged. "Whatever floats your boat."

He glanced down at the file, his voice quiet. "Not my decision."

Sandy threw him a glance, then continued. "I've arranged a car at your disposal. The hotel will provide an extra one or two if needed. Dinner is arranged and booked the first night. Maddox has organized the tickets for the show. The rest of the itinerary is up to you."

"Excellent." I beamed at her. "Thanks, Sandy."

"I'm booking myself an all-day spa package. You three are treating me. I added the champagne lunch because I knew you would insist."

We all laughed. "Enjoy it," Bentley told her, standing and kissing her cheek. "You deserve it."

She looked at him as if he were an idiot.

"I know."

She turned and patted the pile of manila files. "If you're interested, here is some real work. All the paperwork for the Port Albany property is complete. It's yours, so now you can plan what to do with it."

"Great. We'll meet with the team when we return."

"All right." She walked to the door, pausing before she left. "I'm glad to see you beginning to live, boys." She stared at Maddox. "I never thought I'd hear myself say it, but you need to follow in their footsteps. Life is too short to have only money as company. It doesn't keep you warm at night."

With those words of wisdom, she left.

"Jesus," Maddox muttered. "Look what the two of you have done. She wants me to be more like you? Give me strength."

I slapped him on the back. "She's right. We're awesome."

He picked up his file. "Yep. Awesome."

I met Bentley's eyes. I understood why he'd tried so hard to get me to open up to Cami. The reward was sweet and worth the risk. I wanted that for Maddox. We both did.

I'd have to figure out how to help him.

$\sim$

CAMI PEEKED UP at me, her eyes wide. "This is breathtaking."

I glanced around the luxurious cabin of the plane. It was pretty wicked. Wide, rich leather seats and mahogany tables filled the cabin, surrounded by muted blue and gray tones. Even in first class, I had a problem with my shoulders, but here, I had plenty of room. The liquor was top-notch, and I liked being able to stretch out and get comfortable. I could get used to this sort of travel. I wondered how strongly Bentley would object to the idea of BAM purchasing a plane.

Looking over at how tightly pressed Emmy was to him, I decided he might not object too much. He couldn't have her on his lap in a public plane.

I bent low to Cami's ear. "There's a bedroom in the back. We could check it out once everyone else is distracted."

"Distracted?"

"Hmm," I murmured. "Emmy is about to fall asleep on Bent. He won't move and disturb her, and he's looking sleepy himself. Dee and Maddox have an intense game of Scrabble going. Neither of them will give an inch and let the other win. The whiskey they're pounding back is making them slow anyway. The crew is getting lunch ready up front. We could get up to stretch our legs, and no one will notice." I bit down on her earlobe. "Then I could stretch something else. With my cock."

Her breath caught.

"You wanna join the mile-high club, Sunshine? Ride my dick in the clouds? We'd have to be fast, but I guarantee you satisfaction."

"You're so crass."

"Is that a yes?"

She squeezed my thigh, and I grinned.

I was definitely talking Bentley into buying one of these.

The next two days were a whirlwind. We explored the Strip, ate too much, even gambled, although none of us were big players. The show we went to the first night was entertaining, though I thought the girls enjoyed it more than we did, but that was why we were there.

Our suites were large and lavish, and I loved watching Cami's reaction to the world of luxury. It wasn't how I lived daily, but I found I enjoyed spoiling her. She squealed with delight as she investigated the room, tackling me on the massive bed and having her wicked way with me. I succumbed easily.

The heat, though, was brutal—the kind that sucked the air from your lungs and made your clothes stick to your skin two minutes after you walked outside. Even Emmy was warm enough not to be bundled up in her usual layers. She still carried her wrap with her, slipping it on as soon as we entered the air-conditioned buildings. Cami, however, wore little sundresses that showed off her creamy skin and toned legs. I decided she had the most lickable collarbones in the history of collarbones and proved it often.

We left the girls shopping the second day and did look at a few properties. Once we had returned to the hotel, sitting by the pool under the shade of a huge umbrella, I lifted my drink to my lips.

"I think, gentlemen, we can safely say this is not the place for us. This was a great idea in making sure our initial thoughts were correct, though."

Maddox snorted. "Jesus, you are full of it. As if there was any chance we'd get into the property game here."

"You never know. We've done our due diligence. Business part of the trip concluded."

Bentley chuckled and glanced at his watch.

"The girls will be back soon," I assured him.

"I'm aware."

"They have a car and driver at their disposal. The driver is also a black belt. I made sure of it. They're perfectly safe." I leaned back. "I sent Cami out with a credit card and told her to rack it up for her and Dee. I want her to be gone all day and return with so much stuff I have to buy her another damn suitcase to take it home."

"Listen to you," Maddox mused.

"I want her to have some nice things. She doesn't have to worry anymore." I signaled for another round of drinks. "For the first time, I want to spoil someone, shower her with gifts, and you know why?"

Bentley grinned at me. "Because she doesn't give a shit about them."

"Exactly. She'd love me even if we'd flown coach and stayed at the Travelodge." I shuddered. "Thank God I didn't have to prove I love her enough to do that, though."

We all laughed, and Bentley dragged a hand through his hair. "Emmy wants to go to one of those campy Vegas shows tonight. She says it's something we have to do as part of the experience. You two want to do that with us?"

Maddox shook his head. "There's a whiskey bar Dee and I want to check out. I hear it has some rare bottles we want to sample." He smirked. "You, Aiden? What are your plans tonight?"

"Cami wants to see all the sights. I booked a gondola ride and got a spot for the fountain show. We're just gonna be tourists."

Bentley groaned. "Maybe Cami could talk Emmy into that rather than the show. I'm not sure I'm gonna survive the shit she wants to see."

I clapped him on the back. "Man up, Bent. It's just one night. We'll have dinner, do all the things the girls want to do, and tomorrow we'll meet for breakfast and do the Grand Canyon and Hoover Dam. We'll be gone all day, but the limo will be cool."

He stood. "Okay. I need to go inside. This fucking heat is killing me."

We separated at the elevators. I needed to grab some Tylenol at the gift shop, so I headed across the lobby. Leaving the shop, I caught sight of a small window with an eye-catching display, and I stopped to look. Glittering diamonds and multicolored gemstones sparkled under the lights. One piece in particular caught my eye, and without a thought, I went inside the store. A short while later, I left—with a smile on my face, my bank account lighter, and a small, flat box burning a hole in my pocket.

Cami was going to kill me.

⌒

I HAD ALMOST finished buttoning my shirt when Cami came out of the huge en suite. "Is this okay?"

I gaped at her. "Okay? Sunshine, you're stunning."

She was wearing another sundress. This one was her favorite color, a rich purple that looked amazing against her skin. "You've caught the sun." I traced a finger along her sun-kissed skin, teasing the flirty bow that held up the dress. "I love this."

"I got it today."

"You didn't buy much."

"I bought enough. You're spoiling me, Aiden."

"I want to spoil you."

She turned to the mirror, brushing her hair off her face. I wrapped my arms around her, pulling her back to my chest. I rested my chin on her shoulder. "Let me spoil you, Sunshine."

She leaned back, her expression soft. "I do. But I'm not used to it, Aiden."

"Get used to it. I'm not going anywhere."

"Yeah?" she breathed out.

I held her tighter. I knew she was still worried I would push her away again. The only thing that would change that doubt was time, along with my constant reassurance and love.

"Hold out your arm."

Confused, she did as I asked. Her eyes widened as I slipped a delicate bracelet around her wrist.

"Aiden!"

"I saw this in the window today. It reminded me of your eyes. I wanted you to have it as a memento of this trip."

"A key chain would have been cheaper."

I chuckled. "Nope."

She blinked and smiled, her finger tracing the intricate design of emeralds and diamonds that had caught my eye. It wasn't large and showy, but it suited her perfectly. The saleswoman had been patient, explaining in great detail the cut and clarity of the stones.

"I remember once thinking you needed a bracelet on your arm. I decided to give it to you."

"It's so beautiful."

I spun her in my arms and kissed her. "So are you, Sunshine. So are you."

⌒

CAMI HUGGED MY arm to her chest, laying her head on my shoulder. "What a wonderful night, Aiden."

I grinned. "Yeah?"

"Yes. We've done everything I wanted to do. Dinner with our friends. The night with you. The Eiffel Tower, the gondola ride, the fountains. We've been in and out of every famous casino I wanted to see. It's been incredible."

It had been. Dinner was fun, and seeing her shyly show off her gift had touched my heart. The girls loved her bracelet, exclaiming over its beauty. Bentley shot me a wink while Maddox smirked, and I subtly flipped them off, knowing they were teasing me.

The best part, though, was spending the evening with her. Just the two of us. Watching her reactions to everything I arranged, seeing the fear and worry caused by recent events gone from her face, and her simply enjoying the night was the best reward. Kissing her on the Eiffel Tower and in the gondola. Then again by the fountains as we watched the mesmerizing display. Taking silly selfies. Being able to share it with her. It had been perfect.

Yet, I felt something was missing. I wasn't ready for the night to end.

I glanced around, a cab slowly crossing our path. An ad splashed across the doors in bright colors caught my eye.

The Little Chapel. Open till Midnight. Why wait?

I looked down at Cami, tucked into my side. Where she belonged. I wanted her there for the rest of my life. Like a bolt of lightning, I knew. I loved her. She was it for me, and I wasn't waiting any longer or worrying if I was enough. I was what she needed, and she was all I wanted.

"Cami, there's something else I want to do tonight."

She looked up at me with a wry grin. "You want the midnight buffet at Caesar's Palace?"

"No, it's something special. Something I want only with you."

"Okay. Whatever you want."

"Anything?"

"Anything," she stated. "Tonight has been all the things I wanted to do. Now it's your turn. Name it."

I lifted her hands and encased them in mine.

"It's big. Life-changing."

She looked confused. "Okay, Aiden. Whatever it is, I say yes."

I swallowed the nervous lump in my throat and brushed a kiss to her fingers.

"Marry me, Sunshine."

Turn the page for a sneak peek at *Maddox*—Vested Interest #3

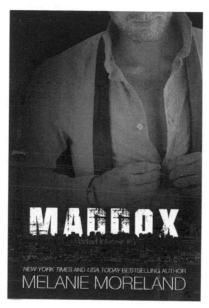

Coming July 2018

CHAPTER 1

WITH THE LIGHTS of the city spread out below me, I stared out the window, sipping my whiskey, enjoying the way the rich flavor rolled around my tongue. The low lights reflected my condo in the large pane windows. Tidy, organized, everything in its place. Exactly the way I liked it. Needed it.

Behind me, I heard a light tap. I hit the button on the remote, unlocking the door, knowing who was waiting. Soft footfalls headed in my direction, and Dee's reflection appeared in the glass. Turning, I offered her a smile and a tumbler of whiskey. I knew she'd like this one.

"Hey, neighbor."

She shook her head, taking the glass from my hand and settling into the club chair. "You are such a dork. I live ten floors below you. I am not your neighbor."

I shrugged. "Close enough." I sat across from her on the sofa. "Seriously, are you settling in?"

She held up her whiskey, studied its dark golden color, then took a sip. Her eyes drifted shut as she swallowed. Her hand swept through her hair, the strawberry color catching the light. She was artless, sexy.

I liked it.

She opened her eyes. "Nice choice."

"I knew you'd like it."

She smiled and reclined her head. "I am settling in. I wasn't expecting to be on my own, but it will be nice to have a home office to work from."

"Still in shock?"

She chuckled. "I shouldn't be, given it was Cami, but I am."

"I think this was all on Aiden, which makes it the biggest shock of them all."

We went to Vegas for a quick trip away. Everyone needed a break, and rather than the girls going on their own, we joined them. The first day was fun with sightseeing and dinner out. We went to a show and even did a little gambling. The next night, we ended up pairing off the way we usually did: Emmy and Bent, Cami and Aiden, and Dee and me.

Bent and Emmy went to another show. Dee and I checked out a whiskey bar we'd heard about, spending a few hours sipping some extraordinary samples and enjoying each other's company.

Cami and Aiden spent the night doing the usual touristy things. They visited the Eiffel Tower, took a gondola ride, and watched the fountains dance. Then, Aiden being Aiden, he had gone for broke and, since we were in Vegas, married Cami.

They showed up at breakfast the next morning, and neither of them said a word. But they looked guilty, yet so happy, and I knew something was up. They simply ordered their meals, talked about the day's plans, and acted as if nothing was amiss. Until Emmy spotted the rings on their hands.

"What the hell? Cami . . . are you . . . oh my God, are you married?"

Four sets of eyes snapped in their direction. Aiden lifted Cami's hand, pressing a kiss to her knuckles. The light glinted off the matching ring on his left hand.

"We are," he stated.

We all gaped at them, shocked.

"Is it legal?" Dee asked, looking between Cami and Aiden. "You really got married?"

"Very legal."

Suddenly, the table exploded. Hugs, kisses, backslaps, and congratulations were exchanged all around. Aiden looked like the happiest man on earth, and beside him, Cami beamed. When Emmy asked if they were going to have a real wedding, Cami shook her head.

"It was exactly what we wanted. Only us." She smiled at Dee in apology. "We thought we'd renew our vows next year and bring everyone to join us."

Dee covered her hand. "That sounds perfect. I'm happy for you."

I had wondered then, the same way I wondered now, if Dee was as okay with the marriage as she seemed to be. In the weeks since we had returned, life had been busy with work, moving Cami in with Aiden, and moving Dee in to her new place in the building where I lived. We'd barely had time to see each other.

Or, in other words—fuck each other.

"You were very calm about the whole surprise wedding."

She sipped her whiskey, contemplative. "I was a bit hurt, but then I realized it was Cami's decision and her life. She was much too happy for me to be upset." She huffed a long breath. "I only hope it wasn't a rash decision they'll both regret."

I scowled, feeling the need to defend my friend. "Aiden loves Cami. He loves her so much it fucking terrified him. When he accepted what he was feeling, it changed him. *She* changed him—for the better. For the first time in his life, he accepted something good for himself. I don't think you have to worry about any regrets from him."

She tilted her head, studying me. "That was spoken with conviction."

I shrugged. "The two of them work."

"They do." She grinned. "That was spoken like a true romantic, by the way. Which you insist you are not."

I chuckled. "I have my moments. I'm okay with romance . . . for other people."

"Me too."

We stared at each other, not speaking. Gradually the air shifted, growing more intense. I stared at her over the rim of my tumbler.

"So, tell me, *Deirdre*, what are you wearing under that businesslike navy suit you have on?"

She loved it when I murmured her full name. No one used it but me, and I only uttered it when we were alone.

She traced the rim of her glass, eyeing me. "I'm sure you'd like to know."

I shifted, my erection lengthening as I thought about it. Wondering what secret I would discover tonight.

Dee was a walking contradiction. Classic, dark suits, neutral-colored blouses. No-fuss hair. Simple makeup. No jewelry.

However, underneath the linen and cotton was an entirely different story.

Lacy push-up bras, tiny triangles that covered silky curls, and a sweet little cleft I knew intimately.

Satin, lace, silk, and sin.

Black, pink, red, every color of the rainbow.

Cutouts and high tops. Thongs, boy shorts, strapless, bustiers, stripes, polka dots, pin-tucked, bedazzled, and sexy.

She had them all. She was sex on legs.

"Why don't you show me?" My eyes raked down her body.

She stood, her fingers drifting to the pearl button under her neck. I settled into the cushions, anticipation waking every nerve in my body.

"Slowly."

She tilted her head.

"I want it slow tonight, baby."

She shrugged out of her jacket, the fabric a dark pool on the floor.

"Is that so?"

"Yes." My cock grew harder as she moved. Slow. Sensuous. Just the way I instructed her.

"Do I get a reward?"

I palmed my erection. "You get me. Buried so deep inside you, you'll feel me for days."

Her blouse joined her jacket, showcasing a cream lace bustier encasing her torso that made me groan. Her breasts were high, ready to spill over the tight fabric. I wanted to bite them. When her skirt fell, revealing the thigh highs attached with tiny straps of lace and a silk thong, I almost lost it.

I widened my legs. "Come here."

She stood between my knees. I trailed my fingers up and down her thighs, tracing the ribbons and lace, teasing the satin of her skin. I jerked her forward, burying my face in her pussy, breathing her in.

She whimpered as I pressed my mouth to her, hard.

"You want me. I can smell how much you want me."

She dug her fingers into my scalp, lifting my face.

"Yes. But the rules still apply, Maddox. Sex. That's all it is. Nothing has changed."

I smiled grimly. "I wouldn't expect it to."

"Then fuck me."

Never breaking eye contact with her, I shredded her panties. Tore them away from her skin with one firm yank of my fist.

I would fuck her. I would fuck her because that was what we did.

To the outside world, we were the same: cool, calm, and collected. Detached.

When we came together, alone, things changed. We were relentless. Explosive and insatiable.

She fucked with my control.

I fucked her to get it back.

That was our game. It always had been.

Until one of us changed the rules and fell in love.

A WORD OF THANKS

THERE ARE ALWAYS so many people behind the scenes when writing a book. They inspire, suggest, encourage, and often lift you up when the words don't come.

Deb, mark another one complete. So many words we have shared! Thank you for everything.

Denise, once again, thank you for your input and encouragement. Your support is so appreciated.

Jess and Jodi, thank you for all your hard work and effort—it is much appreciated.

Caroline, thank you—your keen eyes and enthusiasm are such gifts.

To Beth, Shelly, Janett, Darlene, Carrie, Sue, Jeanne, Eli—you all encourage and support. Share and love. Make me laugh. Add a richness to my life. Thank you.

Lisa, you are a rock star. You went above and beyond and I adore your nerdy side. Hugs!

Flavia, thank you for your support and belief in my work. You rock it for me.

Karen, my wonderful PA, and friend—the dedication says it all, and yet not enough. There simply are not enough words—even for me. Much love.

To all the bloggers, readers, and especially my review team. Thank you for everything you do. Shouting your love of books, posting, sharing—your recommendations keep my TBR list full, and the support you have shown me is so appreciated.

To my fellow authors who have shown me such kindness, thank you. I will follow your example and pay it forward.

To Christine—thank you for making my words look pretty!

My reader group, Melanie's Minions—love you all.

Finally—my Matthew. After all these years, all the laughter, tears, and love, it is still not enough. Thank you for all you are, and all you do.

BOOKS BY
MELANIE MORELAND

Into the Storm
Beneath the Scars
Over the Fence
It Started with a Kiss
My Image of You

The Contract
The Baby Clause (Contract #2)

Bentley (Vested Interest #1)
Aiden (Vested Interest #2)
Maddox (Vested Interest #3 coming July 2018)

ABOUT THE AUTHOR

NEW YORK TIMES/USA Today bestselling author Melanie Moreland, lives a happy and content life in a quiet area of Ontario with her beloved husband of twenty-eight-plus years and their rescue cat, Amber. Nothing means more to her than her friends and family, and she cherishes every moment spent with them.

While seriously addicted to coffee, and highly challenged with all things computer-related and technical, she relishes baking, cooking, and trying new recipes for people to sample. She loves to throw dinner parties, and enjoys travelling, here and abroad, but finds coming home is always the best part of any trip.

Melanie loves stories, especially paired with a good wine, and enjoys skydiving (free falling over a fleck of dust) extreme snowboarding (falling down stairs) and piloting her own helicopter (tripping over her own feet.) She's learned happily ever afters, even bumpy ones, are all in how you tell the story.

Melanie is represented by Flavia Viotti at Bookcase Literary Agency. For any questions regarding subsidiary or translation rights please contact her at *flavia@bookcaseagency.com*

www.melaniemoreland.com

73498678R00150

Made in the USA
Middletown, DE
14 May 2018